D1229160

Walter

The Homeless Man

Walter

The Homeless Man

A Novel

By Tekoa Manning

ISBN-13: 978-0615928012 (It's All About Him, Inc.)

ISBN-10: 0615928013

Walter – The Homeless Man Copyright 2013

It's All About Him, Inc.

All rights reserved:

No part of this book may be reproduced in any form or by any electronic or mechanical means including information storage and retrieval systems, without permission in writing from the author. The only exception is by a reviewer, who may quote short excerpts in a review.

This is a work of fiction. Names, characters, places and incidents either are products of the author's imagination or are used fictitiously. Any resemblance to actual events or locales or persons, living or dead, is entirely coincidental.

Picture on Cover from ©iStock.com/Editorial12

Dedication

I would like to dedicate Walter to two very special friends. One friend, the Ruach Hakodesh, the blessed Holy Spirit and the other, Deborah Testa. If it were not for both of these friends, Walter would have never been birthed and I would not be the person that I am today

Acknowledgements

I started writing this story before I ever became homeless, before my mother grew demented and at times did not recognize my father. Even the song sung by Walter, "Fallen Leaves" was written in this book before it was ever decided by my father to be played at my own mother's funeral. Life is filled with irony and at best can be scribed through bitterness at times. However this crushing of flowers only causes potent perfumes to erupt.

In 2005 I decided to place a couple chapters of this story on a site that was for those suffering with Multiple Sclerosis, immediately people fell in love with the main character Walter, who is named after my grandfather. By the year 2008, I like Walter, had lost is all. My best friend Deborah Testa became a sounding gong as she never forgot about Walter and pressed me over and over to finish this book. When I exclaimed, I am broke and have no gift to send you for your birthday or Christmas, she would say, "All I want is another chapter of Walter" and so the story was written in the course of several years. It was a story that was laid down and picked up and now I pray it touches your heart!

Walter – The Homeless Man

Walter

Chapter 1

Walter Kendal lay beside the tree stump, his head resting behind his arms in a heap of fall leaves. The air was crisp and cool with a freshness that beckoned the sun to come up. Tall evergreens trees towered above and hid the horizon. The woods were faintly dark with slivers of light just beginning to peek through. It was very still, except for the occasional rustling of foliage falling to the earth, and the soft cooing sound coming from the metal cage that held his only companion.

From the wooded area where Walter lay, he could easily watch the small middle class neighborhood come to life. Flickering pools of light brought a warming glow to a scattering of homes. In the distance, he heard the sound of engines warming up to begin the day, doors slamming and voices calling out to greet neighbors. The familiar sights and sounds reminded Walter of a life he once knew.

He had been waiting patiently for the dark blue mini-van to pull out of the driveway on Wildwood Court. The house he had his eye on belonged to Desiree Levite. Through the French double doors of her kitchen, he watched her prepare breakfast for her two small children and knew it wouldn't be long now.

Desiree left each morning at around six thirty. He assumed this gave her plenty of time to cart her children to the sitter, hit the freeway, and begin her shift at Bailsman, Friedman and Stiltz Law Firm. Walter knew Desiree was a file clerk and full time student on her way to becoming a paralegal. He thought her ultimate goal was to become an attorney. He occasionally read a term paper left lying about, and sometimes sifted through her mail.

Walter was thankful that the ground had not become cold and hard yet, and that the arthritis in his joints didn't ache as badly as usual. He crept up slowly and watched the lights of the minivan disappear from sight. Then he counted under his breath slowly from one to fifty, making sure Desiree hadn't forgotten her briefcase, diaper bag, or her oldest son's backpack. Walter had been caught off guard more than once by the forgetful disarray of the sleepy mother. Making his way up the path, he walked briskly to the back porch of the modest three bedroom brick ranch. Then Walter raised the rock that lay next to the welcome mat, retrieved the key and let himself in. Walter had felt nervous the first few times he had entered, peeking through the blinds at the sounds of each passing motorist. The unexpected clank of the brass mail slot had once left Walter frozen with fear, but after a few weeks, he had settled into a routine. He had no excuse for entering. He knew it was wrong, and eventually he would have to stop or fate would rear its ugly head and he'd be a criminal.

"Maybe I have succumbed to this sort of lifestyle after all?" He wished it were all a bad dream, but as he turned on the faucet that belonged to a stranger and raised the ribbed glass to his perched lips, he knew it was far too real.

It had happened by chance the first time, Walter stumbling upon the key. He had merely wanted some fresh drinking water. Walter was headed out of the woods, on his way to a nearby gas station to fill his empty jug in the men's room. The Chevron had bath stalls in back of the service station and Walter didn't have to enter the store to get washed up or refill his empty container. Sometimes they locked them after midnight, he assumed to keep people like himself out. While he was cutting through the neighborhood he noticed the green garden hose. While reaching for the hose he accidently knocked over a decorative rock with the name Levite painted in black. Its only function was to show ownership of the property Walter stood on, and to hide a key. The power to enter lay within Walter's reach. It made his heart pound, he could picture the food and imagine the sound of the thermostat clicking on and blowing warm heat. He longed for a shower, and the company of television. It had been over a year since Walter had felt the comforts of a real home. He had a home three hundred miles away, just before the rich green hills of Kentucky turned into the mountains of Tennessee. A home full of memories too painful for Walter to face.

Safely inside, he slowly exhaled and made his way to the refrigerator for his morning juice. He never took enough for anyone to notice, but instead consumed just one egg, one small bowl of cornflakes, or one piece of toast. Then carefully the sixty-seven year old washed, dried, and returned his plate, saucer and cup, putting everything back in its original place.

Occasionally the phone rang and startled him. Although he used to sit behind a large desk answering calls, he had now become accustomed to sleeping under over passes, across park benches, and in wooded areas. The days of phone calls had been years ago, before his retirement, now they were a distant memory.

After breakfast, Walter took a shower, leaving not a speck of water to be found. The soft green, slightly damp towel was folded neatly back on the rack to dry, his toothbrush was placed into the frayed pocket of his tan London Fog coat. He wanted to shave, but stopped himself for fear that his gray facial hairs would be noticed. He settled for a dollop of hair gel. Walter ran his fingers through his graying hair, relishing the fact that he still had some; although he had lost some on top, all and all he still had plenty. Leaving the bath, he walked down the hall, according to his watch, it was seven thirty a.m. He had at least seven hours before her return.

The small house was tidy and clean, except for an occasional toy left lying about and the many books that lay in heaps. There were educational books on common law, child psychology and the Constitution. There were also hard bound classics, poetry and children's books. Shuffled amongst the collection was a New King James Bible, and from the looks of the worn leather, he figured it had been opened quite often. Walter had never experienced so many books, and at times he found himself skimming through the volumes to pass the day. He had wondered at first if the books were for show, but now believed Desiree had read the majority of her collection.

It seemed funny to Walter that after entering her home for only a few weeks, he already felt as if he knew her. There were photographs of her children on the mantle, scented candles, and the usual displays of potted plants. The one thing that had confused Walter was a recent portrait of Desiree with a dark haired man who appeared to be her husband. He worried at first that the man in the portrait might be a traveling salesman who could abruptly show up and end Walter's only refuge. Then he found the sympathy cards full of kind remarks about the loss of Desiree's husband, John.

Walter didn't know what the future held for him. He was never one to take hand outs and he knew he had to repay this young mother for what she was unknowingly giving to him. Sometimes he did small repair jobs, like fixing the younger child's rocking chair. The leg had been broken at some point. Walter simply glued it back into place. He had also unclogged the kitchen sink when Desiree carved pumpkins for Halloween. On this cool November morning, he didn't see anything needing his handy work. So, after resting a bit on the tweed recliner, he drifted off to sleep.

Desiree

Chapter 2

Desiree peered into the bathroom mirror inspecting her reflection in the morning light. She squinted her eyes, which were darker than most, black actually, to see her pupils was almost impossible. Her nose was petite and shaped solid; her full mouth and straight white teeth enhanced her appearance. Over all she was happy with her looks except for one thing her hair, or the lack there of. The clumpy, bald spots revealed a few desperate follicles, sprouting up like a wiry cactus amongst the array of tresses. Desiree covered them with floppy hats or brightly colored bandanas. She had tried wigs but found them hot and unnatural looking. The shedding had begun following her husband's death. The doctor attributed it to nerves, saying, "Give it time and take some antidepressants, rub the topical ointment into your scalp and it will grow back." That had been over a year ago and as far as Desiree could tell nothing had changed.

She clasped the shower head and stepped into the shower stall. The warm beads of water refreshed her. The shiny silver drain revealed more hair strands. Desiree bent over and grasped the yarn like threads of hair, she glanced at them then tossed them into the commode to be flushed. They reminded her of her son's cruelty the night before. Josh had pulled out all the hair from Desiree's hair brush as well as from her daughter Tabitha's brush. He then balled it up and sat quietly next to her on the couch. Rubbing her head with his hand, he released the hair he had gathered letting it fall onto her lap, exclaiming, "Look Mom! A big clump of your hair fell out again." Tears had welled up in Desiree's eyes, as Josh laughed uncontrollably. "It's a joke. See, I pulled it out of the brushes."

Josh was only seven, but he knew what he was doing. He enjoyed pinching her nerves, and crawling under his mother's' skin. In fact he had become an expert at this since his father's death. Desiree felt somewhat responsible for his manners because of the time she spent away from him while at work and school.

Stepping out of the shower Desiree sat at her makeup chair applying a mask of liquid foundation, eyeliner, mascara, and a copper lipstick to finish. She then parted her hair, combing what she could forward and placed a pink cotton scarf around her head.

Her son, Josh, was screaming from the other room. For fear that he would wake Tabitha, her four year old, Desiree hurried to the bedroom door. Staring her son in the eye, she tried to figure out who this child was and where he had come from. She had carried Josh for nine months, given birth, and yet when they placed him in her arms she had felt nothing. She loved Josh, but had never bonded with him.

He stared back with a joyous grin, stopped screaming, and mouthed, "Oh, you're awake? I was having a dream. I was going down a big roller coaster; I had to scream." He smiled wickedly. Desiree felt her skin crawling. He knew he had gotten to her again. This delighted him all the more. "Juice, juice, juice! I want juice!"

Desiree ignored him. "Here are your clothes, Josh. Put them on, and then brush your teeth, and be quiet or you'll wake up your sister".

But, of course it was too late. Tabitha stood quietly in the doorway, rubbing her eyes with small chubby hands. She gazed at her older brother as if he were an alien. Josh's feet hit the floor kicking, as his fingers wadded the shirt Desiree had neatly laid out for him. The shirt was brand new and had brightly colored soccer balls with the sports logo Nike in blue. "I hate that shirt!" Josh yelled as he threw it against the wall.

"Josh, we're not playing games this morning! Get dressed." Desiree scooped up Tabitha and carried her to the kitchen, plopped her in a chair, where she sat quietly and waited for Cheerios. Desiree spread butter on wheat toast, and then apple jelly, Tabitha's favorite. She looked at her daughter's angelic face, wondering how both Josh and Tabitha had come from the same womb having such radically different temperaments.

Josh came bouncing into the room dressed, not in the soccer shirt Desiree had given him, but an old faded t-shirt with a bleach stain through the hem. He knew this was

11

inappropriate to wear to school, and he beamed brightly as Desiree tried to ignore his effort at getting attention. "What kind of cereal do you want?"

"I want Fruit Loops," he said, placing his face directly in front of Tabitha's, breathing heavily and blocking the path of her own spoon. Tabitha began feverishly swatting at him. Then abruptly, Josh slapped Tabitha in the face. Stunned, Tabitha dropped her spoon and stared red-faced up at her mother. With her bottom lip quivering Tabitha said, "Josh is mean." Josh burst into mocking tears and let out a fake heart wrenching scream. Desiree stood at the counter drinking her morning coffee and felt her anger begin to boil as she screamed. "Josh stop! Don't be spiteful to your sister, she wasn't bothering you."

Josh rose from his chair, anger flashing in his eyes, "You always take her side. She hit me first, almost knocked my teeth out with that spoon." He then pointed to a three day old scratch. "Look! You're just gonna let me bleed to death! You don't care about me! I hate you! I hate you!" He ran from the room. Desiree lifted Tabitha and tried to soothe her tears, she loathed this routine. Shortly she would find him, and then console him in order to get him to school on time, and herself to work by seven.

Once they were all strapped in the car and headed to the sitters, Desiree began to relax. Work sometimes seemed like a retreat, she felt so empty inside. There was so much pain and even more anger since the death of her husband. He was only thirty two, much too young to die. The constant memory of that day spread through her body like a cancer. It rose beneath her skin, self-pity. How ironic, thought Desiree stoically, that such an imaginary cancer should cause her hair to fall out without chemotherapy. With each memory of her husband, with each confrontation from her children, and with each loss of her hair, bitter seeds grew.

Tabitha and Josh became leery of making new friends, wondering if friends would leave as their father had. Tabitha had horrible nightmares, often crawling into bed with her mother. Desiree had told them on more than one occasion that their father was a guardian angel in heaven. "His new job is looking after us," she tried to explain. But that explanation was starting to unravel, strange things were cropping up. Desiree thought about the kitchen sink refusing to drain, clogged with pumpkin bits and pumpkin seeds. It had been stopped up all weekend, but on Monday evening Desiree found it clean and shiny, draining with a swish. She had no answer but thankful all the same. Money was tight during the school year and plumbers were expensive.

The following day Tabitha dragged her white rocking chair into the TV room. Her rosy cheeks and brown curly hair bounced with each tug. It was her favorite chair, together Desiree and Tabitha had painted pink daisies all over it. Then, Desiree had stenciled Tabitha's name across the back in bright green paint to match the leaves. Four year-old Tabitha smiled as she drug the chair over the stack of cars and trucks Josh had left lying in the middle of the room. She blew air out of her cheeks and wiped her brow, after finally reaching the precise place she wanted the chair, Tabitha put her hands on her hip and exclaimed, "No broken." She sat down and began rocking joyously. Desiree couldn't remember if the chair had in fact ever been broken. She hardly had time for either of her children now, but was more focused on work and school. She felt like she was waiting for everything to be over so she could live again. "I'll exhale after I finish this semester, after I get this term paper finished and the children's dentist appointments and John's things removed from the house. There was always

14

something she was waiting for, some event that needed to take place before she could start living life again. Right now she wasn't really living but merely going through the motions.

She wished she could stop and hold Tabitha, stop long enough to make a real day for the children. She wanted so badly to be the mom she used to be before the accident. She wanted so badly to feel again or maybe the dilemma was she felt way too much? She glanced up at John's picture on the mantle and felt her heart ache and her throat close. Focus Desiree, focus.

Ruthie

Chapter 3

Walter sat on the worn park bench. His only worldly possession was a small wire cage with a clasp door. Inside sat Walter's beautiful homing pigeon, Jackie. She had feathers the color of a grey-blue sky when the clouds are thinning. Jackie also had a map inside her brain, a map that no matter where Walter traveled would carry her home.

Walter had always been impressed with homing pigeons ability to travel thousands of miles in only two short days. Some believed these birds have the ability to orient themselves with the earth's magnetic field or even the sun. He stared at the bird's stout body, short legs, and smooth plumage that lay tightly against her skin. Walter knew the truth. He had raised Jackie for years, winning blue ribbons and trophies. First, the bird had to be healthy, with no broken feathers, but the biggest factor in winning was a nest with young babies. Jackie's concern for her young would bring her back in a flash. Yet, it had been a long time since Jackie had any young. Walter thought about this often, because he wanted to return home to his own family. Like a crippled bird, his wings were broken, so was his heart. His own map had become confused and he no longer knew which direction to turn.

The note was still tucked safely in a holding device on the back of Jackie's leg. It had been almost a year since Walter had released his homing pigeon. Almost a year since he returned one last time to collect his bird. No matter how many miles of road was under them, one thing was certain when Walter released Jackie, she would only go home. Now he felt just the opposite, home had become a sorrowful place filled with loneliness. Walter had returned to collect his friend. He stood on the porch and unrolled the frayed message, written in bright red ink, all capital letters, one word, one word that cut through the heart of Walter. The note simply read 'unforgiven'. Walter had placed it back in Jackie's holder a constant reminder of his mistakes.

He had wanted to stay and had tried to stay. At first it wasn't so bad his daughter had helped to look after Ruthie. In the beginning he only had to be concerned with her forgetting the small things, like, if they had eaten dinner, who had called on the phone, or what day of the week it was. But, as her disease progressed, she soon began to forget more and more important things. Once, Walter had found her wandering the streets of the quiet neighborhood where they had lived for thirty years. She had been aimlessly looking for something familiar, not remembering the color of her front door, or the flowers she had planted in the window boxes.

Eventually, Walter had conceded to have Ruthie placed in a facility where she could receive constant care. His daughter, Brenda and son Daniel, visited daily, bringing small items to make her room a little more cheerful. Then the Alzheimer's caused a speedy downward spiral. Walter had come that morning to visit her like any other morning with an egg mcmuffin, small coffee and juice. When he entered her room, she looked at him as if it were the first time they had ever met. She seemed startled, "What's your name? Are you Charles's friend?" Charles was one of the male nurses assigned to her room. "No dear, it's me Walter, your husband." he pleaded.

"I'm married?" Ruthie said nodding. "Oh yes. Did you feed the cat this morning and milk the cows?" Ruthie hadn't lived on a farm since she was a girl.

"Yes Ruthie," he sighed, "it's all been done." He reached for her hand, but she swatted him away and began to sing 'Oh Susanna!' While rummaging through her vanity drawer, she picked up her dental floss, dropped it back in the drawer and was holding her toothbrush and looking at it as if it were a foreign object. She held it up and then she rubbed the bristles across her cheek. She kept picking up the tube of tooth paste and looking at it, finally after giving up in frustration she made her way to bed. There she stared wild eyed at the bars on the window that kept her inside.

Almost as soon as she had lain down, Ruthie pulled herself up again from the bed. She walked to the window peering out into the courtyard where she and the others would sit on sunlit mornings. She began to reach for the picture, Daniel, her son, had brought her. The sterling silver frame was decorated with ropes that formed a bow at the top. It was a studio picture he and his wife had made of their grandchildren, Jessie and Jessica, the twins. Suddenly she turned toward Walter, "What's your name again?" Her brow was creased and her thoughts seemed a hundred miles away. The doctors had warned Walter that she would indeed, begin to not recognize her family members. Eventually, she would not even know Walter, he guessed that day had come.

Walter rubbed his face with his hands. He became abruptly aware of his twisting stomach and the lump in his throat. She was his life, the mother of his children, his soul mate. He met Ruthie when he was just out of the army. He had known from the first moment he laid eyes on her, that God had placed Ruthie on this earth for him to love. To look at her now, the hollow unknowing eyes, to leave her all alone in the bed with just four walls, was too much for him to bear. Walter couldn't take the pain.

He drove away each evening to the home they had shared. The rooms held memories of laughter, heartache, and the love that they had carried for over forty years. Now the walls seemed to close in on Walter. He found the air thick and heavy, just like his heart. The doctors began to warn him that the Alzheimer's would eventually prove fatal. Ruthie would not only forget her loved ones, she would also forget how to swallow and then the unthinkable, she would forget how to breathe.

He sat at home the evening of their anniversary. He had visited her at the nursing home that morning, bringing a dozen yellow roses. They were always her favorite, since the first one he had given her only one month into their relationship. He remembered it as if it were only the day before. They had been to the lake, with a picnic lunch and they had spread his wool green army blanket under an old huge oak tree, talking until sunset. He had almost forgotten the one long stemmed yellow rose taken from his mother's bush. He had wrapped it in crepe paper and laid it under the lunch in the cooler to stay fresh. Ruthie had been so appreciative. Unlike the other girls he'd dated, she was content just to sit with Walter, enjoy nature and listen to him talk.

They held hands and walked along the bank of the lake. Walter had not even dared to kiss her yet, even though they had been together for a whole month. Walter knew Ruthie was special and these matters take time. "You can't rush love," his father always said and Walter didn't dare tarnish their relationship. Ruthie had placed the single rose in a book to press. She had kept it all these years. Walter wished terribly that he could have that Ruthie back, but she had died some years ago leaving behind a shell, a demented Ruthie, who was often crazy.

Walter sat in the living room and remembered the day's earlier events with sorrow. He had carried the bouquet down the corridor and held the yellow cut roses out to Ruthie. "Happy anniversary," he sang. Ruthie had stared at the bouquet and smiled at Walter. Taking the roses in her arms, she inhaled their aroma. His heart leapt, she remembers, he thought! But then she turned toward Walter with that faraway look. Her once auburn hair was now gray, muffled and boisterous. Her lips looked as if they had been colored with lipstick. She was wearing one of the terry cloth robes her daughter had brought her months before. It was pale blue, and seemed to match her eyes. Walter had always loved the color of Ruthie's eyes, her eyes reminded him of the bright blue sky, the color of a rainbow, when violet mixes with green. Still, it wasn't so much the color but the love that radiated from them. Now, no matter how hard he searched, he could not find any connection in her eyes. She continued to stare at him blankly, and spoke frantically that she would call the police and have him arrested for trespassing on private property. "This is private property, you know," she stated matter-of-factly. Walter could not find words to say and instead sank into a chair and pressed the call button for a nurse. Charles brought Ruthie a sedative and she quickly fell asleep. Walter lay caressing her back on the bed as he had for so many years, holding her close to him and longing for her to know him. "Oh Ruthie, I miss you so. I miss your spirit for life and your ability to restore the most dejected creature's joy. I miss you more and more each day. I don't want to live without you Ruthie." He patted his hand so softly over her hair and down to her cheek.

"How can I live without you? How can I wake up one morning without you?" He looked at her lying there peacefully and wished it could be like it was.

It's no use he thought, she will only get worse and I can't stand to see her like this. He ran his hands over her face and kissed her cheek. He said his goodbyes and made the decision never to return, not even for the funeral. No one would understand if he came back then. No, there was nothing else to do to stop this agonizing pain of seeing her this way. As he spent his last night in the home he and Ruthie had shared, he thought of nothing but escape.

The Bitter Root

Chapter 4

Tabitha liked playing in the sand box outside, her father had built it especially for her. She loved running her fingers through the warm grains of sand and scooping them up with her bright red shovel. She also liked playing in the woods behind her house, there was a small creek and she could make mud pies or chocolate brownies. Sometimes, she'd take her mother's old kettle pot and fill it with water from the creek, then she would add rocks, grass, and dandelions for flavor. A big wooden stick helped her stir her concoction she referred to as rock soup. Josh usually left her alone when she played chef. He wanted instead, to ride his bike through the woods, up the dirt trails to his secret hideout. That's what he called it.

"It's got a bed and everything." He told his mother all about his discovery during dinner. Desiree didn't know whether to believe him or not. He had fabricated so many stories, it was hard to tell when he was telling the truth. Desiree convinced herself that it was probably the clubhouse of another neighborhood child. Still, Josh swore he had seen an elderly man lying on a dirty quilt one day as he rode by. Desiree's over worked mind began to spin. Could someone be living out there, behind my property? Surely not. She dismissed the idea quickly, thinking of all the homeless shelters, police officers, and the neighborhood watch. Goodness gracious the neighborhood watch would notice something. More than likely it was just another one of Josh's stories. Still he did seem animated when he talked about it.

She worried about Josh and his fabricated tales. Desiree had taken both children to a counselor after their father's death. She had continued with their visits faithfully. Both children were asked to draw a picture of their family unit on their last visit. It had been quite some time since John's death and Desiree wondered what their little hands would create. Would their pictures still hold an image of their father or would he be gone. She pondered how life could change so drastically and how all it took was one day.

Desiree picked up her son's drawing. Josh's artwork displayed his father much larger than anyone else in the picture, yet he was lying on the ground. He placed images of his mother, Tabitha and himself next to a large tree, holding hands. Everyone was smiling and seemed to be enjoying a day of sunshine and blue skies. Desiree looked at the image of John he'd drawn and felt a stab inside her heart.

Tabitha had drawn her father as well, only she drew him much smaller than her mother. Desiree looked at the huge shoes she had placed upon her feet, they were bright green and looked clownish. Tabitha had given Desiree hoop earrings and a mane of hair she coveted. She had also sketched a house like structure in the background and a small creature that resembled a cat, but Desiree couldn't be sure. She then drew Josh outside her circle of family, giving him no feet or clothing. He was only a stick boy with eyes and limbs, limbs with no ability to walk or reach. When she inquired about this, the counselor said, "I think she likes the idea of him squirming in his nakedness, with no feet to carry him. He must pester her a great deal!" She smiled as she said it, but Desiree wondered if she knew the extent. The psychiatrist had continued to assure her this was all normal behavior. "They are just having a difficult time dealing with such a loss. This is still in the healing process. Your children will be fine. Get them involved in activities. Meet new people." She then turned her expertise upon Desiree.

"Maybe you should start to date, it has been way over a year. You have got to get out there and start living life again, you and I both know John would have wanted you to. Desiree, when the children see you healing and becoming excited about life again, they too will relish in it."

Desiree's thoughts flashed back to her husband, her role as wife and mother. She was still grieving him. She seemed to not be able to get away from his ghost. She even steered clear of one of her professors who wore the same cologne as John had. So many things still stirred her emotions, from movies they watched together, to a song on the radio that took her back to a moment they had shared. Each photograph was still in place, his clothing still hung in the closet of their bedroom. She knew it was unhealthy, but she hadn't had the strength to deal with her emotions. She glanced down at the solid gold band still wrapped around her finger and knew it was time. Could she make new memories with someone else? Each time a man seemed interested, all she had to do was mention her children and he seemed to disappear. Her mind wandered to her thinning hair. Do men even find me attractive? What if the children hated them and her for trying to replace their father? She didn't need that now. Her mind raced and raced and she began to tense up just thinking about it all. Could she love again?

"I'm fine," she said rather abruptly, and then fought back the tears that were welling up inside her. Desiree left the office with one thing on her mind, she'd focus on her goal instead. She wanted to become an attorney, to punish the man who killed her husband, to put behind bars forever the one person that stole her life. She knew where he lived, Desiree even knew where he worked. He had been careless, stupid, and downright selfish. She reasoned that anyone who would get behind the wheel of a car drunk must be all those things and worse. She didn't know how she would pay him back, but she would die trying. He didn't see her children's faces as their father lay lifeless in a casket. He wasn't there when his body was lowered into the cold hard earth.

"The bugs are down there." Josh had said, "Don't put my Daddy down there with the worms and spiders! Why can't he stay in your room in his coffee?" Josh thought his father had fallen asleep and just needed time to wake up again, like the fairy tales he'd heard. What do you say to a six year old who's just had his father ripped from him?

Tabitha had been too young to gather it all in. She cried for her father every night for the first three weeks. She kept asking Desiree, "When will my daddy come back?" How does one answer such questions?

Then, Tabitha began drawing pictures of him with wings hovering over everyone from heaven. Anger and rage began to well up inside of Desiree. Why should Benjamin Stewart walk the streets free just because he was a juvenile at the time of the murder? Desiree wanted her own justice. She was only waiting for his next mistake.

Benjamin had cried in the courtroom that hot August day, his arms and legs shackled inside the bright orange jump suit. He had plead his case. His words had evaporated into air. He had stolen her husband's life and for what?

Desiree had been raised in church. She knew the words Jesus had spoken. Her parents had taken her to Sunday school each week. She had memorized countless verses, winning prizes for her commitment to the knowledge of the word of God. "Forgive and you shall be forgiven. Love your enemies. Pray for those who persecute you. Or was it prosecutes?" The verses and chords rang through her. The verses came across often, but she could not let go of the anger. She knew Christ words about forgiveness, He said, "If you don't forgive others, your heavenly Father won't forgive you of your sins." Well, that was just a chance she'd have to take. If she rotted in hell so be it! Sometimes the pain and hatred was so bad she'd cry out to God, "How can you expect me to forgive him? Help me to want to forgive him, because I don't want to and I think it's unfair for you to ask me!"

The bitterness had sucked away all her joy and was tugging at her health, mentally and physically. The roots of the seed of hatred she had planted for Benjamin had begun to go down deep. She had just one goal, and that was to pay back Benjamin Stewart. She wanted him behind bars and the others who so carelessly drove drunk and took innocent lives. She wanted him to lose his life just as her husband John had lost his.

The Note

Chapter 5

Walter placed the small steel cage on the ground. In his worn coat pocket, his hands fumbled with the grains of corn and wheat for Jackie to eat. He let the grains run through his fingertips for a minute, and then he opened the door slowly and reached into the cage and placed Jackie on the ground. Jackie began to eat the seeds he had sprinkled and wander under the shade of the trees. Walter then reached into his other side pocket of his coat for a small notebook and pen. Sometimes, he wrote notes to his deceased wife to clear his head, other times he just recorded his thoughts. On this day, he did not know what to write. He had plead for forgiveness. He had read the obituary column daily, looking for the name

31

of his beloved wife, until the dreadful day came. He had hitch hiked the three hundred miles home. Even though he swore he'd never return, he knew he had to. Stopping at a florist he pulled his credit card out to purchase the yellow bouquet of roses. The clerk had shaken her head, saying, "This card is expired, do you have another one?" Walter had tried to explain his situation. Feeling sorry for the old man, the young girl at the counter placed a single rose in Walter's hand. "Here sir, you can have just one for free. If I give you any more, I'll get into trouble."

Walter took the single yellow rose as he had so many years ago. He thought about how history does indeed seem to repeat itself. He stumbled down the cobble walkway of the florist to the sidewalk that headed towards the town square.

He waited patiently all day for family members and friends to leave the funeral home. His heart was so heavy and a part of him just wanted to come clean, apologize and make his presence known, but he had left everyone else to deal with something he should have been man enough to deal with. He had walked out on his family and his wife, at a time when they needed him most. Oh, if only they would understand. He felt like the most wretched man alive, nothing more than a coward, a weakling, and he was repulsed by his condition. He wished he could go back, but life did not allow such indulgences and now he wished it was him lying there.

"Oh God, why didn't you take me first. Ruthie would have done such a better job being here for the children. Why did you keep me here and let her leave? You said the two would become one flesh, it's in your word, and yet here I sit without half of myself! I am incomplete without her, just take me home." Walter lowered his head, and sat sulking until the sun had set.

The rose still looked somewhat fresh as he made his way to the parlor. The front door of the funeral home was locked, but Walter made his way to the back and tapped on the door lightly. A stooped man, with kind eyes, greeted Walter. "Good evening sir, can I be of some assistance to you?" But, before Walter could speak, "The viewing has just ended for Mrs. Ruthie Kendal, but you can resume seeing her tomorrow at 10 am. We will be conducting the funeral at that time, sir."

Walter reached for his wallet and pulled out his license. "I am the husband of the deceased and have travelled some distance to get here, can I please just have a moment?" Walter pleaded with his eyes to the man, waiting, and holding his breath.

"Certainly sir," the man nodded and opened the door. "Right this way sir," Walter followed him down a long hallway and then up some steps to the viewing area. "You have 10 minutes sir, please see yourself out the way you came in."

Walter nodded and thanked the man. Each step he took towards the casket felt like concrete blocks were encrusted to his shoes. He choked up at the sight of her, his lovely Ruthie, finally at peace. He placed the single yellow rose in Ruthie's hand tenderly and kissed her cheek. Her pretty blue eyes were closed now and he knew she was better off. He also thought his daughter Brenda, and his son, Daniel, would see the rose and know that he had come to see Ruthie one last time.

Walter knew that he had left them with a heavy load to bear. He could only imagine what it was like towards the end. He thought that somehow they would understand his pain, but then he had retrieved Jackie the following week. Jackie held the note that carried so much pain, 'unforgiven'. His daughter was angry and Walter knew it. She was too angry to forgive him and he guessed he didn't blame her, but would she stay angry forever?

He tried to think of people in his life that he had held a grudge against. He tried to think of instances in his past that he had never forgotten, wrongs and deceit that lingered and hurt. His brother had once borrowed five hundred dollars from him when Walter really couldn't afford to lend it, but it was his brother and he'd been laid off for some time. Later, after he'd gotten a job at a larger company, he had never offered to repay him. Even when he knew Walter was having tough times. He smiled, remembering what Ruthie had done to correct the problem that was slowly driving a wedge between them. She waited until Jack, his brother, had an almost brand new riding mower for sale and phoned his wife Jill. "You know, I think Walter could really use that mower Jacks selling. With Jack still owing us the five hundred he borrowed last May, we thought maybe we'd just call it even. Lord knows Jack's plum forgotten about that or he'd of paid Walter back by now, and Walter's just too kind to bring it up." They received a check in the mail the following Monday, but that was still different. Walter couldn't think of anyone he knew doing something this terrible.

Walter placed Jackie back into the cage and folded the small spiral note pad over and placed it back in his pocket. He had no words to say, what could he say? The memory of visiting Ruthie one last time lingered as he made his steps towards the soup kitchen across town

Benjamin

Chapter 6

Benjamin Stewart lifted the box of French style green beans, and then proceeded to place them in even rows on the shelf. A hurried younger lady with two children unknowingly rolled her cart into the heel of his foot. Benjamin grimaced and shot her a look of pain.

"Oh, I'm so sorry. I didn't…" Her words muffled into the distance and she continued on, turning the corner. Benjamin looked at his watch; twenty more minutes and he'd have to do his community service work at the school for the Blind. It had been sixteen months since the accident and he was still having nightmares. Benjamin had not yet driven. He had completed the alcohol classes. He had worked to pay each fine. Benjamin knew he should have been charged with murder but his alcohol levels seemed to have been dismissed. He hadn't driven since. Just thinking about getting behind the wheel of a car, made his mind freeze. He'd feel dizzy and nauseous. Benjamin had flashbacks where he could hear the tires screeching, the glass shattering. He could see the body of a man lying ever so still. He knew he'd have to live with this memory the rest of his life. He clocked out at the computer and made his way out the back of the grocery store. The rear of the store was lined by dumpsters and truck deliveries; Benjamin turned down an alley between two of the businesses. He took the joint out of his cigarette pack taking long draws, he held the smoke deep in his lungs. Yes, that's better, he thought.

He walked down Gardner Street, and then turned the corner of Huet Street. He entered the Dunlap School for the Blind, signed his name on the visitor log sheet and waited for the director to give him his assignment. The assignments usually consisted of Benjamin passing out the lunch trays, mopping the corridors and emptying trash bins. Two girls walked down the hall, staring straight ahead, tapping their canes in a similar motion. Benjamin wondered what it would feel like to live in total darkness, at times he wished he were blind. Then he wouldn't have to see the blue minivan that followed him home some evenings. He wouldn't have to read the horrible letters she sent to the school or stare into the eyes of the children who would never see their father again because of him. Benjamin felt the anger rising, his pulse quickening as his temples throbbed. He hated her almost as much as he hated himself. She knew nothing about him. He paid for his mistake each day. Benjamin walked down the hallway and spotted Marcie Owens. She was the one good thing about the Dunlap School for the Blind, she was also there to pay a penance, and Benjamin always looked forward to seeing her.

"Hello Benji!" she said, as her words curled around her thin paper lips. She never called him Benjamin. He liked the pet name she used. Marcie wore a pink cashmere sweater that day, revealing cleavage Benjamin could appreciate. Her long blonde hair was thin and straight, charged with static from the cold. The small wire rimmed glasses framed her green cat like eyes. Benjamin thought they gave her a look of sophistication.

"I brought the ink-dot pictures you wanted to see and Kenny picked up a six-pack of beer for us. Do you want to go to the park when we're finished here?" Two more girls rounded the corner their canes outstretched leading them. Marcie jumped in front of them and started doing a silly dance, waving her hands frantically she stuck out her tongue making faces at the girls that they would never see. Benjamin tried not to laugh, remembering that it wasn't their hearing which was impaired. He knew Marcie meant nothing cruel by it, she just liked having a good time.

"So are we on for the park?" she asked once more. Benjamin felt his cheeks turn three shades of red as Marcie smiled one of her brilliant smiles.

"Sure," he said, "sounds great."

They left the Dunlap School at four and hopped in Marcie's 73 Super Beetle, which to start needed a hill and a push to pop the clutch. Benjamin's tall lanky frame lowered into the passenger seat. His brown wavy hair was pulled back into a ponytail with strands left unkempt, which blew in his face. He brushed a strand aside and looked at Marcie who shifted into third gear. "What a knockout," he thought. If she knew the truth about my past she'd never speak to me again. She felt Benjamin's eyes upon her and turned to meet his gaze.

"What?" she said, rolling her lips into an almost invisible smile that made Benjamin wonder?

He picked up the portfolio she brought and studied the black ink pictures she had drawn. They were dark yet stunning, all the tiny dots forming a male torso, his muscular body etched in skilled fashion. He was faceless, and she had started the picture at the neck then worked her way downward. He flipped the sketch pad and studied the next drawing; it was a grouping of sunflowers, their petals tumbling downward. "Sweet," he said, turning towards Marcie, not knowing if he meant the pictures or her.

They reached the park, grabbed the beers and walked down a worn path that led to a huge rock nestled in the creek. In the summer time it was a happening location, but on this cool November evening, pure solitude. They made their way jumping from stone to stone, careful not to slip into the icy waters; until they each climbed atop the massive boulder. Marcie uncapped her beer bottle first and felt the cool liquid begin to calm her nerves. Benjamin followed suit, his breath clearly visible in the chilly air. The time they spent together felt so comfortable to Benjamin, it was as if they had known one another in a previous lifetime. She had been the first person he'd opened up to since the accident.

"Look!" Marcie said, startling Benjamin out of his daydream. "There's an old man over there by the trees."

Benjamin turned his head just in time to witness the pigeon take flight across the crimson sky. A piece of paper floated peacefully through the breeze, traveling north in their direction followed by a peculiar old man with gray hair and a scraggly beard. The old man's head was lifted upward and he began to walk more briskly, until eventually he was standing directly in front of the two youths. In one hand he held a cage, his other cupped his eyes as he peered towards the bird.

"You lost your note." Benjamin said, eyeing the faded paper. Walter didn't speak, his focus was on the beer bottles and the fact that his mouth was as dry as a cotton ball.

"Sure is cold out here," said Walter, as he flapped the long trench coat, flipping up the collar to break the wind. Marcie uncapped a beer bottle and presented it to Walter who seemed very thankful.

"Do you live around here?" She asked quizzically, adjusting her glasses which had left a red ring upon her nose. She guessed he was homeless by the looks of him, but one could never tell. Marcie once had a professor who looked every bit as homeless as this man. She gazed upward at the homes which lined the cliffs surrounding the park.

"No I'm just," Walter stopped, not knowing how to answer. "I stay here and there," he said, taking another swig from his beer bottle. About that time, Jackie landed by his feet and began to coo. Walter knelt down and placed her in the cage. Then he ran his fingers through his silver hair and tried to recall the last time he savored a beer.

"So are you from here?" asked Marcie.

"No, I am from a little town called Barkley, if you blink you'll miss it. It's in Tennessee, that's where I'm from originally. I'm just visiting here awhile."

Benjamin's thoughts at the mention of home shifted to his own place. He had a one bedroom loft he rented from a friend at the grocery store. The old lead painted walls were peeling. The kitchen windows view was a concrete brick building. To say the least, it left much to be desired. He wanted to have Marcie over, but had been too embarrassed. Maybe after he finished with his community service work, he could get a second job and spruce it up a bit. But, with his track record, it had been hard enough to find employment at the grocery store.

The old man finished his beer and placed it back into the empty slot of the beer case. "Well thank you," he said. "I must get going now, it's almost dark and I have a six o'clock appointment. I volunteer over at the homeless shelter. Always take my bird, the kids love her."

"It was nice to meet you," said Marcie, as she introduced herself and Benjamin.

"Names Walter Kendal and it was a pleasure as well," and with that they watched him disappear into the woods, the cage swaying as he walked. Benjamin glanced at the ground where the tattered note still lay.

"Wait, sir, you forgot your ..." But it was too late, Walter was already out of sight.

Benjamin reached down and picked up the paper, his cold fingers began to unroll the worn note. He could just faintly make out its letters bleeding together, forming one word, one word that left Benjamin perplexed 'unforgiven', was all it said. 'Unforgiven', Benjamin almost laughed at the irony of how one word could describe his life. How could he ever be forgiven for murdering a man? Yes, the word seemed to sum up his circumstances. He stuffed the crinkled paper in his pocket and pondered his future.

Bradford

Chapter 7

Desiree opened the thick manual and began to study for yet another exam. It was Saturday and the children were keeping her distracted with their frequent interruptions. She hadn't gotten far into the first chapter when the phone rang. It was Bradford Stiltz, one of the three attorneys she worked for at the firm. "Sorry for bothering you at home," he said, "but I have some information I wanted to share with you, and was wondering if you could be of some assistance? I'm dealing with MADD, mothers against drunk drivers and since you've witnessed it firsthand I brought your name up. They're looking for another spokesperson for their June conference. You know we never seem to know who to go after, the person pouring the drinks, the cashiers selling to underage teens, or the careless drunk drivers. I was just thinking about your particular circumstance and thought you'd have a lot to offer!" Desiree was moved by his interest in her situation and by the idea of meeting others like herself. Desiree also felt he was a sincere man and did not reflect the other partners at the firm.

"Bradford, I think a support group may be just what I need. Except I didn't lose a child to a drunk driver, I lost a husband," she glanced at the mantel to study the framed portrait of John then quickly shifted back to the text in front of her.

"That doesn't matter," he said. "Every case is different and just as valuable to the group. Would you like to meet me for dinner and we could discuss the format?" Bradford secretly hoped she'd say yes, he wanted to get to know her better and had always found her refreshingly down to earth.

Desiree watched as Josh stuck his feet on the back of Tabitha's rocking chair and began to push her forward. Tabitha held on to the arms and let out a squeal, "Stop it, Josh!" Desiree eyed an orange Kool-Aid stain on the carpet and a trail of Lego blocks that Josh had dumped in the middle of the room. She sure wasn't getting much accomplished here and decided to take him up on his offer. "Okay Bradford, I need a break anyway."

They were to meet at Christy's, an upscale restaurant in the older historic area of town. Desiree made a quick call to her grandmother then went straight to her closet. She strummed through the slim pickings, making sure not to cross over into John's clothing. She had tried to make herself go through them and box them up for the thrift store, but hadn't had the strength or the time. Finally, she decided on a sweater dress with matching jacket. The jacket was short waisted with a white collar and matching cuffs. She then chose a pearl necklace and earrings John had given her on their third wedding anniversary. She clasped the strand around her neck, combed what hair she had forward and grabbed her black beret off the dresser. Her stockings were snagged but she was able to stop the run with clear fingernail polish and a blow dryer. A pair of black pumps and an hour later she pulled the minivan into the parking lot of Christy's.

The spaces lined with Mercedes and Volvo's told a lot about the clientele and the establishment. Desiree let out a sigh and hoped Bradford was buying. She watched a blonde with a short chic haircut get out of her sports car. The woman looked exquisite in a red wool coat and matching scarf. Desiree looked down at her outdated dress then waited for the blond to enter before she stepped out of her old mini-van. "I don't fit in here," she thought, as she studied her reflection in the mirror of her compact. She applied fresh lipstick and tried to reassure herself.

Bradford Stiltz was already seated at the table. A candle flickered in the dim lighting, casting different angles across his face. Desiree made her way across the bar towards the table. On spying her, he quickly rose from his seat and pulled out her chair. She lowered herself, crossed her legs and let out a sigh of relief to see Bradford dressed so casually. He wore khaki pants, a blue button down oxford, and leather slip on loafers with no socks. She found this to be peculiar in winter, but also a tad bit sexy. His rough yet handsome features seemed to stir up desire in her she'd lost somewhere.

Bradford cast a glance over Desiree appreciably, "You look very nice tonight."

"Thanks, Bradford so do you," Desiree blushed in spite of herself. She was not used to seeing him outside the office atmosphere.

The waiter approached the table and greeted Desiree. "Can I bring you a drink, perhaps a glass of wine?"

"Ice tea, please."

"Make that two ice teas," Bradford told the waiter, who nodded as Desiree smiled with approval.

Desiree felt at ease with Bradford, he was charming and talkative, showing a genuine interest in her personal life. She had rarely seen this side of him at the office due to the hectic schedule he kept, and it was a nice change of pace. Although there had been times when he stopped by her office and chitchatted, Desiree had too much on her mind to pick up any vibes. The server returned with the ice teas. They were raspberry flavored and garnished with fresh peaches. "We'll have an order of calamari and the baked Brie for starters, how's that sound?" he looked towards Desiree for agreement.

"Sounds great. "She said.

"So, are you sure this is something you're interested in? I mean it's not too soon?" Bradford raised his eyebrow and looked at Desiree contently. "I wouldn't want you to feel obligated if it's going to bring back memories you can't handle right now."

Desiree shifted legs, uncrossing with the left. Her hand rubbed the shiny pearl strand ... "No, it's alright," she fumbled for words and before she could finish her train of thought Bradford began again.

"I can't even imagine the pain you and your family have been through." He looked at Desiree candidly, "You're one of the bravest women I know, to have been through so much and yet able to keep your head on straight, raising those children alone and school, your work at the firm...it's so unreal how you've managed." He continued to talk about her until she was blushing. After what seemed like only minutes, the waiter delivered the appetizers, refilled their teas and was gone in a wink.

Desiree shifted uncomfortably, and took a bite of her calamari. She wasn't used to compliments. "Strong woman, brave...Wow! He's something," she thought. "He's smart, sensitive, and just plain sexy." She eyed the gorgeous blonde she'd seen in the parking lot and remembered why she was there. It's just a business dinner, she kept telling herself, not a date. Plus, there was the stupid hat atop her head. She swallowed the apple slice dipped in the warm brie and felt her cheeks flush as his olive green eyes met hers.

"No, I think it`s a great opportunity. If I can just stop one person from getting behind the wheel intoxicated or make the laws tougher on those who have, then I've done something."

Suddenly, Desiree wanted to be out of the spotlight, "So tell me, Bradford do you have any children?" She had already noticed the empty ring finger on his left hand. "Stop it!" she said to herself. "What are you doing?"

"As a matter of fact I don't, but I'd like to one day." There was a long pause. "Well, actually Desiree, that's not true. I… well in my first year of grad school my fiancée, Patti, became pregnant. She was working on her masters, and well, we just decided not to keep it. You see, her parents were strict Catholics and she gave it up for adoption. That being the lesser of the two evils. She had a son. I guess he'd be just about grown by now, I think about him often. After he was born, I couldn't even look at a baby without wondering if it was mine. Patti never was the same. Although it was her decision, somehow I think she still blamed me. I offered to go ahead and move up the wedding date, but she said she wanted to finish school, teach and not be tied down with a baby, 'for Christ sakes I'm only 23 she'd said'. By the time I thought I'd convinced her to keep it, she changed her mind and moved in with her aunt."

"I'm so sorry," Desiree spoke from her heart, pain and loss was something she knew first hand. Wanting to change the subject again she inquired on the conferences, where they'd be held, and if her schedule would allow. After briefly going over the details, Desiree remembered her grandmother. She talked and talked, the time escaping her in such great conversation with Bradford until she glanced at her watch. "I really must get going." She said, "It's getting late and I need to relieve the babysitter. It's my grandmother, she's getting up in age, but still able to chase them around. She just loves the children. I don't know what I'd do without her. Listen, keep me posted about the conference." Desiree stood up and placed her hand bag over her left arm and held her right hand forward to shake hands. "It's been a real pleasure Bradford. Thank you for dinner."

With that, Bradford took both her hands in his. With the softest brush of his lips, he kissed one and then the other. "No, no, the pleasure was all mine," he said.

Secrets

Chapter 8

Josh rode his dirt bike up the steep hill and followed the trail he'd worn until he came upon the area where Walter stayed. He leapt from his bike letting it crash abruptly to the ground. He then pulled the cotton hood of his sweatshirt down and scratched the top of his head, while he surveyed the area like a sniper. He reached down lifted a water jug, inspected it and then placed it back on the ground. He walked a few more feet to the wool blanket folded neatly by a tree. "Evidence," he thought. "Now she'll believe me." An old rusty can sat next to the jug. Josh quickly inspected its contents, "Hum? Seeds, bird seeds?" Josh wasn't sure. He sat the can down and picked up a flannel shirt, underneath lay a bag of butterscotch candy. Josh pulled one out, he

54

knew he wasn't supposed to take things especially from strangers but he thought only one wouldn't hurt. With his mother away for the evening, he planned on hiding out until Walter returned. He was going to catch the old geezer if it was the last thing he did, then his mother would believe him. He knew he lied a lot, but he told the truth as well. His mother was always referring to him as 'the boy who cried wolf'. Well, he was going to put an end to that, he'd show her. Josh picked up his bike and slowly walked it behind two tall oaks, raised the kickstand, then bent down and lowered his rump onto the cold ground. He unwrapped the piece of butterscotch, popped it into his mouth. "Now, then, I'll just wait," he said to himself.

Walter was tired from the day's activities. He wished it was spring and he could finally make his way back home. He missed his children, and especially his grandchildren. It was time, Walter was lonely and he longed for Ruthie so much. Sometimes he wished he were already dead, lying under the earth next to her.

Walter had been working at the soup kitchen across town. It was volunteer work, of course, but Walter didn't mind. He enjoyed preparing sandwiches and soup for the hungry, plus he got a hot meal and a fresh cup of coffee to boot. The soup kitchen gave him something to do until nightfall. He crossed Brier Street, then Oak Wood Dr., making his way to the path just behind Wild Wood Circle. He wished he had some whiskey to cut the wind that was sharply nagging at his bones.

Walter had tried to sleep at the shelter on several occasions when the weather was unbearable. It was always over crowded, with small children crying and the musty smells of body odor and urine. Walter liked the woods, they were quiet and peaceful. He passed a large stone, stepped over a fallen branch, and caught sight of what he thought was a possum out of the corner of his eye. He finally arrived at the spot where he'd been staying. He set his birdcage down and spread the blanket over a section of earth that was flat. Then taking off his shoes and wadding a shirt up under his head, he stared up at the sky that was just starting to darken and closed his eyes.

Josh peeked through the tree limbs, his heart drumming in his ears. He could see the old man lying on the blanket. Somewhere in the distance a sycamore tree was unpeeling its skin and Josh moved closer. The snapping of a tree branch caused Walter to raise his head a bit, just as Josh jumped from his hiding spot. "I caught you," he said.

Walter jolted from the unexpected voice and the sight of a small youngster with unruly hair. He sat up and eyed the child who had a familiarity Walter couldn't pinpoint right off. This caused a small fraction of annoyance in Walter, like the name of a movie you can't recall or a distant acquaintance you can't place. Then he remembered the photograph framed in silver, sitting atop the mantle next to his younger sister's. He had also witnessed his temper tantrums in the mornings, as his mother tried to coax him into his seatbelt. He was a Levite, all right.

"What are you doing here?" Walter asked.

"Spying on you," Josh sang, as he raised his eyebrows in Colombo fashion. "I caught you and I'm telling my mother!"

"Telling your mom what? Is it a crime to go camping?"

Josh looked confused. He had been camping before with his father but they had taken a large tent, sleeping bags, and a stove to cook on. "You're camping?" Josh asked quizzically.

"Well, sure son, I like the woods. Plus, I brought my pet bird, Jackie."

Josh was intrigued, he wanted a pet, but his mother refused. She said they'd have to wait till she finished up her schooling. "What kind of bird is she?" asked Josh. "Can I pet her?"

"Well, I'll tell you but it is a secret. I bet you can't even keep a secret."

"I can too," screamed Josh.

The old man turned his back towards the boy, bent down and released the catch on the cage door.

"Jackie is a homing pigeon with beautiful blue, gray feathers. See those seeds over there? You can feed her right out of your very own hands, if you don't tell anyone you've seen me?"

Josh had to think for a minute, he had never fed a bird before. Did he want to tell his mother and be right for once or meet Jackie? "I won't," Josh said, wondering if he could actually keep a secret. He knelt down by Walter and put the pieces of corn in his hand. "It tickles," he said as the bird's head bobbed up and down. "When are you going to be done camping?" asked Josh.

"Soon," said Walter. "Real soon."

"Where do you live?" asked the boy.

Walter hung his head and reached deep into his pants pocket, pulled out a knife and unfolded the small blade. He then chose a branch that was twisted like a snake and began to whittle. The wood shavings fell in a pile at Walters's feet. Josh watched as the old man began to carve snake eyes with the pointy tip of his pocket knife. He held it out for the boy to inspect. Josh ran his hand over the creamy smooth wood.

"That's nice," he said. "Will you be here tomorrow? Or are you going home?"

"Well, Josh, it's not that simple. I'm not sure I can go home right now. I'm afraid I've done something I terribly, terribly regret. I've made my children very angry. Haven't you ever done something that made your parents angry?"

Josh looked sad. He knew he did lots of things wrong. "But you're the father," Josh said, "you can't get into trouble. The children always get into trouble, not the parents."

"Not in my case, that's why I had to leave."

"Oh, I see," Josh's forehead crinkled up like a paper bag. "My father had to leave too."

"Where did your father go?" Walter had wanted to know for some time now what exactly had happened to him.

"He's in his coffee, in heaven, some bad man hit him with his car."

"Oh," said Walter, "I bet you miss him very much." Walter laid the branch down, reached into his back pocket and pulled out a picture of Ruthie. "This is Ruthie," he showed the boy, "and she is up in heaven with your father."

"Oh," said Josh. "Maybe they're friends?"

"Maybe," thought Walter.

A loud voice echoed through the trees. "Joshua Levite, you get home right now!"

Josh jumped to his feet and scrambled for his bicycle. Walter then put his right hand out, "It was very nice meeting you Josh, and I'm Walter, Walter Kendal."

Josh clasped the old man's hand, uncertain at first. Then he looked deep into his eyes and felt safe, a feeling he hadn't felt since the death of his father. Josh hopped upon his bicycle. "See ya, Walter. I've gotta go."

"Bye Josh, remember our secret."

"I will!" The boy smiled as he pedaled off towards home, thinking about how neat secrets were.

That night, Desiree, stood in front of her full-length mirror. She twirled around naked, inspecting her calves, thighs, buttocks, and waist. She allowed her eyes to travel upward to her breast, which she now held in her hands. She had forgotten that she was still a woman with desires and emotions and what it felt like to be attracted to a man. "Could someone like Bradford find me appealing?" she wondered. Smiling at her reflection in the mirror, she then untied the striped scarf from her head. Running her fingers through her thinning hair she decided to cut it all off in a short spiky style she had seen in a magazine. Feeling sexier than usual she slipped on a silky black chemise instead of the flannel PJ's she normally wore. She crawled into bed, and then drifted off to sleep, with thoughts of Bradford Stiltz's soft lips upon her hands.

The Lie

Chapter 9

Marcie pulled her long blonde hair back and twisted it upon her head in a sterling silver clasp. She chose a pale green turtle neck and brown corduroy pants, sprayed on the perfume she'd stolen from Banana Republic and surveyed herself in the mirror. Her stomach was upset and fluttering with anticipation as she grabbed her car keys and headed for Benjamin's place. He'd finally invited her for dinner.

Benjamin was stretched out on the plaid sofa in his living room. He decided he had made a mistake inviting Marcie over for the evening. "She's too good for me," he thought. "She's from a wealthy, educated family. What could I possibly offer her?" He chugged the beer bottle, his sixth, and felt uneasiness inside. I'll just tell her I'm a murderer, I'll just throw it all out there, and then she'll go away. Yes, that would be easier than pretending I'm something I'm not. Once she finds out about all my mistakes, she'll see me in a different light. The doorbell rang and Benjamin stared through the peephole. It was her alright, looking quite sexy with her hair pulled back. Benjamin messed up his own tresses and opened the door slowly, acting as if she had just awoken him from a deep sleep.

"Hi Ben!" She walked right past him, plopped down on the couch and silently counted the line of empty beer bottles. "So this is your place?"

"Yah, it's my castle." He smiled showing the small white teeth that looked like a babies. Marcie's eyes skimmed the room, while Benjamin faked an unnatural yawn. There was a poster of Jim Morrison and a recliner that looked like it had seen better days. The kitchen was small, with a glass table and two chairs that didn't match.

"I thought you were cooking dinner for us?" Her eyes gazed around the room, noticing each detail, a candle in a decorative glass bowl, a black and white framed picture of John Lennon, and a bookshelf filled with cheap paperbacks.

"Oh well, I drank a little too much last night. I don't think I'm up for anything."

"We could go out and get something," she said, her heart hoping.

"I'm not really hungry," Benjamin lied.

Marcie walked to the kitchen opened the ugly green refrigerator and uncapped a beer. 'You're not getting rid of me that easy,' she thought. She sat down in the worn recliner and smiled at Ben, who was trying to act as if he didn't notice. Benjamin reached for the remote and strummed through the channels nervously. He ran his fingers through his long stringy hair and lit a cigarette. He hated the fact that he liked her so much. He never thought a girl like Marcie would go for him.

"Yeah, let's go out," he said abruptly, grabbing his boots. They were black with chunky heels and zippers on the inside that went up to his ankles. He wore black pants, a dress shirt that was silky and buttoned down, a black leather coat, hat and gloves. Marcie had noticed he always wore black, his signature color. He was eccentric, mysterious and she was intrigued by the fact that she couldn't figure him out.

She grabbed her keys and they hopped in her Volkswagen, "Where to Ben?"

"I don't care, you pick the place." He hung his head down and wondered what he was getting himself into.

"Do you want to drive?" asked Marcie, thinking that would get him in a better mood. She wondered why he didn't drive, maybe he just couldn't afford a car. She knew he'd been in trouble with the law, drugs she thought. Her niche was thievery and it had stumped her parents, considering she could have whatever she wanted. But stealing had been a thrill for her ever since she'd watched "Breakfast at Tiffany's."

"No, I hate driving. I get sick and dizzy, the road seems to buckle under me, and I feel as if I can't breathe."

"Really," Marcie was shocked. Most guys loved to drive, most guys loved cars. "What happened, were you in a really bad wreck?"

Benjamin's thoughts flashed to the man he'd killed, his mangled body, and the sirens flashing. Oh how could he tell her? "My fiancé died in a car wreck." He seemed to blurt the words out from nowhere.

"I'm so sorry, Ben. I didn't know. What happened?"

"Some guy ran a stop sign, hit her head on. I was driving."

"Oh my God, Ben! I'm so, so sorry!"

"Yeah well, that's why I walk everywhere, plus I drink too much now to drive anyway."

Marcie pulled into the pizzeria overwhelmed. She wanted to hold Ben and comfort him. She couldn't imagine how terrible that night must have been. "So how long ago did this happen?"

"Over a year ago. I just moved here to get away from it all. Been in trouble ever since. My parents had this big wedding planned. She was Jewish, like me. They were so happy for us." He pulled a strand of hair out of his eyes and cleared his throat. "So what are we having, pizza or calzones?" He was out of lies and wanted to talk about something else.

Marcie's mind was running a thousand miles a minute. She was starting to understand all the answers to the many questions she had. So that's why he walks everywhere and drinks so heavily. They entered the restaurant and ordered a veggie pizza to go. There was a silence between them as they headed back to Ben's place. All Marcie wanted to do was console him, make him feel better. They entered the apartment and Ben grabbed some plates and a couple more beers. He took off his coat and took a baggy out of his side pocket. He pulled out some rolling papers and went to work at twisting up a joint. Marcie was relieved, they needed to break their sullen moods. She hit the joint, inhaled deeply, and then laid her head on his shoulder. Benjamin rubbed Marcie's thigh through her cords, thinking what a great story, this might just actually work. It had been a long time since he'd seen any action. He looked at her eyes, her pale creamy skin and said, "Gorgeous."

"What?" Marcie's nose crinkled up as Ben placed his hands on her face.

"I said, you're gorgeous, absolutely breathtaking!"

Discoveries

Chapter 10

Walter lifted the rock and retrieved the key, then walked through the hallway and flopped down on the leather sofa. Not feeling as well as usual, Walter picked up the remote and strummed through the channels, he'd noticed his hands were swollen that morning, along with his feet. He felt dizzy and decided to get some orange juice out of the fridge. There was a good five hours before he had to head to the soup kitchen and he needed a nap.

Along the mantle he noticed a picture of Josh. There was a studio portrait of both the children with their parents. Walter peered into the eyes of Josh's father, what a sad situation, thought Walter, to be so young and lose your father. The man looked friendly and he had a kindness in his eyes. Since the startle of Josh's first visit, Walter had twice now seen the boy. It had been after he came home from school in the evenings. On one of his visits, Josh had brought him a snack and they had sat and chatted about heaven and what John and Ruthie were doing. Walter remembered his little hand reaching into his coat pocket and pulling out two very smashed fig cookie bars. Walter didn't hesitate to shove them in his mouth and thank the little guy.

"Hey Walter, whatcha doing?" He had said as he held out the cookies.

"Thinking too much Josh, what are you doing?"

"I wanted to come see you and Jackie." His hair was a rumpled mess and his face was rosy from the wind.

Walter chewed the fig bar and looked at the small boy's excited face. "Well, come on, you can talk to her."

Josh sat by Jackie's cage and peered in, "Hello Jackie, it's me Josh, remember me?" The bird cooed and did a faithful hop around the cage as Josh giggled.

"Where's your mom, Josh? Does she know where you are?" Walter wanted to make sure Josh had not talked about their previous meeting.

"She's studying. But she can always look out the back kitchen doors and keep an eye on me. That's what she does, plus she's always got homework and anyways she lets me ride my bike back here all the time cause I'm bigger now. See?" He stood up as tall as he could and mustered up a look of adulthood.

"I see, you are getting big." Walter chuckled at the boy's personality.

"I can count to a hundred! Do you want to hear?"

"Not right now Josh, I have to get going."

"When are you going?"

"Soon Josh. I will be going home to see my grandchildren and you sure have made me miss them."

"Oh," Josh crinkled his nose and thought about how he had just met Walter and Jackie and how he really wanted him to stay. "Will you come back sometime?" Josh asked.

Walter didn't know how to respond and felt it best to change the topic. "I have to go into town now Josh. You run along home and back to your yard, it will be very dark soon. Your mom will be looking for you."

"Okay," Josh hung his head and told the bird bye, then waved at Walter as he made his way back down the trail. He had such great spunk considering all he'd been through.

He knew he was asking for trouble but truth was the kid had lifted his spirits a bit. After conversing with Josh, Walter missed his grandchildren something terrible and wanted more than anything to be home again. He snapped out of his daydreaming and sat the picture frame back on the mantle and eyed the telephone. He wondered if his daughter Brenda still had the same number, he picked up the phone and dialed the operator. "Yes, I'd like to make a collect call to a Brenda king."

"City and state?" The operator took his information and said, in her pleasant phone voice. "One moment, please."

Walter heard the rings and then his daughter's voice, "Hello."

"Collect call from Walter Kendal, will you accept the charges?" Walter heard the phone click and then the friendly operator's voice, "I'm sorry did you want to try your call again? We seem to have been disconnected."

"No, that's okay." Walter laid the phone in its cradle, 'disconnected'? He flicked through the TV channels once more.

"Tonya smith, come on down. You are the next contestant on the Price Is Right!" Bob Barker smiled cheekily, "Welcome Tonya." Two models in bikinis stood next to two Jet Ski's, their manicured fingernails and slender hands, brushed across the bright blue items. Walter shifted on the sofa, oblivious to the models that smiled at him from the television set. All he saw was a picture of his daughter and a far off voice saying, "Hello. Hello." Walter couldn't take it anymore, he needed to get home. Maybe his son would forgive him, treat him differently.

He walked to Desiree's bedroom, opened the closet and picked out a pair of navy blue dress slacks size 34 waist. A little loose now thought Walter, but that had been his size before he'd left. He chose a black pair of dress shoes, a pinstriped oxford shirt, dress tie and a matching belt. Walter peered inside the shoes. It looked like a 10 and a half, a little big for Walter, but nothing a couple pair of socks wouldn't fix. He ran the shower and looked through the medicine cabinet for some shaving cream. He was in luck. It looked as if this lady had kept everything he thought, as he lathered up his full beard. Walter showered and combed his hair back then put it in a rubber band behind his neck, at first glance it looked as if he'd just had it freshly trimmed. He splashed on some after-shave lotion and wadded his old belongings in a trash bag. Thirty minutes later, Walter peered into the mirror at his reflection and saw a man who'd been hiding for way too long.

Desiree picked up the phone in mid-ring, "Bailsman, Friedman, and Stiltz, how may I direct your call?"

"Ms. Desiree Levite, please."

"This is she speaking, how can I assist you?"

"Yes, this is Mrs. Platt, Josh's teacher. We've got him down in the office. He's complaining about his stomach and he feels a little warm. I had the nurse take a look at him."

"Oh, I see, well thank you Mrs. Platt, I'll be there as soon as I can." She made a quick call to her grandmother to let her know she was leaving early, and then headed for the school.

'All that bike riding in the cold air,' thought Desiree, 'and I have class tonight, besides my hair appointment.' She shoveled through the mass of children lined up for recess and made her way to the sick room. Josh was doubled over moaning, his hands holding his stomach. 'This better not be one of your pranks,' she thought.

"Hey Josh, what's the matter?"

"Oh, my tummy hurts so bad!"

Desiree smoothed his hair back and placed her hand on his forehead. "You do feel clammy. Come on baby, let's go home and put you to bed."

The nurse smiled then patted Josh on the head, while Desiree signed the check-out sheet. She guessed she'd have to miss class. By the time she picked up Tabitha from her grandmother's and called the pediatrician, her evening would be full. She arrived home ready to get Josh in bed and make her phone calls. Tabitha was carrying her bags and

Desiree had Josh's heavy little body slung over her shoulder. It took her a minute to get the door unlocked, balancing Josh and her purse.

Desiree hadn't noticed Walter until he sprang upward, his face contorted with disbelief. Desiree let out a heart wrenching scream that sent both children in a run, blaring as well, then Josh heard the man's voice.

"It's okay it's me, Walter. Don't be frightened, Josh."

Josh looked confused. He had Walter's voice but he didn't appear anything like the Santa Claus looking man Josh had befriended and he was wearing his father's clothes. Josh looked at the man, studying his eyes trying to make sure it was Walter, but Josh's skin was bumpy and chills were running over him. He felt a wave flutter in his stomach. Josh felt saliva rising, filling his mouth and then the vomit spewing all over the living room rug. Desiree stood motionless, she felt like she was in a state of shock. She didn't know whether to help Josh or run to the phone and call the police, plus she couldn't figure out how this man knew her son's name.

"Mom, it's okay, it's my friend Walter." Josh stated as he spit and gagged over the puddle in the rug. At this point, Walter was already scrambling to the back door running. His hands and feet were still swollen and he was out of breath. He was halfway into the wooded area behind Desiree's house when he fell, hitting his head on a large rock. The next thing Walter remembered was the ambulance driver putting him on the stretcher and raising him into the back of the van. There were police cars lined down the street and Desiree was holding Tabitha, crying and screaming, "What has this pervert done to my son? I need my little boy checked out, this man knew his name for God sakes! He could be some kind of child molester!"

Awakenings

Chapter 11

Walter awoke with a stabbing pain behind his eyes and a throbbing in his head that he hadn't felt since his younger days. Not that he drank much, but it reminded him of a bad hangover. He blinked several times and tried to focus on his surroundings. There was a beeping sound and several electrodes stuck to his chest. He could faintly make out a figure sitting opposite the room, it was a large police officer.

His eyes were widening now and it was all coming back in pieces, like a slideshow. Clips of Josh and Desiree, then of him running through the kitchen and out the back door. I must have fell, thought Walter. He moved his hand over his chest and up to the place on his head and touched something that felt like a giant mushy plum.

The police officer looked up from his field and stream magazine, he had a crew cut and black shades propped on top his head. Although it was winter, he looked as if he had just come from the tropics. He walked rather stiff and unnaturally, almost robotic and then in a cocky tone he looked at Walter and said, "Are you alert?" Walter shook his head as to nod yes and wished he hadn't.

"I asked you a question old man, do you understand me?"

"Yes, sir." Walter said with a sinking feeling in his chest that had nothing to do with the EKG machine he was hooked up to. And then Walter heard words he had only heard watching crime shows. "You have the right to remain silent, anything you say can and will be held against you in a court of law. You have the right..." his words became barely audible, then floated off into the distance.

The police officer then turned around and walked robotically back to his chair, picked up his jacket from the chair next to him and removed a can of Copenhagen. He snapped the can between his fingers three times, pinched a wad between his bottom lip and gum, picked up his Field and Stream magazine and proceeded to act as if Walter wasn't there.

Walter's mind began to catapult backwards remembering more and more. He touched his smooth shaven face, so close to new beginnings he thought. Then he wondered what would become of Jackie. Funny how that bird had become a part of him. Jackie knew every secret he had and all his inner fears. Walter had confided in her every trepidation, worry and loss he'd felt since the death of his beloved wife.

Walter knew now, he had far bigger troubles to overcome than his bird. The police officer was reason enough for him to wonder what would happen now. He knew he was guilty of breaking and entering, but other than that he wasn't sure. He wondered if Josh had retrieved Jackie or if the police had taken her. Poor Josh, what a great little guy. Walter thought Josh must have missed his father about as bad as he missed Ruthie.

The officer picked up a Styrofoam cup, spit twice and walked to the door of the corridor, "Excuse me miss." The nurse, a young girl extremely plain with an almost Rapunzel rope of hair braided down her back turned towards the officer. "I'm Officer O'Connell, and I was wondering since he is alert now, Mr. Kendall that is. I need an approximate release date, as close as you can get. I mean, besides his head, he's alright?" He leaned in closer to the woman and whispered, "That there is probably one of the worst child molesters I've seen, can't wait to get him in a cell if you know what I mean."

Walter heard the words 'child molester' and felt nauseated. A sharp pain jolted through his temple. Oh no, he certainly hoped they didn't think he could ever hurt Josh! Walter remembered the last words he'd spoken, "It's okay Josh, it's me Walter." What a foolish thing for me to do, he thought and now his mother is probably worried sick.

"O'Connell was it? "

"Yes, ma'am"

"Well no, officer, his heart is fine but his blood sugar levels are off the charts and we're still waiting for the CAT scan results of his head, not to mention the vitamin deficiencies."

O'Connell picked up his cup spit twice, reached his fingers in between his cheek and gum and with a flinging motion plopped it into his cup. Some of the excess prune looking juice slid down the side of the cup. The nurse looked repulsed and whispered under her breath, "You're probably the biggest child molester this side of Jackson County." She walked to Walter and asked if he needed something for pain.

Before Walter could reply the officer interrupted sharply, "I need an ETA," he said sternly looking at her with a controlling stare.

"Excuse me," she glared back, her eyes lifted with disgust.

"I gotta call the captain and give him an ETA, estimated time of his arrival. "

"As soon as I know something, I'll let you know first." She spoke to him as if she was speaking to a three year old and wondered how he managed to remember letters and codes like ETA.

Janice walked to the cart inspecting the bags of glucose, potassium and B12 that were feeding through Walter's veins. She grabbed a cup and filled it with water from the pitcher on the stand next to his bed and after helping him wash down a pain pill, she tucked him in gently and patted his hand. "I bet your noggin is killing you." He was so thin and so pale, he reminded her of the homeless she seen in the winter months. If he hadn't been dressed so nicely she'd have bet on it. Janice eyed the officer coldly and left the room.

Jackie's New Home

Chapter 12

Josh felt better after he'd thrown up, at least his stomach did. His mom kept asking him questions about Walter, she kept acting like Walter was a bad man. Josh was still confused to how Walter found his house and how he had looked so different from the night before. Josh had been jumbled up at the voice, it was Walters but it didn't match the face. But then he had peered into his eyes intently and he knew it was Walter. Walters's eyes had a twinkle in them that made Josh feel warm and safe.

He had been a little upset that Walter was wearing his father's suit. Josh remembered his father getting dressed in it for church. It was Easter Sunday and Josh's mother had bought him a matching suit. It was a nice, blue one. Josh wore a black bow tie with his. His father had on the special tie he and mommy had picked out for him, it had sail boats drifting on the water. Walter had the same tie on, tucked neatly in a Windsor knot. But deep down in Josh's heart he knew Walter was probably just borrowing it, after all he had snuck into Walters's campground? He was probably just waiting for him to see if it was okay to borrow it. Josh remembered that his children were mad at him and he probably just wanted to look nice. Then his thoughts flashed to Jackie. Who would take care of her now that Walter was gone? Josh could picture the bird all alone cooing in the darkness. He would have to ask his mother. Josh pulled back the covers and crept through the hallway. He could hear voices coming from the kitchen. As he tip toed, peering around the corner wall there were three police officers sitting at the kitchen table.

His mother was twisting her necklace back and forth, her fingers tightening and releasing. She was nervously chewing on her bottom lip, a habit she had picked up of late. Josh looked at her scowling brow and angry eyes. She looked more upset than ever, Josh let out a sigh. It's just like the day his father died, thought Josh, it's the same look. Josh walked through the kitchen just as the large police officer who had asked him so many questions cleared his throat rather loudly.

"Mom, I need to go get Jackie!" Desiree looked at him wondering what had happen to her son, she couldn't bear the thought of it all. "Mom, I need to go get Walter's bird, her name is Jackie and she's all alone!"

"We've already taken care of that little fellow." The officer with the deep voice said kindly.

"Well, where are you taking her?" Josh demanded.

"We will take good care of her, don't you worry."

Josh began to shout and yell over the other officers who had been there for hours, waiting on a full background check and inspecting the area.

"Can I keep her, please, please, please?" He pouted, his lower lip stuck out as he tried to activate tear ducts that had cried so much earlier that they were dried out now.

Desiree didn't want anything that belonged to that perverted old man. Anger penetrated through her very being. 'This is his fault. It all goes back to him! If Benjamin

Stewart had not killed my husband, my son would never have met this crazy old man and he sure as hell would have thought twice about breaking into my home,' she thought.

"No, now go back to bed Josh!" She felt sick inside, she'd have to call the pediatrician, her psychiatrist, and talk to an attorney from the firm. She instantly thought of Bradford and how only a couple nights before she was enjoying herself having pleasant conversation with a handsome mysterious man.

Josh stomped his foot and ran from the room, jetting straight towards the front door. You would have never known he'd thrown up three times that day as he ran towards the police cars. His mother and the officer with the deep voice and curly hair followed him. Josh pulled on the police doors but they wouldn't open. His mother grabbed him by his pajama top and gave him a quick jerk, "Listen here Josh, I know you are upset, we all are, but you can't keep the bird!"

Desiree started feeling guilty. She didn't know what all Josh had been through. She didn't even want to imagine the sick possibilities. She peered up at the officer, "Is the bird evidence or...." she hadn't finished her thought when he interrupted her.

"You want to take a look Josh, and see what your mom thinks?"

"Yes, yes," Josh jumped a foot off the ground his stomach did a flip flop and he felt a little nauseous, but only for a second.

The officer bent down into the back of his parole car and lifted the wire cage out. He gently sat it on the driveway for Desiree and Josh to see. Jackie cooed and jumped up and down like Josh had earlier. "What kind of bird is it?" Desiree asked, as if the officer would know.

"Looks like some kind of pigeon miss, not really sure though."

"Could it carry diseases?" She'd always been leery of bird droppings, ever since her puppy got infected with parvo when she was a child. She had never forgotten how sick he'd gotten. He wouldn't eat or drink, just laid there dehydrated and throwing up. Her mother kept saying, the bird droppings, that's what caused it.

"I don't know Ms. Levite, but I am sure you can take it to the vet and get it checked out. Strange thing about this bird, it's got some kind of holding device attached to its leg, as if to carry something." Officer Rolland said, he thought it was a homing pigeon.

Oh yes, Desiree had heard about them but couldn't remember what specifically, "Okay Josh, but only if everything checks out okay at the vet."

"Yes, yes, thank you, thank you!" Josh grabbed the handle of the cage and tugged, but it was useless he couldn't lift it.

"Hold on there Josh, the bird stays in the garage until it checks out! Got it?"

Josh agreed, he knew Walter would be happy when he got out of the hospital to find out he'd taken such good care of her! Josh just knew they would be very good friends. He kept telling his mother that, but for some reason it seemed to upset her more and then she got that look on her face that reminded Josh of the worst memory he'd ever had. He could still picture it as if it were yesterday, it was the black shiny coffee with his daddy inside and the men were lowering it into the ground. Josh decided to go in his room and be alone for a bit. He wished Jackie could sleep next to him but at least she was safe in the garage. Josh closed his eyes and tried to picture all the neat things he could teach Jackie, until finally after a day full of exhaustion, he was fast asleep.

Marcie

Chapter 13

Marcie felt so many emotions lying next to Benjamin. She always knew it would be like this, now that he had opened up to her about the car crash. If only she could get him to forget about his fiancé. She just knew, in time, he would become so engrossed with her, that he'd completely lose himself. She smiled thinking about how upset her father would be when she brought him home. She hated all their snooty, uppity friends and had spent an entire summer during her freshman year rebelling. She wore gothic clothes, black nail polish, heavy black eyeliner and shaved her head except for a row down the center that she died florescent pink. Then she pierced her nose, belly button and ear cartilage. But she soon tired of this and subsequently, she decided in her sophomore year to appease her father by playing the part of a well groomed CEO's daughter, which earned her a credit card with a hefty limit. If Benjamin would have known her before the transformation, would he have loved that girl, the rebel with a Mohawk? She ran her fingers across his hand and pressed in even closer to his body. She knew her mother and father would disapprove of Benjamin and that gave him that much more appeal.

Even though Marcie loathed her parents, her grandmother had made up for them immensely. Marcie found herself spending countless hours listening to her grandma Lilly reminisce about her past. She would help her with her flower gardens and with filling the countless bird feeders that lined her property. She even learned to enjoy hot tea and classical music. Lilly would serve tea in delicate china cups on a silver platter. There was a cream pitcher and a bowl of sugar cubes with silver tongs. Unlike her father, she didn't live in a large cold home but a warm inviting cottage, with a large yard and old trees that lined the property, giving character to its already charming surroundings. She couldn't wait for Benjamin to meet her.

"Benjamin, what are your grandmothers like?"

Benjamin shifted his leg and trapped her with it, over lapping her legs. He smiled up at her and wondered how to even answer that question. "What grandmothers? I don't have any."

"You mean they're both dead?" Marcie squinted up at him and held her hands up, "Well?" She wondered if Benjamin had any warm happy stories to tell, as she waited for his response.

"I'm not sure I even remember Marcie. My father's mother died before I was born and my mother's, well, I was young when she passed too. Let's see, I can faintly recall her hair, it was dark and always in a twisted bun. She would come out to the car and greet my mom when we came to visit, which was rare because Larry never liked to let mom out of his sight. Grandma always had a box of candy canes. They were yellow and blue and green striped, not like the Christmas canes you'd get during the holidays, but different. She died though when I was around 9 or 10, so I don't have a lot of memories of her, sorry."

"What was her name, Ben?"

"That I do remember, because it was so unique. Her name was Reedafae, but mom just called her Reeda. Why do you ask?"

"I was just thinking about how much you would love my grandma Lilly,"

"We never had much company, due to my dad."

"Why's that?"

"He's a first class jerk." Marcie looked into Benjamin's eyes and saw a fear she hadn't seen before.

"My father's a pretty big jerk himself," she said raising her eyebrows upward.

Benjamin wondered how long before this whole situation blew up in his face. He couldn't confide in her about his messed up childhood, she'd leave for sure then. He had to stop giving her pieces of himself. He was mixing lies with the truth, lies about an imaginary lover who had died violently. Benjamin knew that the man he killed had a wife who was telling a very different story. He hated himself, how could he let anyone love him when he couldn't even love himself.

"My dad can beat up your dad." Benjamin said poking her in the rib playfully.

"Stop it, Ben!" Marcie squealed.

"Somebody's ticklish?"

Marcie settled back beside him her thoughts multiplying. What was so evil about Benjamin's father?

She knew that her father was an important man, even as a small child she felt the power of his presence. Maybe it was the way his posture rose up and towered over you or his eyes that held yours and made you look away first. Yes, her father had the ability to make you want to impress him and yet you knew that it was useless. Her father had another side and it was this side that came out to charm, becoming the main focus even in a room filled with attractions. Marcie was always invisible, even to her mother who seemed to have lacked any nurturing qualities. Marcie raised up on her elbow and peered down at Benjamin, curiosity filling her. "Benjamin, what was your mother like?"

"I don't know Marcie, she was your average mother I guess. What is this History 101? You writing a book or what?" He frowned and wished the conversation would go elsewhere.

"Sorry, just trying to get to know you better." Marcie, wasn't sure why the men she chose always had walls so high and so thick. Now she felt a twinge of rejection, but of course this is what drove her. It was all she knew.

Marcie had learned how to gauge the emotions of those around her. She became an expert at their posture, gestures, eyes that dropped down and wouldn't look up at you. She had learned shiftiness, lips that pursed, pouted, and twisted, yes she had learned. Now she wondered how long it would take her to learn Benjamin and to become completely bored like her father with the countless nannies and secretaries he seduced and discarded. She'd get him to open up and then what?

Benjamin shifted on the couch, leaving Marcie alone with her thoughts. He knew she had fallen for the story about his make believe fiancé and he felt like he had found a way to cover his secrets. Marcie lingered over his long lean body and stretched out next to him. He rubbed her shoulder, then her arm, slowly caressing her. She could feel his breath on her neck and she was slowly becoming aroused, but it was different this time. Marcie finally felt like she had met the only other person who had suffered as much as she had. In time, Benjamin could be the person who she could let into that secret place. She had let him look into her eyes, clear down into her soul without shifting, without acting. She like him, had lived in that undisclosed space, covered brick by brick, and now with each caress she felt the tower beginning to crumble.

Benjamin slid his arm into the opening of her sweater and brushed his hand across her stomach. Her skin was so soft, he found himself pulling her towards him. His lips tasted hers and softly, slowly he lingered over them teasingly. Everything felt so right, it was as if her skin was licking up his, melting into him, morphing and changing into one. He didn't want to love her, he wanted to use her like he did the other girls, but with Marcie something seemed different. She'll eventually find out the truth, he thought, and then where will that leave us? He removed his hand from her top and placed it around her waist, then closed his eyes, he pretended to be content.

Marcie felt his spirit pulling away from her, even though he was holding her, something had changed. Marcie smelled his fear. She then began to wonder what his fiancé had looked like, she knew her name had been Debbie or Deborah, but that was it. Needing some space, she removed his arm and shuffled towards the restroom. She was so close to getting him to want her, she knew it, he was just scared.

"Do you care if I stay here for the night, I'm kind of buzzing?"

"Sure no problem." Benjamin's words made her heart jump, she knew now exactly what to do. Giving herself away had become a habit for Marcie that often left her feeling empty and used. If sex was what they wanted, why did they leave her afterwards? She had pondered this time and again, but with Benjamin something seemed different. If she didn't do something quickly, he might leave her and find someone else, but she needed him desperately. Everything would be different with him. She could help him get over his past and give him the courage to live again.

She sat down on the commode and peed, then looked into the medicine cabinet mirror and rubbed a spot of smudged mascara from underneath her eye, then unclasped her hair and let it fall. She then pulled off the turtle neck sweater and unclasped the second item, her bra. She pulled off her corduroys and socks, leaving on nothing but the black sheer lace low rise panties that held on to her hips. Marcie opened the bathroom door, not realizing that her body was sacred and not an offering of appetite. She walked past the back of the couch and made her way to the fridge. "You want another beer, She said?' "Sure, sounds good," Benjamin mouthed the words, wondering how the night would end.

Marcie strolled into the living room holding one beer bottle, which she uncapped rather seductively tossing the cap over her shoulder. Benjamin was suddenly more awake and more aroused than he thought he'd ever been in his life. Marcie tilted the beer bottle letting some of it drip down her concave stomach. She looked past Benjamin's eyes and said, "Thirsty?"

Promises

Chapter 14

Bradford Stiltz jolted from sleep and poked at the alarm clock that showed four fifteen am, before realizing it was the phone on the nightstand that was making such a noise. He fumbled for the receiver, dropping it once before getting the ear piece on his ear. On the other end, he heard a frantic voice sobbing in between sighs, it was Desiree and he wasn't able to make heads or tails out of what she was saying.

"Calm down Des," he said before he realized he had given her a pet name. "Slow down and take a deep breath." He heard her blow her nose into a tissue in the background, as her breathing began to adjust.

"Gosh Bradford, I am so sorry, I didn't even realize how early it was. I haven't been to bed yet." Then she heard his calm, but firm voice.

"It's alright Des, now tell me what's going on?"

Desiree did not know where to begin her mind was swooning and her thoughts were spinning. "Someone broke into my house and they were here when I came home with the children and they were wearing…" She began to sob uncontrollably and Bradford was shocked to hear this strong woman he had just had dinner with the night before so vulnerable.

"Would you like me to come over there, Des? I can move some appointments?"

Desiree wanted Bradford to come over more than he knew, she wanted any man who was strong to come in and rescue her at that very moment. "Oh God, Bradford, I am sorry, I need to calm down and get my head on. I have to be at work in a couple hours and I have to take Josh to the doctor," and she began to ramble on and then stopped herself. "Oh crap, how am I going to make it to work?" She wiped her nose again and panicked, "Yes, do you mind, I really need someone?"

"I'm on my way," he said reassuringly. Desiree hung up the phone and wondered what she had gotten herself into. She raced to the bathroom and peered into the vanity mirror, her eyes were swollen and there were dark circles under them. She washed her face and brushed her teeth and grabbed her baseball cap off the dresser. Her worn blue jeans and jersey t-shirt was a far cry from the dress clothes she had to wear for the office. She rushed through the house picking up toys and straightening up books, then put a fresh pot of coffee on and picked up the cups from the officers that had left. Then she plopped down in an overstuffed chair her mind racing from all the events. Letting out a much overdue sigh, she drifted off to sleep.

Bradford pulled his jeep Cherokee out of the garage and headed across town to Desiree's. He stopped at a bagel shop, ordered two breakfast sandwiches and an assortment of donuts for the kids. He knew she had two children and he'd heard a lot about them. Desiree had been a great co-worker and a friend to him in the work place. Bradford was used to dating women with children, he was the only person he knew over forty without any. He immediately thought of Patty and felt heartache, but that was the past and there was no changing it now. He knew he had a son and he knew he was out there somewhere. Maybe someday they would meet. Bradford had read the countless stories of twins separated at birth that had found each other. There were plenty of adopted children who ended up meeting their real birth parents, some out of pure mishap and others went to extreme measures to find their real parents. Some just wanted to know why? Others wanted to get medical records and some were angry at being discarded and feeling unworthy to be kept. It was sad and yet so many people were unable to bear children and loved these babies as if they were their very own. He hoped his son had been raised with love and affection.

Bradford turned into the subdivision and noticed the small houses that lined the street. Most of the homes were adorned with a welcome mat and a porch swing. Bradford missed the warm feel of his childhood home. He hated the large, cold neighborhood he lived in, with the neighborhood police as he liked to describe them. If his yard were brought under the scrutiny of the board and it wasn't the perfectly manicured image they had set they sent out someone to correct it and then shot you the bill. Everything is up for discussion, from the size of your fence and the type, attached or unattached garage, the length and type of your pool and the pool house. It was all too much for anyone to really enjoy. Bradford had bought it because most everyone at the firm lived there and they all convinced him that it was a good investment.

But when Bradford shut his eyes and pictured where he longed to be, it was an old home that had been restored. A home with character and enough land to fish and ride a dirt bike. He wanted to buy a head of cattle, even if he didn't know one thing about them. He wanted to grow gardens on that land and walk up and down the length of it and throughout it, and stand upon it and appraise it and say, "Bradford Stiltz you got you a little piece of heaven!" But so far he'd only had the courage to buy the jeep and he had taken a good beating on that from the guys at the firm, they didn't get him.

Bradford pulled in the drive, walked up on the porch and knocked on the brass door knocker, engraved with the name, 'Levite'. A small boy with rumpled hair and spider man pajamas cracked the door and peeked out a small split.

"Hello there, you must be Josh," the door opened wider as Josh peered upward at the tall man standing on the door step. "Is your mom around, Josh?"

"Yes, she is wanna see?" Josh opened the door a little wider and displayed a modest living room. Desiree was curled up in fetal form on an overstuffed chair, a white laced pillow and a crocheted afghan covered her body.

"Well do you mind if I come in Josh, she is expecting me and we work together, my name is Bradford," and he smiled at the boy who he'd heard had a horrible temperament.

Josh jumped up and down, "I gotta a new bird, and her name is Jackie wanta see?"

"Sure Josh, but let's be quiet and let your mom get some sleep." Josh took off flying down the three steps that led down into the den and then up three more that led to the door entrance of the garage. A large cage sat in the corner and a peculiar bird hopped up and down as Josh opened the door and began to reach in and pull her out. "Hold on there, buddy, are you supposed to let him out of the cage."

"It's a she," shouted Josh in a voice way too big for his body. "Her name is Jackie and I am watching her for Walter."

"Who's Walter?" Asked Bradford in a curious gesture. He knew about Desiree's deceased husband John, but he had never heard her mention a Walter.

"Walter is my friend," said Josh. "He used to live behind my house in the woods. He was camping out back there."

Bradford creased his brow and took hold of Josh's arm, "What happened to Walter?" Bradford asked sternly, frightened for what Desiree must have been through.

"Let go of my arm," Josh said, shoving him.

"Josh answer me. What happened to Walter?"

"The men took him away in the truck with the lights, he was wearing my daddy's tie."

"He was?" Bradford felt an alarm go off inside of him. "Walter was your friend you say?"

"Yes, I already told you and that's Walters bird Jackie. Walter had to run away because he did something bad."

"Oh is that so Josh? Well why don't you tell me all about what Walter did that was bad?" Bradford took his hand and began to describe the jelly filled donuts and the chocolate sprinkled ones, as they walked out to his jeep to get the box out of the seat. Bradford was trying to figure out how to go about this. "Josh was Walter ever mean to you?"

"No," said Josh with his head down.

"Did Walter ever touch you anywhere or do anything that scared you or made you feel uncomfortable?"

Josh looked at Bradford's face and decided he didn't like him or anyone else who was trying to get him to say bad things about Walter! "NO! I hate you! I hate you, leave me alone." He raced through the garage door and into the house before Bradford could stop him. Josh had even forgotten Jackie and had left her to be placed in the cage by Bradford, the bird squawked almost as much as Josh, and Bradford wondered what he was getting himself into.

He walked into the living room and gave Desiree a small pat on her arm and then began to brush the hairs out of her eyes. "Hey you," he said as she began to come out of her hard slumber.

107

"Oh God. Oh Brad, how long have you been here? Gosh Brad, I am so sorry. I laid on the couch here by the door so I wouldn't miss you...Who let you in?"

Just then she heard heavy stomps coming down the hall and a familiar voice yelling, "Mom, I hate him, make him leave!" Bradford smiled and told Desiree he had already picked up breakfast and called the office to notify everyone that they would not be in today.

"Oh God. Oh no. my grandma, I totally forgot to call her back," and with that she jumped up and grabbed the phone out of its cradle and before she could finish her sentence, began to cry again. Bradford was completely baffled at the complexity of it all and at the emotions he was seeing in a woman that hadn't displayed this much fear when she lost her husband John. "I'll have to explain later Grams, okay I'll drop Tabitha off shortly," and with that she was back in control. "Would you like some coffee Brad?" she asked, as she made her way into the humble kitchen.

"I would love some," he said. Just as he proceeded to follow her, a sleepy eyed beauty came tumbling down the hallway in a long pink nightgown, smiling at Bradford as if they were old friends. Hum, thought Brad, this might prove to be interesting.

Bradford reached for her hand and to his surprise she accepted. They tottered into the kitchen and he placed her into her chair as if it were the most natural thing in the world. Desiree turned and placed the cups of coffee on the table and asked Bradford if he needed cream or sugar, he looked into her eyes that were watering and said, "Desiree, I know you didn't wake me up at 4 in the morning to see if I use cream or sugar. What has happened, you say you have been robbed and the whole house is spotless, nothing turned or dumped out. Then Josh tells me some man was in your house and he was his friend and to top it all off, you have a strange bird in your garage with a holding device on his leg? What on God's green earth is going on here? I mean I am here for you, but you have got to fill me in. I am an attorney you know, and I want to help you, but what is this all about?"

"Oh God, Brad, that's just it, even I don't know what's going on. For weeks Josh kept telling me there was someone camping out behind our house and that he had seen a blanket and a can with seeds in it. Well Bradford, I just brushed it off, he has such a vivid imagination, if you catch my drift."

Josh ran to the box of donuts and pulled them off the counter into the floor. He grabbed a chocolate one and shoved it in his mouth abruptly. Desiree tried to pick up the mess and get Josh to go play in his room. "I'll make a bet with you Josh, okay? If you can go in your room and play quietly while Brad and I talk I will let you stay home from school today and I'll even let you take that bird to the vet."

"Really?" Josh said, his eyes huge. This was too good to be true thought Josh. "Okay," said Josh, "but you promised?"

"Yes Josh, and I never break my promises."

"You did that one time." said Josh.

"And just when was that?" Desiree peered into his big almond eyes.

"When you promised Daddy would take us to the zoo."

Desiree had forgotten all about the promise to the zoo and all about the ingredients she had sent John out to get so she could finish packing up the cooler full of treats for the children. "Josh go play in your room for Mommy, please."

Josh sensed a sound in her voice that he would not argue with this morning, a sound of fear. He turned and ran, then abruptly stopped at the hallway as his socks slid clear across the shiny hardwood floor. Desiree followed Josh and made sure he was willing to make good on their bet. He grabbed his Lego bucket and dumped it out in the middle of the room. "I am going to make Jackie a new cage," Josh said as he began to pick up pieces.

She came back up the hall and found Tabitha holding something soggy that used to be a donut, jelly was smudged on her face and she seemed to be enjoying her new found friend. "Hi Mommy!" Tabitha waved and smiled up at her.

"Hi, my sweetheart!"

Bradford had poured milk into the Sippy cup Desiree had set on the counter and they seemed to be having a good time together. "Carry on now," Bradford said, with his brows raised to show he was still waiting for the rest of her story.

"Well Bradford, like I said before I never thought anything about it. Then Josh gets sick at school and we arrive home early to find an old man wearing John's suit and tie sitting on my sofa as if it were the most natural thing in

111

the world. To top it all off, Josh knows him and even calls him by name, Walter or something. I swear Brad if that sick perverted old man touched one hair on my sons head, I'll have him castrated, even if I have to do it myself!" Her voice was cracking and Bradford sensed that underneath her tough exterior was a woman about to break.

"Come here Desiree," Bradford got up out of his chair and held his arms out to her and she held on to him as if she were on the sinking Titanic.

"Oh God, Brad, Oh God, what if he touched my son, what if he hurt him?" Tears streamed down her face and her nose began to run. Bradford continued to rub her back and pat her head.

"It's alright Des, it will be alright, I will see to that. That's a promise." He pulled her face towards his and looked into her striking dark eyes and said, "I never break my promises!"

Visions

Chapter 15

Walter sat up in bed and waited as the doctor pushed on the knot that was still the size of some type of fruit. Walter realized they always described it that way, tumors the size of grapefruits and cyst the size of oranges and the knot on his head a few days before had been the size of a plum. Now the doctor said, "Looks like you took a hard hit by the size of that walnut on your head." Then he smiled at Walter as if they were old friends and as if Walter wasn't an accused child molester. "Alrighty, the MRI looks fine and so does the CAT scan, so I guess as soon as we get your sugar straightened out, you should be on your way." He smiled again and then chuckled, adjusting his wire rimmed glasses and combing over his few strands of hair with his stubby fingers. "Yep, you'll be on your way home."

Walter found it amusing that he kept implying he had some nice quiet home, on some nice quiet street to go to, like the police officer with the black shades wasn't sitting across the room just waiting to cuff him. Walter thought about his options and he had weighed them carefully. He could call his daughter Brenda and beg for her to forgive him for deserting her and leaving her with Ruthie to care for all alone. Yes, he had even left her to bury Ruthie, "Ruthie." Walter said her name again, "Ruthie," the word seemed to glide across his memory like a wonderful movie screen and she was the star of the film. Each clip was a precious moment in history. The first kiss they shared and how he had went home that night and replayed it in his mind over and over again. The look of her eyes, the touch of her hand, her smile and then clips of her enjoying her iris garden. She wore a hat and gloves and carried with her an array of tools, she always wore dirt smudged on her face. Oh, she looked beautiful with those flowers as a backdrop.

Then there was the excitement of her first pregnancy. She had gone out and bought a baby rattle, two to be exact a pink one and a blue one, then she had gift wrapped them and placed them in his briefcase for work. He remembered opening the first one at his desk after getting her on the phone and asking her what the gifts were for. "It's not my birthday," he had said. Oh the excitement in her voice as she cried, "Open it, open it, and hurry!" And before he could say a word she had cried, "Walter, you're going to be a father!"

Walter snapped out of dream land and back into reality as a candy striper sat his lunch tray before him. It held salisbury steak, mashed potatoes, green beans and peaches in juice along with juice in a plastic container that he was far too familiar with opening for Ruthie at the home. Walter began to think about option number two, his son. But if the truth be told, Walter had always been closer to his daughter. He never had to compete with her, never had to impress her. He loved his son Daniel but he always felt so inferior to him. Daniel had the corporate job, the big home and the degree that Walter never had the opportunity to achieve. They were more like pals, but Walter needed an attorney and in a bad way. He couldn't even remember all the charges he had against him and now the mistake of talking to the child, what in the world was he thinking? Walter hadn't meant any harm and besides, the child was spying on him and not the other way around.

The police officer moved his sunglasses, placed them on top his head and glared at Walter as he began to eat his dinner. "Ole man you got it comin, you understand. We don't play them pedophile games here. You'll get whattcha got comin, hear?"

"But I never did anything," Walters's eyes pleaded with the cold, officer as he shifted his eyes away from him.

The officer looked at Walter as he made his way to the bed, "We'll just see about that, old man. We will just see about that."

Walters's steak and gravy traveled back up into his mouth, he forced it back down and waited for the officer to leave his bedside. There was another officer with copper red hair and a much kinder manner who came on Tuesdays and Fridays. Walter looked forward to those days, but it looked as if he would be leaving now. Walter wondered where he would be going, as he forced another bite of food down.

Walls

Chapter 16

Benjamin shifted and felt for his arm that had gone to sleep. He smelled a fragrance of apricots and tobacco as he placed his nose into Marcie's hair. With memories of the night before still fresh in his mind, he felt a sensitivity he hadn't felt in so long, he did not know how to react. He began to panic and then slid his arm out from under her, slipping quietly out of bed. He walked into the living room and grabbed his boxers. While putting on his jeans, he picked up his wrist watch and looked at the time, eight a.m. He never liked rising early and couldn't wait until his community work was complete and his friend Clark could hook him up with a restaurant gig, cooking over at Frank's

Steakhouse. He needed night hours and late mornings to lounge.

He walked back into the bedroom and peered down at Marcie. Man she was hot and a smart chick, not some dumb girl that couldn't take care of herself. No, Marcie was tough, he knew that from the first time he met her. He was not at all in her league, not even close. He had heard about her big shot father and she wanted him to go to her house for dinner? What was he thinking, he wished the whole thing had never transpired and now he needed to get rid of her. He wasn't good enough for her and once she found out the real truth about his past she'd hate him anyway.

He decided the best thing to do was refuse to get out of bed. She would want him to go out and get breakfast or mingle with society and he didn't mix with anyone. He pulled off his jeans and thanked a God he didn't know for Sundays, and then crawled in next to her turning his back toward her and facing the wall. He heard her stirring and closed his eyes pulling the covers over half his face. She slid her arm around his waist, rubbed his chest and pulled her body next to his closely. He tried to think about anything he could to keep himself from becoming aroused. 'Why did I let this happen?' He thought to himself, 'Why did I let her into my life, my miserable life?'

Marcie was wide awake now. The sunlight was coming through the cracks of the dark sheet over the blinds to keep any warmth or trace of morning light from entering. He blocked it all out and pretended to drift back to sleep. Marcie walked over to the window and pulled on the sheet.

"What are you trying to do blind me?" He rose up wincing at her and trying not to look into her gorgeous eyes or at her muffled hair and beautiful skin. Oh God, he hated this. He laid back down ignoring everything and pretended to be off to dreamland again.

Marcie lit a cigarette and inhaled deeply. This was going to be harder than she'd thought. She blew the smoke out and thought about their evening of lovemaking and how many times he had told her, "You are so gorgeous, so stunning." But then as the night became longer and she became more relaxed and sure of herself and their relationship, he had begun to talk about his fiancé that died and had even compared her to Marcie. She had brushed it off because he was a little drunk, but the more Marcie thought about it the more it bugged her; she crushed the cigarette butt into the ashtray. Would she always be compared to a dead lady and would he ever love her as much? She walked to his side of the bed and moved his arms and slid right in next to him and let his body cradle hers, then she drifted back to sleep. It wasn't until one o'clock in the afternoon that she had become tired of his charades and tired of laying there waiting for him to rise from the dead. She knew this was some kind of game and she was tired of playing it and upset that he would treat her this way.

She had shaken him twice getting only a grunt and a slight movement, now she was just finished. Grabbing her clothes, she went to the restroom to get dressed. His cell phone buzzed several times and he acted as if he slept that way every day. She knew better, she could feel his cold vibes. Grabbing her purse, her keys and her lighter she closed the door a little too hard on her way out. I hate men she said to herself as she climbed into her car, I hate them all. She rolled out of the parking space and popped the clutch, then reached for another cigarette to start the day.

New Beginnings

Chapter 17

Bradford lightly turned Desiree around to face him, "Now I want you to go shower and get ready, we have a long day to fill." He pulled her baseball cap down and covered her eyes flirtatiously and gave her a playful shove. He wanted to make all of this go away. "I'll get the children taken care of, now go on." He pulled Tabitha out of her chair and sat her on the counter and began washing her face and hands in the sink.

"Do you sand?" She asked smiling, "I have a sandbox wite out back and we can build castles and make stuff wiff it." Bradford thought she was the cutest thing he'd seen in a while.

"Maybe next time," he smiled and placed her down on the floor, patting her head. "You go play for a while until Mommy gets ready, okay?"

Tabitha headed in the direction of Josh and Bradford started making phone calls. He felt more like a man than he had in years, he felt needed. Desiree had given him a sense of being a part of something. He had had his eye on her for a while, truth was ever since the funeral, he knew those feelings weren't good. It was too soon and her heart needed time to heal. He had always been attracted to needy women, but Desiree wasn't the same, she was bold, strong, intelligent and such a caring mother. He wondered if she would ever want more children. He knew he was thinking too far ahead and he wasn't even sure of what she truly thought about him. But Bradford had a theory, if you go out on a date with someone, you are automatically trying to see if they are marriage material. He wasn't being deceitful about their last date. It was about MADD and Desiree speaking on behalf of those who had lost a loved one to drunk driving, but it was also a way for him to get her alone.

He knew Thomas Friedman, his partner at the firm was divorced, yet content to wine and dine a new beauty every evening. He told Bradford he had been taken so badly by his ex-wife Jenny that he'd never trust another woman, "Nope, no sir, no more alimony for me," he'd said. "As soon as I feel a tinge of emotion for one, I move on to the next. You can't trust these women today Brad, they are a whole new breed, leeches that want to suck you dry." Bradford somehow got a feeling that Desiree was different.

He sat down at the kitchen table and pulled out his appointment book and began to make calls. He had called the county circuit Judge's office but there was nothing on the docket for a Walter Kendal yet. After getting his background check something didn't seem exactly right, Walter Kendal wasn't your typical homeless man. This man was sixty seven years old and had no criminal history, not even a traffic violation. He was an honored veteran of the United States Army and a retired insurance salesman who had worked for the same company for forty years. Married forty two years to a Ruth Ann Kendal, he had two children, a son, Daniel Lee Kendal and a daughter Brenda Ann King, both of Barkley Tennessee. Something was wrong here, but what? Bradford called the police department and found the man he was looking for at a local hospital. "Walter Kendal, I'm not so sure about you," Bradford said aloud as he scratched his head and made a mental note of the charges.

Desiree yelled from the other room, "Almost ready Bradford, just let me get the children dressed." She pulled a sweatshirt over Tabitha's head and helped her step into her fleece pants. After getting both children ready, calling the child psychologist, the vet and her Grandma back she assured Bradford she was ready to go.

"Well let's go get Jackie then, okay Josh?" Josh looked up at Bradford and wondered if he could trust him. He seemed nice enough, but why was his mother being so kind to him, he wasn't sure if he liked that. "Okay," said Josh, skipping down the hallway. Bradford picked up the handle and lifted Jackie into the back of his jeep. Desiree fumbled with Tabitha's car seat and carried it to the jeep. They finally got everyone in and were headed to her grandmom's house.

Desiree was feeling a little embarrassed that she had let Bradford come over to rescue her. This was something foreign to Desiree. Even after John died, she hadn't burdened her family or friends, night after night it was all she could do to pull through without having a break down.

124

Desiree never was much on making friends. She was content to spend time with John and the children, Sunday dinners at grandmom's and an occasional outing with John's business partner Allen.

John and Allen had owned a sports shop that sold mainly items for the local high school. There were jerseys with their team's logo's, football and basketball equipment and uniforms. It was a small town and Allen and his wife Janet had been old friends. Janet was older and her children were already wearing the high school jerseys, while Desiree was still busy chasing hers around. Desiree didn't feel they had much in common and she had lost touch with her friends from the office after she had Tabitha. It was more economical for her to quit, stay home with the children and help out at the store than to pay for daycare.

She wasn't sure what Bradford could possibly see in a widow raising two children, most men scurried when she told them their ages. Wondering if she would be able to retain her composure throughout the day, she glanced at Bradford. Every time she looked at Josh it was all she could do to not shake him and ask him what that old man had done to him. She knew from reading her child psychology books that this was not the route to take, but she wanted so desperately to know what had gone on. Hopefully today would bring a relief of some sort, she had checked and double checked his little body for bruising in the tub the day before, but she hadn't seen anything.

Bradford asked her for directions from the freeway and she wondered how her grandmom would react to her bringing a man over. She hadn't confided in her about Josh, just that someone had broken into her home and had assured her that nothing much was taken and that the predator had been caught. The first appointment she could get for Josh wasn't until noon. Her trusted psychiatrist who had held them together after the death of John suggested Desiree take Josh to a friend who specialized in this type of counsel. They were going to the veterinarian's office for starters and the situation with Josh would have to wait. That darn bird she thought, why in the world did I agree to keep it? She secretly hoped it was sick or not meant to be domesticated.

Bradford pulled in the driveway and unbuckled Tabitha. Desiree decided that he could meet her grandmom another time and told him she'd just be a minute. She grabbed Tabitha's bag and opened the front door. "Grandmom, we're here." Her grandmom came into the room smiling as always. The lady never ceased to amaze Desiree, she was always positive and always cheerful. She dressed neatly, wore lipstick, made sure she set and rolled her hair each night and forever had something baking in the oven that filled her home with a savory aroma. "How's my best girl," she said as she opened her arms to Tabitha.

"Bradford is outside and he wought me donuts!"

"Is that so," Grandmom raised a curious eye towards Desiree and said, "Bradford Stiltz is outside and you didn't invite the likes of him in? Now I know I raised my granddaughter with better manners than that!"

"I know Grandmom but we have appointments and he's helping me with errands today."

"Well that doesn't excuse your manners and after all the nice things you've said about working with him." She raised an eyebrow and smiled her gentle smile, "I guess I'll have to go outside to meet him myself," and she marched right past Desiree towards the front door with Tabitha on her tail.

"Well hello there, you must be Bradford," she said, as Bradford stepped out of the jeep. "I'm Linda, but everyone just calls me Grandmom."

Bradford reached for her hand and said, "I sure have heard a lot of nice things about you Linda."

"Just call me grandmom," she said smiling and not missing a beat. "Now I'm making a peach cobbler, do you like peach cobbler Bradford?"

Bradford smiled and said, "Grandmom, I don't know anyone who doesn't like peach cobbler!"

He'd won her heart at that very moment, "Then I'll expect you to join us later for dinner?"

Desiree loved her grandmom so much, she was her rock. "Bye grandmom, bye Tabby girl," she said, kissing the top of Tabitha's head.

Grandmom peered into the back seat and waved at Josh, "Hi there Josh, how's my best boy today?"

Josh jumped up and tried to get out of his seat belt, "Grandmom, I got a new bird!"

"You do," she said, just as Jackie cooed and hopped around the cage. "Well you sure do and a big bird at that." Grandmom looked at Desiree and raised her brows, "What is all this about?"

Desiree raised her shoulders and let them drop as to say, 'I haven't a clue'.

"Bye bye, Josh!" Grandmom waved and took Tabitha by the hand and led her into the house.

Desiree felt her cheeks flush. "Josh you weren't supposed to tell her about Jackie, we don't know if you can keep her. It was supposed to be a secret."

Josh's heart sank, he missed Walter and their secrets. He missed talking to him about his father, he had never met anyone who had a family member in heaven with his daddy. He sure hoped Walter got better soon and he hoped they could be friends again.

Escape

Chapter 18

Walter heard that he would be released the next day. He had tried to call his daughter again but to no avail. He wanted to call his son but he just couldn't muster up the courage to try and explain it all. It would have to start with why he deserted his mother and then move on to breaking and entering, then charges of possible child molestation. Walter would rather rot in a prison cell, he just couldn't put this on his friends or family, they wouldn't understand, plus it had been over a year since Walter had spoken to any of them. Even if he could get a hold of his daughter, he could not handle the shame and humiliation he would cause the family. He just knew Daniel's wife would probably never let him come close to the twins now. Oh the shame of it all! How had everything gotten so out of control?

He wished he could go back and do things differently. He wished he could go back and stay till the bitter end but he just couldn't bear to see her like that. Ruthie was the one reason he woke up in the morning. Most couples grew comfortable together, he had listened to his buddy's at the insurance company as they talked about their old lady or some even referred to their wife as an old nag or hag. Walter just never could use such adjectives when he thought of Ruthie. With each wrinkle and each grey hair she became more beautiful than the first day they'd met. He enjoyed raising their children, but truth was, he enjoyed watching her take on the role of mother and the excitement in her eyes over each new discovery the children made. She was incredible. Ruthie lit up over it all, whether it was a first tooth, or a first step or even a first word, watching her was the true thrill for Walter. When she stopped breathing he stopped breathing.

He knew what they did with child molesters and at his age he didn't stand a chance. Glancing around the room, he noticed his clothes that had been placed in the plastic bag.

The guard in charge today was Officer Don, the red headed friendly man who never made snide remarks to Walter. He looked at his arm, there was still one drip bag, but thankfully he had been removed from the heart monitor. Walter knew that this officer usually dozed off in between the nurse checking his blood pressure and temperature. Feeling unsure about making it past the nurse's station, he decided it was worth trying. He had formulated his plan, he figured if he got caught it would be just one more charge against him. What did he have to lose?

He waited until the nurse left, and then he moved his IV cart to the side and slowly removed the clear adhesive tape from his arm. Easing the needle out gently, he raised his arm up, pressing down firmly until the bleeding stopped. He then tiptoed to the restroom, changed into the suit and dress shoes as quickly as possible, then opened the adjacent bathroom door. The room next to him had an older woman with several monitors hooked up to her. Walter slid over the floor tiles like a cat and peered through the doorway, two nurses were sitting at the desk conversing and rummaging through papers. It was early morning and the doctors were making their rounds. The hospital was filled with the bustle of food carts and visitors walking down the hallways. There was a dirty laundry hamper by the door filled with soiled items. Walter scurried down the corridor, his heart beating in his eardrum. He turned the corner and pressed the elevator button and waited impatiently for the doors to open. Walter had rehearsed up until the parking lot, then his plan became blurry. He figured he could hitch a ride with someone. His head was still pounding as he walked under the street lights that lined the parking garage. Keeping his head lowered, he continued to make stride clear across the parking lot to the express way. "Here goes," he sighed as he held out his thumb and never looked back.

The Messenger

Chapter 19

Desiree and Bradford pulled into the veterinarian's office and pulled the cage from the rear of the Jeep. There was an elderly gentleman with a Boston terrier on a leash walking and waiting by a tree for him to do his business. They entered the office and signed the registry log. There was a cage full of feisty kittens in the corner peeking in and out of the maze inside. Josh ran to the cage and repeatedly said, "Mom look, look Mom, can we get one please, please." His eyes begged and pleaded and his lip puckered.

"Now Josh, you and I know that cats and birds don't get along." Just then Jackie squawked as to say she agreed.

"Jackie Levite" the receptionist called, as if Desiree had already made her a part of the family.

Bradford picked up the cage and carried Jackie into the room and sat her atop the table. The receptionist looked inside the cage and snarled her nose to imply that she found Jackie to be a dirty pigeon and rather disgusting. "Dr. Waters will be right with you," she said and shut the door.

An elegant older lady with white hair piled on top her head greeted them. She wore mosaic rimmed glasses, hanging from a chain around her neck. She smiled at them and introduced herself then she peered into the cage as she open the wire door. "What an amazing creature," she said, as she pulled Jackie out of the cage and propped her on top her arm. "I see you got ya a little racehorse of the sky."

Desiree had no idea what they had, it just looked like one of the birds she considered a nuisance, one of the birds that liked to defecate on her car at work. But now Dr. Waters had her attention. "We just recently found the bird," said Desiree. "We were hoping you could help us out with it. We noticed the round tube attached to the leg, but weren't sure how it was used."

"Oh that is a holding device, and right over here should be a chip. Hmm, I don't feel a chip, but today most these birds are fitted with a band that has a tiny RFID chip in it which can be read when the bird comes home. At the home loft, the electronic scanner records the bird's arrival. Do you know these birds saved hundreds of lives during World War 1, if not thousands? Some even had cameras inserted to photograph the enemy and deliver messages to military planners." She raised her eyes at Desiree and Bradford, "What do you think about that?" But before they could answer she began giving them even more information. "These birds have been studied by university after university. Scientist believe they can navigate with the earth's magnetic field and find their way back, others believe they follow the same pattern you would follow in a car. They have been bred to find their way home from extremely long distances. For instance if you were to release this bird right now it would more than likely return to its home, be it hundreds of miles away. It's just fascinating. Yes indeed. But of course if you want to keep the bird that is up to you. "She raised her eyebrows at Desiree, then glanced at Josh who was surprisingly quiet. He knew now if Jackie were released she would go back to wherever Walter had come from. Yes, she would fly all the way to Walters home.

Dr. Waters carried Jackie to the sink and began to turn the faucet on slowly. She placed her finger under the water and splashed some towards the bird. Jackie jumped from her arm to the sink and began to take a bird bath soaking up the water and splashing uncontrollably. "These birds make terrific pets, but she shouldn't be kept in this cage much. You should let her out to fly around your neighborhood, she shouldn't run off unless you release her in a manner that will suggest returning to where she's come from, say an open field setting with arms lifted skyward. Do you have any idea who the owner could be?"

Josh spoke up in his loud voice, "She belongs to my friend Walter, but he's sick right now in the hospital." His eyes were smiling as he watched Jackie enjoy the water and splashing in the sink.

Desiree's heart sunk at the mention of his 'friend' Walter. She had had enough of Walter and could not wait to get to Doctor Lord's office and get to the bottom of what had transpired between them. The friendly Dr. Waters turned back to Bradford and Desiree and began to fill them in on how to care for the bird.

"You may purchase special pellets for Jackie filled with healthy grains and if the bird becomes inactive or sickly don't be scared to give her a little Gatorade and of course always fresh water in an area where water is available for her to splash in like she is now. Any other questions?" She placed her arm next to the sink and Jackie hopped back on and she placed her back into the cage.

Bradford looked at Desiree and then turned to Dr. Waters, "What kind of shelter should we build for the bird?"

"Well you have to be careful with that as well, nothing outside that would allow squirrels or raccoons access. But something tall and screened and of course as I have suggested let her fly around the neighborhood a couple times a day."

"Thank you Dr. Waters."

Desiree smiled just as the kind older vet opened a cabinet and handed them a bag of bird feed, "There you go, that should last you awhile." She turned and opened the door to leave. "Good day," she said and left them with their eyes on Jackie.

They had seemed to look at the bird in a whole new light and with a whole new respect. "So Mom, can I keep her?"

Desiree looked at Josh beaming at the bird and just couldn't say no, not after all he had been through. "Sure Josh."

"Yes, yes, yes," he chimed and grabbed her leg and waist holding on with glee. They loaded the bird back into the jeep and headed to Dr. Lord's office. Desiree held her breath almost the whole way there. She was so frightened and so unsure about so many things. She felt so many emotions and so many fears, yet she was grateful for Bradford and was thankful that God had brought someone strong into her life to help her at this moment.

Catnip

Chapter 20

Benjamin crawled out of bed and headed to the shower. He couldn't wait until he finished up his last two weeks at the School for the Blind, then he wouldn't have to see Marcie anymore. He felt sick at his stomach and sick of his life. If he had any spine or back bone he would have already finished himself off. He had thought about taking his life after the wreck and had been placed on suicide watch while in jail. Sometimes he thought about going back home and looking up some of his friends, but it just wasn't a home anymore after his mother died of cancer. His parents had adopted him. They had tried repeatedly to have children but had no luck at it. "That should have been their first signal from God that they weren't meant to be parents," he thought.

His father, Larry was an alcoholic and his mother was an Edith Bunker type who instead of repeating, 'Oh Archie,' said 'Oh Larry' constantly. She just worried herself sick. She spent her days trying to make sure his father didn't become upset, in hopes he would not turn into a monster, which had backfired more times than he could count. It was like waiting for the plot in a horror movie, you just never knew when it was going to jump out. Anything and everything could cause explosion. "Ben, did you drink the last of the milk? Benjamin did you just use the last of the hot water in the shower? Dammit Benjamin, If I've told you once I've told you… ahhh hell forget it, I would have to pick the stupidest child at the adoption agency!"

And then his mother would chime in, "Oh Larry, don't say that, that's a horrible thing to say Larry! Don't listen to him Ben, Don't listen."

And then his father would throw something, "Shut your pie hole, Grace, before I shut it for you." Then he'd stumble across the room towards Benjamin's mother and proceed to tell her the only thing more worthless than his son was her.

Benjamin couldn't wait to leave home. He couldn't wait to get away from it all and then his mother got sick with cancer. He couldn't leave her alone with that jerk, so he stayed until hospice came in and his father had to help wipe her bottom and wait to destroy his liver with his scotch after the nurses left. Benjamin had stayed and watched her waste away to nothing. He loved his mother but he had begged her time, after time, to leave Larry, she just didn't have it in her. He wished he knew where his real father was because he'd love to find him and just beat the living crap out of him. It was always the men who didn't want the kids, Benjamin knew that much. He had seen friends at school go through hoops to get the abortion money for their girlfriend so they wouldn't have to deal with the responsibility. He wondered where his real mother was. His real parents were probably able to finish up their degrees and get those cushy jobs, able to buy the big nice home in the suburbs and take a nice trip to Disneyland once a year. Yes, without the burden of raising him they could have such wonderful lives. He could still picture the home where he was raised, the screen door torn and the ceiling fans covered in dust that spun too fast. The blades always looked as if they were going to fly right off the fan and decapitate someone. It was hard to stay cool

142

in the summers with one window unit to cool the shotgun house. The walls were paneled and the sinks dripped. The sound of water going plink plink plink, would keep Benjamin awake at night, that, and the sound of his father forcing himself on his mother. Yep, he wondered what his other life would have been like, but instead he had been given this life all wrapped in paper and neatly placed into a loving family of freaks.

Every time Benjamin tried to remember something special and caring, it was instantly replaced with a swift kick or hurtful words. Like the time he brought the stray cat home he had found. He didn't know it had just had babies and was sickly. His father had grunted, "What the hell you got Ben?"

"Um it's a cat dad, can I keep it?" Benjamin's voice was trembling and so were his fingers as he reached for a bowl and began pouring some milk in it. Ben could smell the liquor on his father's breath as he continued to provoke him.

"You think I got money to spare so you can waste milk on some damn cat? You think money just grows on trees, is that it? Huh, huh," he slapped his head hard with an open hand. "Well, why don't you go pick some milk money off one of them there trees," he said sarcastically. Ben's heart sank and fear had replaced excitement, why had he thought any different. Was it because sometimes his father surprised him? Yes, sometimes he could confuse Benjamin with his actions. There were those hopeful words his father could use, he could still hear them.

"Benjamin wants a cat aye, well let's have a look at the little fellow." He picked it up and began stroking its fur, the cat had even begun to purr. "Nice kitty, you're a nice, nice kitty aren't you?" Benjamin had felt a twinge of hope and then his father had walked to the sink in front of the window, all the while stroking it and speaking friendly hopeful words. "What a good pleasant girl," he said as the cat rubbed her head along his arm purring. He kept stroking it and talking to it. Then the evil voice that Benjamin was too familiar with took over, "Benny wanta kitty? Ahh does little Benny wanta kitty?"

"Stop it," cried Ben, but it was no use and then his father held the cats head under the sink full of dirty dish water. He held it hard struggling with it, until his father's arms were clawed and bleeding from the cat fighting for her life. He remembered his father throwing it against the wall and Ben guessed what people say about cats was true, they do have nine lives or at least this one sure did. That was the last time Benjamin had asked for a pet of any kind.

He stepped out of the shower and tried to decide if his conscience could handle lying to Marcie. He knew she was a gold mine, with money to spare. If he could play his cards right, he could possibly come out ahead. But his past would always be there to haunt him and a man like Marcie Owens father would certainly do a background check. What if he continued with his story and only changed a few details. It was possible that he could convince even him, they did it in the movies, why couldn't he? He pulled his t-shirt over his head and popped the lid off a beer bottle, white cold smoke hovered off the top. "Breakfast," he said, as he raised the bottle in the air. "Cheers dad!"

Buddy

Chapter 21

Walter was astonished at how quickly he received a ride. A black semi-truck with orange and yellow airbrushed flames pulled over to the side of the road in the darkness. A large bellied man sat behind the wheel. He had a long graying beard and he startled Walter as he hollered out the window, "Where you headed old timer?"

That's the thing, Walter really didn't know, but he knew he needed a ride desperately. "Where you headed?" Walter asked the trucker sheepishly.

"Well I'm headed to Nashville, but first I'm headed to a diner up the road for some eggs, you interested."

"Sure," said Walter. He was feeling overdressed in the suit pants and dress shirt and was thankful he had grabbed his coat from the hospital bag. He was a little embarrassed that he had no money for breakfast, but maybe he could get a biscuit or at least a cup of coffee out of the man.

"You like the South Side Café?"

"Never heard of it," said Walter.

"Never heard of it!" The man looked at him like he was the strangest character he'd run across.

"No sir," said Walter. "Is it good?"

"Is it good?" Walter could see that the man was going to answer each question with the same question and it struck him as funny. They pulled the big rig into the truck stop at the next exit and Walter immediately noticed a couple police cars in the parking lot and wondered if the guard from the hospital might be in there.

"We haven't been properly introduced," said the trucker. "I'm Buddy," he looked towards Walter who had to think for a minute about whether he should give his real name.

"I'm Clay," he said. "Nice to meet you Buddy, thanks for picking me up."

"Not a problem," he said and climbed down out of his rig.

Walter didn't know what to do now. He glanced across the truck and spotted a black toboggan. "Do you mind," said Walter holding it up.

"No, Clay you go ahead, I think it belongs to the last guy I picked up. I don't pick up many anymore, can't trust people these days like you used to." He glanced at Walter and eyed him up and down, giving Walter uneasiness. "What are you dressed for old timer? I mean it's early and you look like you're ready for church," he chuckled and kept walking, not waiting for Walter's reply. He grabbed a booth in the front and Walter sat with his back to the restaurant, after glancing about and spotting an officer or two towards the back.

The booth wasn't greasy, but more coated with oil, dust and some sort of film that caused you to stick to it. The table was covered with a red and white checkered table cloth that had a plastic vinyl top for easy clean up. The menu was plastic and one page, with breakfast on one side, lunch and dinner items on the other. A lady in a checked polyester blouse that said 'South Side' in stitching above the pocket, grabbed Buddy and placed his head into her bosom, hugging him and smiling. "How's my favorite trucker," she said standing back now and smiling widely. Her teeth were overlapped in the front and her figure was straight up and down, no curves, just busty. If she noticed Walter at all, he couldn't tell. She never acknowledged his presence, until Buddy ordered two coffees before Walter could protest.

"Thanks Buddy, I appreciate it." Buddy nodded still gazing at the waitress with the boyish shape. Walter knew he needed to eat something and quick, his blood sugar was acting funny and he knew one cup of coffee wasn't going to fix it.

The waitress came back and set the two steaming cups of coffee down and Walter noticed her name tag, 'Donna' it said. Walter figured she looked like a Donna, with her bleached blonde hair and pink pastel lipstick smeared across her overlapping teeth. "Whatta ya having, Bud, your usual?"

"Naw, think I'll switch it up this time, give me a ham and cheese omelet with hash browns and a side of biscuits and gravy. Oh what the heck, give me a slice or two of that thick bacon too." Walter eyed his belly that was pressed against the table, tiny holes in his t-shirt struggled to keep from splitting apart. Donna looked at Walter. Walter stirred his coffee and acted as if he didn't feel her eyes upon him. "Whatcha havin, Clay," Buddy asked.

"I'm good," said Walter.

Buddy's voice perked up, "Oh no you don't. You never been to South Side Café and you ain't getting nothing? Give him an order of Biscuits and gravy Donna, and put it all on my ticket!"

Walter smiled and thanked Buddy. His bladder was on the verge of bursting and the restroom sign was calling his name, but the police officers were sitting right next to the entry way. Walter pulled the toboggan down a little lower and excused himself and made his way to the restroom. His heart was beating strong and hard. He knew at this point that there was a special bulletin on all the news channels with a photo of him to view. He walked past the two men in uniform and stood at the urinal just waiting for the trickle to become a stream. He was just beginning to feel some release when he heard the door open and watched the shiny military shoes standing next to him. Walter didn't have to look up, he would know those pants and shoes anywhere. "Morning sir," the officer said looking towards Walter who was zipping up his fly.

"Morning to you," Walter said politely and left without washing up or looking in the mirror. He made his way back to the booth and was thankful the truck stop was old and outdated and had no TV in sight. Walter just couldn't take looking at his photo and hearing what a dangerous criminal he was. He wondered if his son or daughter would see the report and what they would think about him now. Walter shuffled back to the booth and slid in.

"So tell me about yourself Clay, you got family here?"

"I sure do," said Walter, forgetting for a moment that he went by the alias Clay.

Buddy crinkled up his forehead and looked at Walter funny. "Then why they letting you hitchhike in this cold air?"

Walter hadn't thought his plan through enough. He could see he was going to have to come up with answers for this Buddy character and fast. "Buddy you ever been in love?" Buddy shook his head and waited. "Well, I recently lost the love of my life. The only woman I have ever loved and ever will love. After my wife was buried I got lonely, depressed, and at times just crazy. You ever felt like that Buddy?" He looked intently into Buddy's eyes.

"Yes, Clay, I have. I been out on this road so long I forgot what it was like to have my family. After spending three weeks, sometimes four away from home at a time Sheila, I guess got lonely and started looking elsewhere. I would have never thought she'd do it. I thought we were golden." He kept talking about Sheila and Walter let out a sigh of relief, it would take him a while to come back around as to why Walter was hitching a ride. To top it off Donna was bringing the plates. She sat a hefty size portion of two biscuits halved and smothered in thick sausage gravy in front of Walter and then a smorgasbord of plates in front of

Buddy. Everything looked so good to Walter after eating the hospital food.

He started bragging right away to Buddy. "You sure do know how to pick a place," Walter said, taking a bite of his gravy encrusted biscuits.

Buddy held out a piece of bacon towards Walter. "Try this bacon, you ain't never tasted thick smokehouse bacon like this before. Go on," he said holding it up in front of Walter, dangling it.

Walter took the piece, anything to keep conversation on the food was fine with him. "Sure is good Buddy and you're right, I don't think I've ever had bacon this thick or this good."

About that time Donna came over and poured more coffee into their cups. She smiled at Buddy and started talking about her tips and the lack of them on third shift. "Hell if it wasn't for my breakfast bunch, I wouldn't be able to pay my bills. Course you always take care of me," she said rubbing her hand along his back and pressing her large bust into his shoulder.

Buddy wiped most all the gravy out of his beard and smiled up at Donna. Walter felt a little like he was intruding on something. Donna kept talking and then shared with Buddy how the last trucker that stiffed her said, "If you want to get your tip, it's in the bed of my truck. Can you believe that Buddy?" Only she said it with a delightful mixture of poor pitiful me and please take me outside Buddy and show me your rig.

Buddy almost blushed and then said, "Darling, you know you can come on the road with me anytime, shoot ole boy like me gets lonely."

Walter had about all the stickiness he could take. He ate his food in silence and drowned out Donna, Buddy and the police officers. That is until they got ready to leave, Donna brought the tab and with big eyes looked at Buddy and said, "Be careful who you pick up. Marty and Hank over there, said they got a report in of a criminal who escaped Floyd Memorial hospital." Buddy looked as if he'd heard it plenty of times, but Walter wished he could disappear at that very moment and crawl under a booth.

Buddy placed a twenty on the top of the bill and told Donna to keep the change. "Remember Bud, be careful out there."

Buddy grabbed her by the arm and pulled her close to him and said, "Maybe what I need is someone like you to protect me." Donna giggled and shoved the ticket with the twenty in her pocket and moseyed off to the next booth to cuddle up to another lonely driver.

Brenda

Chapter 22

Brenda King was getting ready for her job at the bank where she had been a teller for almost twelve years. She had just stepped out of the shower, wrapped a towel around her head and was brewing her morning coffee when she turned on the six o'clock news. She was patting her long red hair and checking the weather report to see if rain or snow was in the forecast, when a picture of her father appeared on the screen. "Burt," she yelled, "come quickly!" Her husband, who worked second shift at the Frito Lay plant, wasn't used to her making a commotion and since he hadn't heard his ninety pound German shepherd bark, he gathered himself and stumbled into the living room. He arrived just as the reporter was finishing up, "The man was last seen wearing navy blue slacks and a white dress shirt, leaving Floyd Memorial Hospital, he is believed to be on foot, police say the suspect is unarmed." Brenda was pointing at the television set but not making a sound.

Calm down Brenda, Burt said and rubbed her back. "What's he wanted for anyway?"

"I don't know Burt, something about breaking and entering and possible child abuse, case pending further investigation, I think." She was sobbing now and completely shocked.

"But Brenda, we both know Walter is not capable of such allegations."

Brenda looked at Burt and wanted to believe what he was saying was true. She loved her father, he had always been a good father but something had happened to him after her mother became ill. She knew he had loved her mother more than her or her brother Daniel that was obvious. To just run off and not even stay and help care for her, well, Brenda still had anger and rage in her heart against him. He had not been there for her. He had left her all alone to deal with all the suffering and heartache. He wasn't there when her mother, Ruthie would peer into the mirror at the nursing facility and say, "Brenda that woman is staring at me, make her stop. I don't know why she's in my room, please make her stop." Her mother had held the bristle brush in her hand, raised at her own reflection as if she'd never even laid eyes upon herself.

No, her brother Daniel had not witnessed most of their mother's antics. Nor was he there when Ruthie had taken her fist and the hard brush, striking the glass until she had shattered it and cut her fists and arms all the while screaming, "Quit staring at me, I said quit looking at me!" Brenda remembered the horrible, long visits with her mother gazing into space, not really even knowing her own self, let alone Brenda. Occasionally she would notice a bright color like Brenda's shirt and comment on it, "That's pretty." Sometimes she would tell Brenda to leave, "Why are you here, nobody asked you to come." Sometimes they restrained her wrist and her legs and all Brenda could do was watch her thin frail crazy mother, try to break free. Brenda knew it was hard for Daniel, but he was not there regularly and the worse her mother grew the less he came. After her father left, Daniel rarely showed up at all. "Well we're busy you know," he'd say, "we have the twins to take care of," as if to imply it was easier for her and Burt to deal with it all.

These comments only felt as if he were picking a scab. She ached over her own inability to bare children. She just couldn't take it all, the pressure and the guilt of caring for mom and the worry over her father who had just vanished. She had been worried sick until she hired the private investigator who had found him in Kentucky, sleeping in motels with that damn bird and running up charge cards for all his meals. All the while, here sat Brenda at her mother's side, watching in horror as she gasped for each breath. She had practically dwindled to skin and bones. Oh, she had had enough of all of them! If it weren't for Burt being so kind and loving and supportive she'd have gone off the deep end. The funeral arrangements had been the last straw and who else but Brenda to greet all the family members and try to explain her father's strange disappearance. She never once told Daniel or any of her closest relatives that her father was fine. I mean what was she to say, "Oh Daddy, well he's just great. He's staying at the Red Roof Inn and has his homing pigeon for companionship, not to worry!"

Burt looked at his wife and was completely at a loss for words to comfort her. The last two years had been more on Brenda than he could possibly know. Between losing her father, burying her mother and then the constant fertility treatments, well it was all too much. He wanted so many things for her and now this. "The police will be contacting us soon." He shifted his eyes from Brenda to the telephone and wondered if she was up for it all.

"I better call in to work Burt, Janet will have to come in today," she said, as if she were preparing herself for the next twenty four hours.

Her freckled skin was covered in hives and she repeatedly rubbed her eyes, a habit her mother had warned her would cause wrinkles. She could still see her now, showing her how to apply the under eye lifting cream. She slumped to the bathroom and began to blow dry her massive thick red hair. It was the color of a campfire, warm and glowing and she had enough to cover several heads but Brenda always thought it was her glory. Her friends at the bank had short bobs and hip new looks, they were forever after her to update her style but Brenda was quite content. Burt had always loved it, so she figured, as the old rhetoric goes, 'If it aint broke why fix it'. She hated that saying actually, but what else could she say.

Brenda walked out of the bathroom and poured herself a cup of coffee. She walked to the refrigerator and opened the milk cap then poured a splash of liquid in to her cup, as long as it looked like mud she could drink it. About that time the phone rang and Burt yelled from the living room, "Its Daniel, Brenda you better take it."

"Oh, give me the phone!" She was half put out with him anyway. She picked up the phone and without saying hello spoke into the mouthpiece, "Yes Daniel, I seen the news bulletin." She heard her brother on the other end blabbering about his job at the office and how Jessica and Jessie had contracted a cold at the daycare. Finally, she decided to stop him in mid-sentence, "Daniel you go on to work and leave this to Sandra. The police will stop by, I am sure, and possibly put a trace on any incoming phone calls, so calm down." He stopped and was silent for a moment then started whining about how he wished he had a normal family like Sandra's.

"Come on Brenda, you know I'm worried about Dad, truth is I was glad to see he was still kicking, just we went through so much with Mom and now this." Brenda could hear his voice repeating over and over the word we, but she knew it was really her that went through so much, he wasn't even there at the end, well how convenient.

"Okay Daniel, well just call me if you hear anything or see anything. I've taken off today or should I have said, have Sandra call me if she hears anything."

Daniel stuttered something and then said, "Brenda, I sure hope Dad isn't really guilty of all those things. I am sure there must be a mistake, but of course now Sandra's all upset and saying even if he is found innocent she doesn't want him around the twins, well not alone anyway. She keeps saying if he's sick like Mom he won't be able to come here and live. I just don't know what's going on, I mean Dad was fine until Mom got sick."

Brenda had heard enough, "Okay Daniel, I'll be in touch." She walked to the kitchen and opened the bottle of aspirin and shook out three or four not counting and tossed them down. She couldn't stand snobby Sandra, hey come to think of it that should be her nickname thought Brenda, 'Snobby Sandra'! And to top it all off she was at church every time the doors were open. I mean really. This is why people don't bother with organized religion anymore everyone seems so fake, she thought. The things that lady complained about, please, she had had enough. She used to call Brenda over the smallest problems, hell a six year old could have figured them out. Her nails were manicured and so were her clothes. She had to get her roots done every six weeks and she kept the twins dressed to the nines. She had a maid and a membership at the country club. They took a vacation every year and went on a cruise boat once a year as well. She was a selfish spoiled baby who had never grown up and Daniel treated her like one, he was worse than her own father had been towards her mother.

Brenda was thankful she was a strong woman who could tend to her own problems without medley mouthing to others for pity. She walked to the bedroom and changed into a comfortable sweat outfit with a zip up jacket. It was still rather cold outside, but now that she was off she thought she'd walk Sam, their German shepherd and have Burt go back to bed. He usually didn't get in until mid-night or later since the overtime at the plant had steadily increased. He never went directly to sleep but watched television, sometimes until two or three in the morning. She put on her socks and sneakers and grabbed Sam's leash, the sun was beginning to come up in the distance and she thought a brisk walk would do her good.

Destination

Chapter 23

Walter climbed into the truck and with his belly full and a hot cup of coffee to go. He was ready for a nap, but he had a feeling Buddy was a talker. The knot on his head had gone down tremendously and he felt better than he had in months. He took the toboggan off and settled back in the seat.

"How far you want to go Clay?" Buddy asked as he shifted gears.

"Take me as far as the Tennessee line, if that's alright?"

"You got family there?" Buddy asked, eyeing Walter. Walter didn't know what to do. He knew the police were looking for him and he knew that his info would be coming across that CB radio. He knew Buddy was naive when it came to women, but he had a feeling Buddy would put two and two together before long. But where else was there to go? Walter knew he couldn't go to Daniel or Brenda's homes. He knew the police would be looking there. He thought long and hard about what he should do and the best he could come up with was go wherever Buddy was going, live like he had for the past year and pray that the truth would come out in the end. Walter looked at Buddy and decided to be honest.

"Well I used to have family in Tennessee. Truth is I've been running from my mistakes for a while."

"Well, you never did tell me why you were dressed so well, or why you were hitching a ride?"

Walter went to scratch his head and felt the bruise that was healing giving him an itch. "Well Buddy, I lost my wife over a year ago. When I lost her I just didn't find anything exciting anymore. The sun wasn't as bright and the sky wasn't as blue, food didn't taste as good and breathing became a chore. I woke up each morning and reached for her like I had for years and she wasn't there, Buddy. I guess I been trying to hurry up and finish this life so I can go be with her. The home we shared became a prison and I feel like I have lost my compass. So to answer your question, I don't know where I'm going and can't deal with what I lost. You ever feel as if you are wishing your life away?"

Buddy looked at Walter and thought he was one of the most honest, raw men he'd ever met. Most men he knew would never admit to loving a woman that much. Buddy thought about his grandparents, they married during the great depression, never had much, but love. He remembered after their fiftieth wedding anniversary his grandfather, Stewart had taken his grandmother Daisy's hand and looked her in the eye, knowing that his time was short, he said, "Daisy how about we just get in that ole pickup truck of mine and drive off the road. That way I won't leave you behind, and you won't leave me?" Buddy ran his finger through his beard and thought about how much he missed them both and how much people take other people for granted while they are here.

"Yes Clay, I understand how you feel, I miss Sheila every day. I am so sorry for your loss. The way you describe your wife brings up memories of my grandparents. Now that was true love. They don't make it like that anymore. Nope, sure don't make um like that."

Walter laid his head back and asked Buddy if he cared if he napped a bit, then closed his eyes and tried to drown out the CB radio. The truck hummed along the interstate and Walter had left Buddy with plenty to think about.

Daniel

Chapter 24

Daniel hung up the phone and felt hurt. He could sense the tension in his sister's voice. He wished she had not had to go through so much. He wished he could explain why he hadn't been there for her during their mother's horrible death, but Sandra just didn't want to worry Brenda. Sandra had insisted that it would be too much for Brenda to take in and she didn't feel the time was right. Ever since the doctors had diagnosed his wife with Multiple Sclerosis their lives had changed from being care free and enjoying their twins, to living in complete stress.

Brenda didn't understand that the reason his wife called and repeatedly asked her the same questions was because her memory was failing. The truth was, he was scared to leave her with the twins alone, that's why he had put them in daycare, but Brenda just felt Sandra was being lazy. She didn't understand that she had caught the kitchen on fire and almost wrecked the car with the twins inside. She didn't understand that the few times she went to the nursing home to see Ruthie; she had become so fatigued it left her in bed for days afterwards. Brenda did not know that his wife's bladder refused to empty and now at thirty five years of age she wore pads in case of accidents.

He felt as if he had three children now to look after. Thank God for Beanie their neighbor, who checked in on her while he was at work? He hated going to visit his mother because it hurt so bad and made him only think of what he might have to go through later with Sandra. He was starting to feel a secret bond with his father that he'd never before shared, it was a bond of common suffering. He tried to get Sandra to let him confide in his sister, but she just said she wanted to wait until after the funeral. Then she had told her parents and her brother Don.

It seemed instead of this helping the situation, it had made it much worse. Sandra felt that it had only been a burden on her parents. Her brother was forever sending her organic diets to try and telling her that all she needed to do was exercise. Then Daniel had to listen to Sandra cry for hours, because her brother Don was always telling her she looked fine and that she would feel better if she would get out of bed and get some fresh air and sunshine. He was unaware that the sun and the heat could put her in the hospital and had done just that, leaving Sandra for two days on a steroid drip, the two days right after his father had disappeared. He couldn't leave his wife, she needed him and he needed her. He missed his old wife, the woman he had married. She was carefree and full of energy. They had no sex life now and honestly he was tired of hearing about her aches and pains. He was sure that she felt by telling him over and over again it was her way of saying, 'Daniel I am sorry I am such a horrible wife'. He felt that in his spirit, and picked up and detected the little jabs she spoke. She felt like such a failure as a mother and a wife, she had even told him that she wanted to die.

But the worst was when she told him to just go ahead and find another woman, because she was not a wife anymore. She had said there was no reason for him and the twins to suffer with her. "Go meet someone else and get out there and enjoy life, this is no way for a young handsome man to live." He hated the way she talked. Of course she would get out of bed and read to the twins and watch a movie with them on good days, but they seemed to be few and far between. The neurologist said it was an exacerbation period and that she would come out of it, but Daniel felt the stress of his mother's death and his father's disappearance had not helped matters.

Daniel had pressed Sandra while she was in the hospital to tell his family, but she just kept saying that's way too much for your sister to bear. Plus she never felt as if Brenda liked her. She always felt underneath that Brenda was a little jealous that she could pop out two children with no planning, while Brenda had tried everything possible to conceive, only to fail. She knew Brenda would think she had premeditated it all so that Ruthie wouldn't get all the attention. So Sandra had told him that she felt it was no use and that Brenda would just think she was lazy or wanted attention.

Daniel dressed the twins and packed their bags. He knew he couldn't leave Sandra to deal with the police so he called in to work as well. He walked up the stairs and kissed his wife on the head, told her he'd be back shortly and headed out the door with the twins by his side. He had something he had to do, regardless of what happened, he knew it was time. He sighed heavily and longed for the comfort of his mother but that was out of reach.

Friends in Heaven

Chapter 25

Bradford and Desiree stepped into Dr. Lord's office. It was actually a historic home with large windows, high ceilings, and a wraparound porch. The inside felt warm and inviting. There were plants and huge paintings of tropical birds and fish, the couches were red and the walls were the color of burnt squash. Dr. Lord had drawing tables and chairs with colorful paints, markers and crayons. She had black hair and warm inviting eyes. She smiled at Josh and knelt down to his height. "Hello there! You must be Joshua Levite." Josh looked kind of embarrassed and smirked sheepishly. "I'm Dr. Lord, but you can call me Clare if you like? Well, let's all take a seat," she said motioning at the bright red couches. "Now I am going to speak with both you and Joshua and then I'll ask you to wait in the adjacent room for a bit," she said glancing towards Desiree. "I also need you to sign a paper giving me permission to video the meeting. Will that be alright with everyone?" Josh walked to the table and picked up some construction paper and pipe cleaners. He fumbled with some foam cut outs of animals, unsure why he was here.

"Now Josh, come sit over on the couch for a bit." Josh didn't want to. He had gone to a similar place after his father died and all they did was ask him questions that made him feel sad inside. He stumbled over with his head down and scooted his butt onto the sofa. Dr. Lord was jotting something down on a clipboard. Her hands were chubby and so were the legs that stuck out of her skirt like two softball bats. She was short and seemed anxious that Josh wasn't cooperating as quickly as she would have liked. "Now Josh, tell me what you like to do?" Josh didn't know what she meant, so he shrugged his shoulders. Dr. Lord smiled, but it didn't seem as genuine as it had at first. "Oh come on Joshua, what do you like? Do you like riding a bike or roller skating?"

"Yes," Josh said, shaking his head.

Dr. Lord sighed and began to jot down more information. "So Josh, do you have a lot of friends at school?" Josh felt bad because he knew he really didn't. He was always playing jokes and pranks and getting into trouble.

"No," he said, lowering his head.

"Well Josh, I heard you have a new friend that you met recently. What's his name?"

Josh looked up at Bradford and his mother, he knew his mother did not like Walter, but he didn't know why. "Walter," he said sadly.

"Walter, well that's a fine name," Dr. Lord said with a bit too much enthusiasm. "And where did the two of you meet Joshua?"

Josh once again looked at his mother then back at Dr. Lord, "I met Walter in the woods behind my house. He was camping out there."

"Oh, I love camping," said Dr. Lord. "Did he have a tent?"

"No," said Josh, "just a blanket and a plastic clear thing to keep the rain away. But he has a really cool bird and I get to keep her," said Josh excitedly.

"A bird? Well Josh, your friend sounds really neat. What did you all talk about?"

Josh didn't want to tell Dr. Lord about Walter. He didn't want her not to like Walter too. "We talked about Jackie."

Dr. Lord raised her eyebrows in confusion and asked, "Who is Jackie?"

"She is my new bird," said Josh. "Wanta see her?" His eyes got big and he stood up waiting for Dr. Lord to answer, but she just kept writing more and more on her papers.

"Uum, well not right now Josh, lets finish our conversation. What else did you and Walter talk about?"

Josh thought back to the night and remembered the stick Walter had whittled with the eyes that looked like a snake. It was so silky smooth and Josh wished he would have taken it home. "Walter had a knife," Josh said as Desiree gasped and Bradford leaned forward interested in where this was all going.

"Oh, I see," said Dr. Lord, "and did he try to hurt you with it?"

Josh wrinkled up his forehead and looked at Dr. Lord angrily, "NO! Walter would never ever hurt me!" His eyes flashed with anger.

"Calm down, Josh." Desiree said, breathing a sigh of relief.

"Well, what was Walter doing with the knife Joshua?"

"He was whittling," said Josh, excited that he remembered such a big word. "The wood was so smooth without the bark pieces and he let me feel it. Then Walter cut eyes out and made it look like a snake, it was cool." He hopped up and down with his butt on the sofa. Desiree did not want to hear about knives and snakes and she was certain she'd heard enough.

"What else did you and Walter do together, Joshua," asked Dr. Lord smiling again now, with a look of concern.

"Nothing," said Josh.

"Oh come on, you must have done something else, now think, think hard."

Josh closed his eyes and thought but he just couldn't think of anything else.

"Okay Desiree, I am going to ask that you and Bradford wait in the next room for a while okay?" She said, as her fat legs walked them to the adjacent room.

"Josh, Mommy will be right here, okay?"

Before Josh could answer his mother, Dr. Lord was crouched again at his level. "Now Josh, I'm going to let you draw a picture of your favorite friend Walter, would you like that?" She smiled and pulled out the small desk chair and asked Josh what he would prefer to use. Josh chose markers and was happy that he finally didn't have to answer any more questions for a while. He decided to draw a picture of Jackie eating bird seeds out of his hand and Walter smiling. He was really getting into his picture and had almost forgot Dr. Lord was even in the room when she came and sat beside him.

"Whatta ya got there, Josh? Tell me all about your beautiful drawing."

"Well," said Josh, "this is Walter." He pointed to a stick like creature with a huge smile. "This is me feeding Jackie out of my hand, it tickled," said Josh smiling.

Dr. Lord looked at the picture and wrote some other things down on her tablet. "Josh, did Walter ever touch you anywhere?"

Josh was tired of answering this question and it made him feel weird when they asked it, like he had done something bad. "No," he said, only to shake my hand, like cowboys do.

"Is that right?" Dr. Lord said chuckling. "Josh, I know Walter is your friend, but I have to ask you a couple more questions, okay?" She looked at Josh and smiled again as she removed the strand of black hair from her eyes.

"Okay," said Josh, not knowing why it was such a big deal. All Josh could think of that would have made Mommy so mad was Walter taking his dad's suit, but Josh knew he'd bring it back.

"Joshua, did Walter ever show you anything?" She raised her eyebrows funny. "Did he ever go to the bathroom in front of you?"

Josh just stared at her oddly and wondered why Walter would ever go to the potty in front of him. "No," Josh said rather slowly.

"Did you ever see Walter undressed?"

"No," said Josh again feeling more strange than ever.

"Okay Josh, well can you tell me what made Walter someone you would call your friend?"

Josh didn't have to think about this answer, he knew it, "Walter's wife died and she is in heaven with Daddy and they are friends. I always wanted to have a friend that had someone in heaven like my daddy." Josh lowered his head now and tried not to cry but tears were welling up and he kept wiping them and looking down at his snow boots that he insisted on wearing that morning.

"Well Josh, we are all finished, how would you like to make fun stuff in my play dough factory while your mother and I talk?"

Josh suddenly felt better and he loved play dough so off he went with Dr. Lord to the children's room.

Dr. Lord entered the room where Desiree and Bradford sat and said, "I think there is something you should see."

Desiree's heart sank and she felt as if her legs were unsteady. Bradford took her by the hand and led her back to the bright colored sitting room. Dr. Lord held a remote control and she was rewinding the tape. "I think everything will be okay," she said, looking at Desiree, "but there is something I believe you need to see." She paused the tape and then hit play. Bradford and Desiree peered up at the television as Dr. Lord asked Josh, "Can you tell me what made Walter a friend?" Desiree waited impatiently, she had chewed all her fingernails down into the quick. Then she heard the sweetest, most heartbreaking words, "I always wanted to have a friend who had someone in heaven like my daddy."

A Change in the Air

Chapter 26

Marcie arrived at the School for the Blind and secretly hoped that Benjamin was there. She knew he wasn't worth the trouble and would probably hurt her like every other guy she'd dated, but she just couldn't get him off her mind or out of her heart. She hoped once he had moved forward and gotten over Debbie he'd be fine. She made a mental note to go to the library and check out some books on the effects of losing a loved one or spouse. Maybe if she did some research she could understand more thoroughly why Benjamin kept pushing her away. She climbed up the steps and wondered why a blind school would even have steps.

183

She caught sight of Benjamin out of the corner of her eye and began to walk in that direction. She shuffled past the front desk without signing the register sheet. "Hey Ben!" She said smiling and trying to catch up with him.

"Hello Marcie, how you been?" His head was lowered and he had his hands shoved down deep inside his pockets.

"Good," she answered, "haven't heard from you though, you okay?"

"Yeah fine, I'm fine, just started a new job over at Franks Steakhouse with Clark." Benjamin removed one hand, ran his fingers through his long hair and chewed on his fingernail.

"Oh, that's good. Is it more money?"

"Yeah, a couple bucks more." Benjamin looked at her thin lips and gorgeous smile and wished he hadn't screwed up his life so bad. He wished he was someone good enough for her. "So, what do you have planned for the night?" he asked.

"Not much Ben, what about you?" She waited for his reply, her heart was beating extra hard in her ears.

Benjamin kept telling himself to be kind and friendly, but to just continue walking. 'Don't look into her eyes Ben,' he kept telling himself this over and over again. But his heart gave in and he found himself inviting her into Frank's to have a drink around the time he got off.

"I might be able to come," said Marcie, who was already trying to decide what to wear and how to fix her hair. Then of course what time to show up, not too early, but not too late. She was pumped and couldn't wait to leave and stop at the library to check out some books. "See ya later Ben," said Marcie, smiling all the way to the front desk where she signed in late.

Benjamin was cooking steaks tonight and his only requirement was to make sure the temperature was perfect to order. If it was ordered medium it better be medium, because if it was medium well or well done you couldn't make it pink again.

Frank, the owner, was a heavy set man with an Italian background and a temper that was worse than Benjamin's fathers at times. When he was angry, he was the devil, but when he was having a good day and food cost was low, he was your best friend. He ran a tight ship, but he also let all his employees sit at the bar when their shift was over, they just had to follow the rules. The first rule was a nice clean appearance, which meant a shirt with a collar. The second rule was that there would be no cursing and no getting tanked. Getting tanked is what Frank considered too drunk to handle your booze.

Benjamin knew Frank was sharp, right when he came to work for him. If you let your employees sit at the bar, well they give you back all the money you pay them in wages. The other bonus for Frank was the fact that they got acquainted with the guests and the guests grew to like their company, hence bringing them back time and time again. Frank didn't hire anyone with a sappy personality, which made Benjamin wonder what he had seen in him. Each employee always brought a shirt to change into and sometimes a pair of shoes. If the bar was completely full he'd let the employees sit at the tables around the bar. Once you got to know Frank and his eccentric personality, he was an okay guy. Sure beats this community service work thought Benjamin, just as a young man opened a stall door and knocked his cane from one side of the door to the next.

Benjamin finished sweeping the men's room and reached for the dust pan. He figured he'd just continue his relationship with Marcie until she found out or until it ended some other way. He seemed to change his mind from one minute to the next.

His friend Clark knew about his past and he had known the owner Frank for a long time, so Benjamin was just lucky to get that job. Clark was his best friend before and after the accident. He had a father that had walked out on his mother when Clark was thirteen, leaving Clark with a little sister to take care of and a lot more chores than any other kid his age. He started smoking weed with Benjamin when his mom left for work at night. She stopped working at the gas station and took a job as an exotic dancer to pay the bills. They had all night to party, but his mother was starting to get a bad reputation, which just added more harassment for Clark at school. Sometimes they stayed in Clark's mom's garage and played guitar and listened to music, both of them looking for escape but for different reasons.

Benjamin was scared to go home to his father and all his cruelty. Clark was afraid his father might never come back, leaving him and his mother with a large hole in their hearts.

So they smoked a little more or they'd find some bum in the parking lot, who for the price of a cheap fifth of bourbon would buy their beer too. Life was good, Benjamin missed those days. They both made money selling weed and would have made a pretty decent haul, if it weren't for them smoking up most their profit. Benjamin couldn't afford to do that anymore, not with his past. One more court appearance and Benjamin would be completely finished. He hadn't seen Desiree lately and hoped she had finally backed off. He walked to the front desk and signed the check-out sheet. He opened the door and drank in the sunshine that was pressing through the winter sky.

Benjamin felt like his life was changing. He couldn't pinpoint it, but deep inside he felt a wave of change and an inner intuition that things were beginning to look up. He skipped down the front steps and breathed the air of freedom.

The Makeover

Chapter 27

Bradford's phone had been set on silence during the appointment at Dr. Lord's office, but now he noticed that he had two missed calls from his partner, Thomas at the firm. He stopped at a Starbucks and grabbed coffee for himself and Desiree and some juice for Josh, then checked his messages. He walked back to the jeep and wondered if he should tell Desiree the news that Walter had escaped from the hospital. They were having such a good day and Bradford had a gut feeling that this man wasn't guilty of much more than petty theft. Plus Desiree seemed so relieved after going to see Dr. Lord and he didn't want to spoil it just yet.

"Where would you two like to go before we pick up Tabitha?" He said, wanting nothing more than to pamper her and help her heal. "Josh, how would you like to go to a pet store that specializes in birds and get some things for Jackie?"

Josh jumped up and down and screamed, "Yes, yes, yes!"

Bradford took Desiree by the arm and led her aside, he reached in his pocket and then looked deep into her eyes. "Desiree, I want you to take this credit card and go pamper yourself." She began to protest and Bradford shushed her with his finger by placing it over her lips. "Listen, I don't have any children and I live all alone, it's just me. I want to do something nice for you. So you go to the salon or the mall and pamper yourself. Just drop Josh and me off at the pet store and we'll be fine."

Desiree was forever feeling guilty about letting anyone help her or especially dote on her for no reason. She hadn't let anyone help her after John's death and she felt odd even being placed in this situation. But Desiree also felt that if she said "no" and didn't allow Bradford this pleasure that she would be hurting him. She smiled and finally agreed, dropping them off at the pet store that was located in a strip mall with a sports shop and an ice cream shop as well.

"We'll be fine," Bradford said, pointing out all the locations they could hit. "You go do something nice for yourself."

Desiree left them at the pet store and knew exactly where she was headed. She unclasped her purse and pulled out the crinkled magazine photo of a blonde with short spiky hair and bright red lips. Desiree pulled into the salon and asked the young girl who had called her name if she would be able to create a miracle. The stylist was a little younger than Desiree was used to getting, but she kept saying all she needed was a razor cut and some products. She seemed to think she could help her hair look fuller and thicker. She placed Desiree in the chair by the sink and began to shampoo her thin hair. Then they picked out a blonde colored bleach that would add body and the stylist separated pieces and placed them in foil, then after being under the dryer for fifteen minutes she was ready to rinse and cut.

Desiree closed her eyes and listened to the scissors snip, snip, snip. She felt the razor rip through her hair, held her breath and hoped it would turn out okay. She had fallen in love with the cut in the photo, but more than that she hoped would Bradford like it. It was funny how close she felt to him in such a short time. She knew they had been friends for about a year now while working together, but this was different. She felt sparks and desires that had lain dormant for too long were beginning to stir.

After the stylist was finished blow drying and styling her hair, she asked Desiree to close her eyes. "Ready?" she said as she turned the chair around to face the mirror. Desiree opened her eyes and sat looking at the reflection of a woman she didn't recognize. She looked at least five years younger if not more and her hair for the first time in a long time actually looked thick, it even felt thick. Her eyes filled with tears as the hairdresser screamed, "You don't like it?"

"Oh no, no, honey, it's just the opposite I love it!" She hugged the hairdresser and handed her the credit card. "Here you go, Mrs. Stiltz," she said as she gave her the receipt and Visa card back. Desiree liked the way that sounded 'Mrs. Stiltz', hum she better snap out of it, she thought as she made her way back to the jeep. She had bought all the products the stylist suggested, thickening shampoos and styling gels and foams and sprays. She just hoped she would be able to make it look like the stylist had.

For the first time, in a long time, Desiree felt sexy and more sure of herself than she had in years. She kept looking in the mirror on her way back to pick up Bradford and Josh. She turned the radio on to her favorite classic seventies station and started singing to the music, she raised her hands in the air and sang, 'Your Mama Don't Dance. She pulled into the parking lot feeling like a new woman, peeked one more time into the mirror and applied some lip gloss. Bradford and Josh were headed down a sidewalk that went directly in front of the sports shop, Josh had a bag in one hand and so did Bradford. They spotted the jeep and headed that way. Desiree decided to play it up with all she had and rolled down the window, "Do you boys need a ride?" She said smiling.

Bradford was blown away. "Why pretty lady, I think we do!" She pulled over next to them and hopped out of the jeep just as Bradford grabbed her and ran his fingers through her hair. "You look so beautiful," he said the words slowly and when he came to the word beautiful it was as if he let each syllable run over his tongue. Then he kissed her, right there in front of Josh and the whole world. Even though it was a subtle kiss on the cheek, it made her heart ripple. Desiree could not believe that a handsome attorney would want to kiss her, but she had sensed he had wanted to all morning. Josh pulled on his coat and made a face that said stop.

"Mommy you look different, I did not even know that was you with that wig on your head."

Desiree's face turned red. "It's not a wig Josh, its Mommy's hair."

"Oh," said Josh not pressing it and not causing Desiree any embarrassment.

Desiree was so proud at how well Josh had acted all day. He hadn't thrown a temper tantrum at all, what was that about? As they headed to get Tabitha and visit with her grandmom, Josh told her all about the brand new fountain they   got   for   Jackie.

"It has flowing water and an angel with a light. And we got Jackie some toys and a bell and bird food with vitamins!" He was talking a mile a minute and Desiree knew he needed a nap.

They arrived at her grandmom's and she began to fuss over Desiree's new haircut, complimenting it over and over again. Tabitha cried and didn't want to go to her, not recognizing her at first. Desiree helped her Grandmom set the table and they all took their plate to the kitchen, fixing their own plates. Bradford helped get the children's plates, as Linda watched him with approval. She had cooked pot roast with new potatoes, carrots and celery. She had corn bread cakes and the promised peach cobbler, sitting inside the oven to stay warm. Everyone sat down and began buttering their bread and pouring their tea when finally Grandmom asked everyone to bow their head as she said the blessing. Desiree loved the fact that time could go by and this tradition could end in so many families, but that was not the case with her grandmom. As long as she had breath, she would thank her maker, her Lord.

The television was on in the next room and it was just about time for the evening news. Joshua ate his dinner and walked into the living room just in time to see his friend Walter on the screen, "Mom! Bradford! Walter is on TV come look, hurry!"

Desiree rushed into the living room with Bradford and her grandmom close behind. "And now we take you to the downtown center for the homeless, we are coming to you live with Jennifer Cobb. Hello Jennifer."

"Yes, Tom, I'm here with Sarah Flags, she has worked as director of the kitchen here at the 7th street homeless shelter for nearly nine years. What can you tell us about the escaped convict, Walter Kendal?"

"Well Jennifer, Walter was a lovely man who never ate a meal for free. He arrived at our shelter six days a week, washed dishes, mopped floors and helped prepare sandwiches and soups for the day. If there was anything broken, Walter fixed it. He was the handiest person we've ever had here. Truth is Jennifer, most folks here miss Walter and his pet pigeon. We just can't imagine what he could have done to merit being wanted by the police."

"Well you heard it here first Todd, this escapee it seems, is also a man very much missed."

"Thank you Jennifer, and we will keep you updated on the man who escaped from Floyd Memorial Hospital. The sixty seven year old suspect was last seen wearing dark blue slacks and a white button down dress shirt, if you have any information please contact the numbers on your screen."

The Officer

Chapter 28

Brenda walked into the kitchen and placed Sam's leash on the hook above the laundry door. She felt better after a brisk walk in the cold air and her mind seemed clearer. She threw a pillow off the sofa, plopped down, picked up the remote control and flipped through the channels, wondering how this all would end. Burt was napping on the lounge chair and the coffee pot had gotten cold. She decided she needed another pot and was just rinsing out the grounds when the doorbell rang startling her German Shepherd and making Burt jump. Brenda turned the door handle and told the officer she'd be right with him after she put up her dog. He was holding up a badge with one hand and his other hand was resting on his gun holster. He smiled crookedly and shifted his eyes from her to Sam.

The officer took a seat on the sofa and Brenda offered him a cup of coffee that she hadn't even begun to brew yet. He was young, nervous and eager to take notes on his small spiral note pad. He spoke in a falsely deep voice, and a manner that implied he was important. He even cleared his throat and made his eyebrows arch to add to the overall effect. "My name is uuuhummm, Officer Floyd and as I'm sure at this point you are aware Mrs. King, that your father is an escaped criminal. My job, Miss, is to see if you can help me, uuhumm, help me find him."

Brenda nodded her head and wanted to scream, "Cut the crap and the 'miss' talk and just ask your questions." He couldn't have been over twenty five and she was quite sure she could out shoot him.

"Well Mr. King and Mrs. King, I hate to do this but do you care if I take a uuumm," he cleared his throat again, "look around the place?"

"Of course not, Mr. Floyd," Burt said, "Look away."

"It's Officer Floyd," he said, arching his brow again to imply we better be on our toes. Brenda was thankful for the police and she knew their job was difficult to say the least. She highly respected them, but something about this officer irked her. Maybe it was the fact that she was worried sick about her father and the whole situation.

Brenda walked to the kitchen and placed a coffee filter in the pot and dumped an extra scoop in the filter, she figured she was going to need it by the looks of things. Hell, she hadn't smoked since her mother's funeral, but she just might make Burt go buy her a pack. Burt led the police officer throughout the house and asked him if he wanted to see the room with Sam in it, who at this point was barking uncontrollably. He said it was alright, but Burt decided he'd put Sam outside and let him take a peek so there would be no doubt. About that time the phone rang and it was Daniel. "The police are here now," she said in a whisper, "have you heard anything?"

"Not yet Brenda, but I'm sure I will." He had started to come to her house and bring the twins and fill them in on the truth about Sandra, but had gone back home defeated and unsure of what to do.

"Yep, they are here or I should say Barney Fife is here!" He chuckled and for a minute, she missed him and even felt sorry for the way Sandra had him enslaved. I mean really she can't even watch the children while my brother is at work, she thought. While here I sit with no children wishing I could fill my days with finger painting and book reading. Brenda sighed and walked to the cabinet and grabbed a coffee cup, "I'll keep ya posted Daniel, and you call me if you hear anything."

"Okay, Sis," he said, "will do," and then he said, "Brenda.... I love you."

She was not expecting that. Brenda hadn't heard those words from him even at her mother's funeral. "I, I love you too," she said sounding a lot like the officer who kept clearing his throat.

Officer Floyd took a seat again and asked Brenda and Burt when they had last seen Walter. He asked if he had ever been accused of hurting or sexually abusing a child. Just the words made Brenda squirm, she just couldn't imagine her father ever doing anything to harm anyone, let alone an innocent child. She had so many emotions running through her right now, they were hard for her to get a handle on. Part of her wanted to hug her father and comfort him wherever he was, another part of her wanted to shake him. She ran her hands over her face and rubbed her eyes. Her skin was blotchy again and she felt like this was all a bad dream.

"I'm going to be leaving you two now. Remember, any information that you may have forgotten to tell me or any places or people that you think your father may have contacted, don't hesitate to let me know. We'll be monitoring all your incoming calls. A tracer will be added, with your permission of course." He raised his eyebrows as to see if there was any protest and then nodded his head. "And of course there will be a police car patrolling the area."

Officer Floyd raised up from the sofa then and stood up rigidly stiff, and cleared his throat one last time, straightened his hat and looked at Burt with a serious expression, "If you hear anything Mr. King, or see any strange vehicles don't be indecisive, just call." He held out a business card and made his way down the porch to his patrol car.

Brenda looked at Burt and rolled her eyes, "Police Academy," she said with a grin, "Well Andy?" He grabbed her from the side and pulled her to him, "Marlboro lights?

How did you know?" She smiled and headed to the kitchen for another cup of coffee.

Conversations With God

Chapter 29

Walter awoke with the sun beating down in his eyes and a repeated tug on his shoulder. "Clay, Clay, we gotta talk ole timer."

Walter glanced around the semi and tried to focus on Buddy, but the truth was he was tired. He had never felt so tired. The whole experience, he guessed was catching up with him. He couldn't figure out why he was calling him by the name Clay, and then reality started to click into place. They were pulled over in the back parking lot of a truck stop and Walter could tell by the wild look in Buddy's eyes that it was not going to be good news for him.

"Clay I know we talked a small good bit about you and your past and how you ended up on the side of the road with your thumb out, but I need to know if your real name is, perhaps Walter Kendal?" His face was red and blotchy and he looked like he was about to explode. "And tell me please," he threw his hands up in the air, "if it was you who just escaped from the hospital this morning?" His eyes stared at Walter piercingly. His hands were shaking and Walter could tell he was not comfortable with him being in his truck. Walter figured he might as well fess up, he'd never been good at telling lies and then more lies to keep up with the first. He eased out of the cab and Buddy followed him to the rear.

"Yep Buddy, it's true, I am Walter Kendal and I am wanted by the police. I am sorry if I have been dishonest with you, it's just, it's just I don't know where to turn or what to do." Walter lowered his head and shook it back and forth in disbelief. He wished he would have died first and Ruthie would have lived, then none of this would be happening. "I never hurt that boy. I have children and two precious little grandchildren. Well they were little, but it's been over a year now since I've seen them." He sighed and rubbed his face. "I'm sorry Buddy you don't need this. I thank you for breakfast and for the ride."

Buddy studied Walter suspiciously and tried to discern whether he was being completely honest. Walter could tell he was going to have to open up a lot more if he was going to get anywhere. But Walter was too weary, he turned and started walking down the parking lot towards the restrooms, he had to go something terrible and he had cotton mouth rather fierce. He was so tired of fighting. This was no way to live life, he thought to himself and no way to feel. He might as well turn himself in and let them do whatever they wanted with him. He tried to leave so he wouldn't involve his children and now he was sure they'd seen him on the news, probably even had the police contact them.

He unzipped his pants and waited for his bladder to work, it seemed to get slower each day and a little painful too. As his urine trickled and started to flow he began to pray. He thought maybe he shouldn't pray while he was using the latrine, but it felt right. "God, its Walter again, I know I haven't talked to you in some time and I probably have even been angry at you for taking my Ruthie. You know God, I just figured why do you need her anyways? You got all those angels and plenty of people there and I, well, she was all I really had." He stopped talking for a minute and tried to not cry. Men don't cry. That's what he had always heard, not real men anyway, but as hard as Walter swallowed and choked back he could not stop the tears. They seem to come from some dry place that needed watering. He remembered his mother used to always tell his father, who had referred to Walter as a sissy boy for crying, that even Jesus wept. He wondered why Jesus, the very Son of God would weep? He had forgotten most of that story, but he knew it had something to do with a friend dying. Jesus was able to raise him from the dead. If only I would have had that power, thought Walter. Walter wandered back to the reality of his dilemma and began to pray again.

"Anyways God, I have really gotten myself in a mess and it's so big Lord, I know there ain't no way I can get out of it." He leaned back and let each drop of urine out, then zipped his trousers and walked to the sink, looking into the mirror he continued his conversation. "Lord, if you can help me out of this, I will serve you the rest of my short days. I will do whatever you ask of me." His eyes peered into the mirror searching the truth of his very own soul. Walter wondered where the years had gone and then he realized he should probably ask God to forgive him for his anger and thank him for the good years and the joy he had with his children. He studied his unshaven face and his hair which now looked as if he was a member of a hard core biker club. He rinsed his mouth with water from the sink and splashed some in his face, then dabbed his hands and face on the paper towel and took a deep breath. "It's all in your hands," he said in a soft voice as he pulled open the door.

Walter walked out of the restroom and started towards the restaurant. He didn't know why, because he had no money. As he was just about to step inside the doorway, he heard Buddy's voice behind him. "Hey Clay, uh, Walt, uh look here, maybe we could talk about this. I don't feel right just leaving you here and anyways you have been nice company. I know you lost your wife and I know you been sick or you wouldn't have been in the hospital. Now let's get a bite and you can fill me in on what's really going on and I'll see what I can do."

Walter looked up to the ceiling and said thanks under his breath. They picked a booth in the back and Walter was so hungry he figured at this point if Buddy was going to help the first thing he could do was feed him. He looked at the menu and just the pictures of cheeseburgers and fries made him salivate. He had barely eaten at the hospital and was trying to be nice earlier due to his lack of money, but right now he had decided that this could be his last meal outside of jail. He was going to order the biggest, juiciest cheeseburger on the menu, triple decker if they had it and the whole works, lettuce, onions, tomatoes, pickles, heck, he wanted fries and a strawberry milkshake too. But Walter knew that was wishful thinking. On second thought, Walter decided with his sugar levels and the trouble he'd had lately, to stick with a more traditional meal, roast beef and mash potatoes and gravy. He thought he'd have some dinner rolls and a salad as well. His mouth continued to water as Buddy asked the server for a cup of coffee and a BLT. Walter was expecting him to order a plethora of food like he had earlier, but Walter was determined to get whatever he wanted. 'From now on,' he said to himself, 'I am living my life to the fullest and with or without Ruthie, I am going to try and make every second count!'

He placed his order and Buddy looked at him and grinned. "You hungry, or what?"

Walter knew when Buddy smiled that his eyes showed he believed him and Walter felt like he had dropped a heavy load, after talking with God and clearing his tear ducts. He felt like even if he were handcuffed and taken away that very second, he would be alright.

Walter looked up at Buddy and said, "Do you want the short version or the long one?" Before Buddy could answer Walter asked a question. "Buddy, have you ever made a mistake that was really foolish and then that mistake created the snowball effect and before you knew it you were rolling down hill, out of control with one bad decision after another? Ever notice how all it takes is one day and one decision to change your whole life?" Once again before Buddy could answer, Walter was on to explaining how he had arrived on the highway with his thumb stuck out. Buddy had been so engrossed in the details about Ruthie and the horrible effects of her disease, that by the time he started talking about Josh and Jackie he believed in Walter, hook line and sinker.

"Well, Walter, I guess we need to get you some clothes and a haircut if you're going to be riding with me." He smiled and shook his head, "You know I have done some pretty dense things in my day. Some things that if I'd been caught, I'd been locked up for sure, but this one takes the cake!" He continued smiling as Walter sopped up the last of his gravy with his bread. He shoved one last bite in his mouth, before he and Buddy went to the store aisle on the other side of the restaurant. Buddy purchased hair clippers, razors, shaving cream and a pale blue sweat shirt. Walter went back in the men's room and stood before the mirror he'd cried in front of earlier. He raised his hands in the air and said, "Thank you God!" He splashed water on his face and lathered up. After shaving he plugged the clippers in and added a number three attachment to the end of the shears and began shaving his long grey coarse hair. With each row of hair that fell into the sink, Walter felt like he was leaving behind his old life and lightening his load even more.

Walter, like Benjamin couldn't pinpoint why, but he felt as if his life was beginning to look up. He pulled off the white dress shirt of a dead man named John, and pulled over his head the new light blue sweatshirt Buddy had bought him. He picked up the handfuls of grey hair out of the sink and threw them in the trash bin, then rinsed out the sink.

He was now ready to face whatever came his way. He looked once again in the mirror and was surprised to see a familiar face he once knew. Walter chuckled and with his stomach tight as a tick and his face cleanly shaven, he walked out of the restroom a brand new man. He walked to the back of the truck stop where buddy's big rig with the flames had been parked, but the space was peculiarly empty. He looked high and low and up and down the whole area of Sander's Truck Stop but his friend Buddy was nowhere to be found.

The Angel

Chapter 30

Desiree and Bradford loaded up Josh and Tabitha and headed back to her place. It was a quiet ride and there was a lot on everyone's mind, including Josh. He kept asking his mother why Walter was on TV but no one seemed to give him an answer that made any sense. He knew something was wrong, and kept asking his mother if she was mad over Walter wearing his father's suit. But whenever he said anything about it, she just told him to hush-up. Why were adults always trying to get him to quit talking, he hated that. Why did they seem to think little kids did not know as much as them, it didn't make sense. Josh knew a lot more than they did about Walter and about why they were mad, but they never would listen to him. He couldn't wait to get home and put Jackie in her bird bath. It had been a good day and he was tired from all the places they had been. He closed his eyes and drifted off to sleep in the back of the Jeep, next to Tabitha's car seat.

Josh was thinking about Walter and how he hoped he was okay when he drifted off into a dream that was very different than any other dream he had ever had. It seemed so real, but not like anything here on Earth. In his dream there was a lady and she was very great. Josh had never seen anyone that tall before. Her hair was crimson and long. Her dress was so white it hurt his eyes to look at it and it had a large sash that was made of golden rope. She smiled and motioned for him to come with her. He was leery at first, but then she opened a large gold purse and let him look inside; Jackie was sitting peacefully inside her handbag cooing softly. Josh was still reluctant to come, but she then took him by the hand. Her hand was very warm and as he took it they began to fly. Josh had never flown or been so high above before. He looked down at fields, homes, mountains and streams and then he noticed the lady had huge wing like feathers, which gave her the ability to fly.

They landed softly in a field that Josh had been to plenty of times, it was at the park by his school. Her feet had touched the ground so smoothly, it was as if they had settled on top of the clouds. She then handed him the large purse like bag that held Jackie and said, "Release her." Josh shook his head from side to side, clutching the bag tighter. He looked down at Jackie's shimmery green neck and pale blue-grey feathers. The birds head bobbed up and down. Then she said it again, only this time more sternly, "You must set her free."

Josh gazed up at her radiant face and bright cherry hair, "But I love her so much." His eyes pleaded with hers as he peered into her face.

"I know," the angel said, "but you must set her free, she will come back," she said. "You will see my son."

Josh turned the knob and opened the clutch of the case he had just closed. He gently lifted Jackie out of the handbag and held her close to his heart. He rubbed his hand tenderly over her feathers. He looked intently into the angels face, "Why do I have to let her go? She's all I have now." He lowered his head, "My daddy's gone and my friend Walter

is gone, and I am supposed to be taking care of her for him."
He held Jackie tighter.

The angel smiled at Josh and her eyes sparkled like
crystal. He thought he'd never seen eyes that kind and that
loving. Her voice was like the sound of china tinkling.
"Now Josh, you must release her and set her free, trust me
Josh. She will come back, but first we need her to complete
her mission."

Josh lifted his hands that were cupped into the air and
held them as high as he could and then he felt a rustle of
wings and a flutter of feathers against his skin. Then as soon
as Jackie was soaring above him, he wished he could take it
back and he began to scream, "NO, no, no!" Just then
Bradford was shaking him and asking him if he was alright.
Josh looked out the window and realized he had been
dreaming. The sun was setting in the sky and he was covered
in sweat. The Jeep was parked in the driveway and his
mother was unbuckling Tabitha from her car seat.

"Where's Jackie?" he said frantically, as he climbed up
abruptly to look over the seat.

"She's fine," Bradford said, opening the door and lifting her cage out of the back.

Josh was greatly relieved to see her, but he could still hear the voice in his ears, the voice that sounded like a tinkling of glass, "You must release her and set her free."

What's In A NAME?

Chapter 31

Bradford was thankful that it was Friday evening and both he and Desiree would be off tomorrow. He knew she was concerned about Walter Kendal since hearing of his escape, but Bradford felt in his heart that the man was harmless. He didn't know why, but he just had a gut feeling that the whole encounter was a fluke. He picked up Josh, threw him over his shoulder and thought about how different life was for people with children. He had spent his whole life alone or in relationships that seemed to go nowhere. He wanted to have Desiree over for dinner, but after spending some time at her home and dinner at her grandmom's, his house seemed rather cold and so uncluttered. It was as if no life breathed there.

Bradford and Desiree got both the children out of their coats and into their beds, and then settled in next to the fire place. Desiree made a pot of coffee and as she sipped from her ceramic mug, she thought about the strange old man who had sat right here in her house and felt a chill. She knew Bradford was here and that she was safe right now, but what if he were to come back? Bradford kept assuring her that he would not be so careless as to come back, but Desiree still felt uneasy. She looked at Bradford and thought about the kiss he'd given her in the parking lot earlier and felt a different kind of shiver, a good one.

"Have you always been called Bradford?" she said. She wanted to shorten it to Brad something terrible, but was afraid she'd insult him.

"Well, yes and no, my mother at times would slip up and call me Brad, but my father always used Bradford. He hated nicknames and would scold my mother if he heard her. When I got older and started school my third grade teacher, Ms. Smith, asked all the children in her classroom if they had a nickname or other name they preferred to be called by. So when she came to me, I said Brad. I was all of eight years old, and it seemed like the cool thing to do at the time, until

I received my first report card. I remember the day I brought it home. My father looked over the notes from Ms. Smith that said things like, 'Brad is doing quite well in his studies and it is a pleasure to have Brad in my classroom.' Well, even at eight years of age I could see the vein lines bulging in my father's temple. He kept asking my mother, do we have a son named Brad? Last time I checked his name was Bradford and he was named after my father Bradford Steven Stiltz! My father marched into her classroom the next morning and informed Ms. Smith that if he intended for his son to be called Brad he would have named him that and that my name was Bradford and he expected her to call me by it. So I have always been rather frightened of people who've tried to shorten it ever since." He chuckled and looked at her and thought to himself, 'but I think I'd let you call me anything you want'.

Desiree curled up on the couch and thought about the day's events. Her life had changed drastically in just weeks. She ran her fingers through her short silky hair and realized she hadn't felt this good about herself in a long time.

"So where does a name like Desiree come from?" he said with a smile.

"Well, I was almost Napoleons fiancé, almost, just not quite." She laughed and wondered if he remembered Desiree Clary from his history class. "Yep, good ole Desiree Clary, you know rumor has it she went nuts at the end of her life and was said to go to sleep in the morning and then awake at night and eat breakfast. My mother's family came over to America from France and she found the name unique. I think it's atrocious," she laughed and wished secretly that Bradford would still be there in the morning. Why, she'd stay up all night too, she thought.

Bradford knew it was growing late and he should leave but he enjoyed every second he spent with her and her children. "You know Desiree, I've been thinking and I just want to tell you how much I have enjoyed both Joshua and Tabitha. I never really thought that much about children until watching you with yours. You are such a terrific mother, and Josh, he's so clever and so boisterous. He can be a real piece of work, in a good way, and Tabitha, she's just a doll. You have made me decide to do something I should have done a long time ago. I want to find my son. What would you think about that?"

Desiree didn't know what to think. Every other guy that she'd met since the death of John, did not want anything to do with her once they found out she had two children. She remembered him telling her about being engaged and Patti giving their son up for adoption. "Well Bradford that could be really good if he's receptive or that could be really bad. What if he's happy with his life and doing well and isn't even aware he was adopted? You could really throw him for a loop."

Bradford knew she was right but it was something that he could never get out of his mind. It haunted him and each time he saw a young man, he wondered what had become of his son.

"How old is he now?" Desiree asked, concerned Bradford might get hurt or used in the end.

"He should be around nineteen or twenty if memory serves me correctly. I don't think it will be too hard with public record database websites, it's a whole lot easier than it used to be. I never wanted to pry into his life before he was eighteen, because I just felt if I had adopted a child, I would want the same respect. Leave me alone and let me raise my child, you gave him up. That's what I would have told the father." But it has been over eighteen years and I have had this on my mind for some time now. You have inspired me. I know that the couple that adopted him according to Patti, was Catholic and middle class. It has been so long ago only bits and pieces come to mind. I was so angry about her deciding to give him up that I just tried to block it all out. I do know however, that they lived here in Kentucky. Of course, they may have moved out of state after such a long time, that's possible. I have even thought about how he could be in Iraq serving his country. For all I know he could be dead! When I think about my weird habits, I wonder if he might have some of the same. Does any of this make since?"

Desiree nodded her head and wondered what it would be like to have a child she'd never met. They sat in silence for some time and from exhaustion began to yawn.

Bradford finally decided that he should leave. "Well Desiree, I guess I should be going, it's been a wonderful day and I have enjoyed every minute of it. Your grandmom is amazing!"

Desiree did not want him to go, but she did not want to come across as needy or clingy, so she stood up from the sofa and walked with him outside. "Bradford, thank you so much for all you've done, I mean taking Josh to the doctor's office and sitting with me was huge. How can I ever repay you?"

Bradford smiled as he contemplated the many ways she could repay him. "Well I can think of something you can do, actually two things." He tapped her nose, looked into her eyes, then gently and carefully kissed her. "That was one way and now for number two, stop worrying about Walter and Josh, everything is going to work out perfectly, you'll see."

Desiree was swooning and for a minute she didn't care if the world ended right that second. She was caught off guard that he had kissed her, even though it wasn't an open mouth kiss, it was still a kiss. This was so different than her relationship with John. With John it was more of a comfortable feeling, a friendship, but with Bradford it was like a fiery passion erupting inside of her. Her mind had never once contemplated that all this time, what she thought was just him being nice was actually more. Her self-esteem had gone down the toilet after losing John. How could she have known he was attracted to her, when she felt so unattractive?

She watched his Jeep pull out of the driveway then walked up the sidewalk and into the house. She was still tingling from the kiss from Bradford, when she realized she was all alone for the night. Locking the front door, she walked into the kitchen and looked out the French double doors to the wooded area past the creek. "Walter Kendal, who are you," she said aloud. "Where are you and why did you come to my house?"

Debbie's Shadow

Chapter 32

Marcie was nervous about meeting Benjamin at Frank's restaurant. She had it bad for him and he was playing with her emotions. She knew he liked her and thought she was attractive and intelligent, but there was something strange and dark about Benjamin that she just couldn't put her finger on.

She was so sick of her mother and father trying to control her life and at this point she didn't care anymore. If Benjamin dumped her, she'd get over it somehow. Her hair was freshly shampooed and blown dry and she was wearing a brand new shirt, it was lavender and wrapped around her waist and tied. She had a new brown leather coat and boots to match and when she walked in Frank's, men and women stared at her beauty. Marcie felt self-conscious, but no one else could tell that by looking at her. She walked down to the bar and sat down next to an older man with an indention where his wedding band usually sat. He had dark brown hair slicked back like someone out of a mob movie and he was flicking his cigarette over and over into the ashtray. As soon as Marcie pulled out a smoke, he had a flame waiting.

"Thank you," she said smiling. He never responded to Marcie, but instead motioned with his head at the bartender and said, "Whatever the lady needs."

Marcie was too young to drink, but she wondered if she could get by with her fake I.D. "I'll have a Cosmopolitan," she said. She and a friend got hooked on them after watching the show, 'Sex in the City'. They were actually quite good and this one was free, so it tasted even better. Not that Marcie cared, she had a credit card in her purse with a ten thousand dollar limit, but it was fun to see what she could get with her looks. The kitchen was behind glass and quite a ways from the bar, making it hard to see. She could make out the white chef coats and the tall hats, but she couldn't make out Ben.

It was almost 10:00 and Ben got off at around 10:30 or 11:00, but the bar was open until midnight. Marcie took a drag off her cigarette and took a look around the bar. There were two college guys playing trivia at a game monitor. They were talking too loud and trying to impress a brunette with short hair and a tattoo on her neck. She had a friend with her that looked old enough to be her mother, but she was dressed too young and painfully thin. There were two old men, eating peanuts and trail mix, drinking beer and talking shop and then the mob guy who kept eyeing her up and down.

"My name is Jerry, nice to meet you," before Marcie could tell him her name, he asked her how her drink was.

"Oh, it's great. Thank you, really you didn't have to do that. I'm Marcie."

"Haven't seen you around here, Marcie. You waiting on someone?"

"Yes, I have a friend who works here. You come here much, Jerry?"

"They should have my name engraved on a brass plate," he said, then chuckled. "I'm thinking about doing a little

227

gambling later at the casino boat, you and your friend interested?" He smiled and looked her up and down again. Marcie loved the attention and she could tell he had money. She wondered for a second what her father would think if she brought him around. She stood up and took off her leather coat and watched his eyes travel up to her lavender top and then back to her eyes.

"I'm not sure but I can ask him when he gets off." She knew that would put a stop to her Cosmos but she loved playing hard to get and with Benjamin it was more the opposite.

"Your boyfriend works here?" he said, as he blew his smoke out of his nostrils, tapped his rocks glass and eyed the bartender.

"Yes, he's a chef here." Marcie watched as he smiled and then turned to face her.

"Darlin, what are you doing with a cook?" I can tell by looking at you that you got some class. You could do better than that sweetie, but it's your life."

About that time Benjamin came out of the kitchen wearing a white chef coat with his name embroidered on the chest and a white chef hat in his hand. He looked tired and sweaty, but he took her breath away. "Hi Marcie, I see Jerry's keeping you company." Ben smiled at Jerry and winked. "I bet you didn't think I had it in me, did ya Jer?"

Jerry laughed and motioned for the bartender to bring her another drink. "You better hurry Ben, you're about to lose your little lady out here. I been fighting the men off left and right, but I can only do so much."

Benjamin leaned in and kissed Marcie on the lips in front of everyone, just to mark his territory. "Let me go change and I'll be right back, okay." He looked at her and smiled as Jerry patted him on the back.

Benjamin returned a little later wearing a silk shirt and a pair of jeans. His hair was pulled back and he looked as charming as usual. Marcie wondered about Ben, he came across like a redneck at times, but there was something very distinguished about how he carried himself. She knew he had a rough upbringing, but he didn't act like it.

Benjamin's friend Clark came out and joined them. He had short hair almost a razor shave and he talked like he came from the streets. He was handsome in the fact that he had nice features and had a good build, but there was something about him that bothered Marcie. Pretty soon they were all playing trivia and laughing about who knew more useless bits of information.

Marcie had never been out in public with Benjamin. She had only heard about Clark and the other friends he talked about. She had never witnessed this side of Ben, this was a side of him more open than she had ever seen. He picked her up off her bar stool and swung her around and pulled her tight to him. He looked in her eyes and at one point said, "I want the whole world to know you're with me." Marcie felt so safe again and she had let another wall of bricks crumble. So much so that she ended up back at his apartment and back in his bed.

But, this time it was obvious that she was going to have to compete. There was a framed picture face down on his nightstand and when Ben went to the restroom Marcie pulled it up to take a peek. She was lovely, she had long dark curly hair that traveled the length of the picture. She had dimples, large eyes and an even larger mouth. Marcie put the photo back down on the table just as Ben entered the bedroom. "What was she like?"

"Who?" asked Ben, knowing she'd seen the picture.

"Debbie?"

"She was incredible, beautiful and I loved her very much."

Marcie's heart sunk and she lay there not knowing what to do, she didn't know whether to leave, cry or just let him get it all out. "It's okay Marcie, she's gone and I am with you." He touched her nose and began to kiss her. She felt relieved but there was still a weird uneasiness. She didn't want to be second place in anyone's life.

Benjamin was working on a buzz and he had lost count of the beers and the shots of tequila he'd had at Frank's. He knew he had blown it by forgetting to put Debbie's picture away. Truth was, he had concocted a lie partially, but there was a girl once upon a time before the wreck, who he had loved very much. He felt bad for Marcie, but he was getting drunker by the minute and she should have known what she was getting herself into.

Marcie's mind was spinning and she was replaying the evening. All his charm and complements in front of his coworkers convinced her that he loved her, but she never had to compete with a dead woman before.

He ran his hand across her face and traced her lips. He pulled her to him and began to kiss her softly and before she knew it she was melting into his body, and she was in heaven. He was her soul mate. Then Marcie heard two words that shattered the darkness and left her speechless. Benjamin lips began kissing her neck and inhaling her skin. He was running his fingers through her hair and moaning softly, when all the sudden he began to say two words Marcie would never forget, "Debbie, mmmmn Debbie."

A Familiar Friend

Chapter 33

Bradford awoke with a permanent grin across his face, after a night filled with dreams about Desiree. He honestly felt like a teen in high school again and he loved every minute of it. He wasn't sure how this would go over at work but he couldn't wait to see her. Life was exciting again and he was ready to explore adventures he had all but given up on. As soon as he got to the office, he was going to get right to finding his son. He couldn't wait to start a new chapter in his life after years of waiting and wondering. Now he had Desiree to thank for it. Honestly he couldn't think of a warmer, kinder, better person to bring home to meet his family. The fact that she had children didn't bother him.

233

He welcomed them and had actually had more fun with them than he had on any date he could remember.   The stuffy, flakey women his friend Tom was forever fixing him up with were exhausting. He had finally found a down to earth woman with a big heart and great lips that he'd dreamed about kissing. Just the thought of it made him want to get to work early and see her. He found her new haircut extremely sexy and something about her made him feel so needed and so wanted, but not for his money. This was a new feeling and he was enjoying it.

He showered and dressed, then grabbed a cup of coffee. He walked outside and looked at the beginning signs of spring and thought that nature had never looked so glowing. Once he arrived at the office he went straight to work at uncovering his past. After several hours and several trips past Desiree's desk to catch a smile and a glimpse of her, he had a name, Larry Stewart. He had to be at court at nine a.m. for a hearing and another at one p.m., but after that he was free to take a ride to a part of town he hadn't expected to uncover in his search, but he was still anxious.   Would Desiree consider going with him, he hoped so. He shot her an e-mail and she sent one back.

Desiree, Good morning beautiful! I was wondering if you would like to take a late lunch and go with me to meet the man who raised my son. I have a sinking feeling just from the bad area of town he lives in and I could really use your support. Whatta say?"

Love, Bradford

Dear Bradford,

After all you have done for me in the past few days I hate to refuse, but I can't today. I have a paper to write and it's a final. Please forgive me? I really want to meet your son Bradford and I can meet up with you after class, but I have missed so much school already and it's almost break.

I will say a prayer for you.

Love, Desiree

This relationship at work may be easier than he'd thought. Bradford grabbed his brief case and headed to the parking garage. As he passed Desiree's mini-van, he thought about what kind of car she would look good in. He hoped that his journey would lead him to a place of peace finally and a rest knowing his son, who he gave up was okay.

Future Unclear

Chapter 34

Walter was shocked. The last thing he thought Buddy would do would be to leave him at the truck stop. Walter felt better after eating and having slept a good four hours. He ran his hand over his head and marveled at the strangeness he felt from the absence of hair. He started walking down the parking lot and realized it had been a full day since he'd left the hospital. It was a strange town and he didn't know a soul. He wondered what the next chapter in his life would hold, imprisonment, reconciliation with his family or a life traveling from town to town as a vagabond. When he had reached the expressway, he saw a sign that read '165 miles to Barkley'. About the time he decided to stick out his thumb, an eighteen wheeler blew his horn and pulled over. It was Buddy.

"You're faster than lightening Walt," he smiled and motioned him over. Walter didn't know what to expect, were the cops on their way? Had Buddy gone to the police station? He guessed it was a chance he'd have to take, he trotted up to the truck with the familiar flames, climbed up and stuck his head through the open window.

"I ran down to the K-Mart to get you some jeans and sneakers, but by the time I got back you were gone Ole timer. And talk about looking different, if it wasn't for that blue sweatshirt I bought you, I wouldn't have recognized you!" Walter sighed and climbed inside the truck.

"Now here's my offer," he said looking at Walter seriously and running his fingers through his beard. "I got a load I have to have in Georgia by tomorrow, but I will be going through Barkley if you want me to drop you off there? But if I were you Walter, I'd think hard about that one. They'll be looking for you there for sure."

Walter knew he was right, but he was so tired of running away from his problems. He was so tired of running away from his life and he just wanted to reconcile his relationships with his children and see his grandchildren. But more than anything he just wanted to see Ruthie, he was going to the cemetery and he was going to talk to her about this. He had already talked to God, now he wanted to listen to her voice. She would know what to do, she always did steer him in the right direction.

"I guess I'll be going back to Barkley. I don't have anywhere else to turn and I don't want to cause you any trouble, Buddy." Walter picked up the bag from K-Mart and looked at Buddy, smiling in disbelief at God's grace. "I owe you so much already, my friend."

"Walter, don't you worry about it. You have helped me more than you know. I haven't had my head this clear in a long time. I'm finally prepared to put my priorities in order and make time for my children and the people I love, instead of worrying about money and how fast I can get the shipment to the next city." He turned and looked at Walter with sincerity. "I have you to thank for that, Walter!"

Walter had a little over three hours before he would be home. He wished it could be different, but life had a way of bringing chaos and serenity, calmness and storms. Walter was ready to face his past head on and he was ready to work on his future. He had made things right with his maker and he was determined to make things right with his family, if it was the last thing he did before he died. He looked at Buddy and back at the road and thought about little Josh and his mother and all the other people he owed. He wondered why he had ever entered her house and why he had ever met her son. Everything happens for a reason, but this time he was at a loss. The future for him was full of uncertainty. What could he offer anyone, he wasn't sure but he would die trying. He planned on making things right with the people he loved, if it was the last thing he did. Walter thought about Jackie, he had brought her with him and he should be bringing her back. Of course, he knew she was only a bird, but he had grown to love that bird like a best friend and he sure hoped she was faring well. Life had a funny way of coming full circle and he had a feeling he would end up exactly where he was supposed to be. But for now he was just thankful that a God that he had been so angry with in the past, had heard a man like him pray in a truck stop restroom. Not only did He hear, but He was swift to answer him. Walter knew he could have been picked up by any old trucker going down the road but he hadn't, he had been picked up by someone who had taken care of him and even felt like a friend. As the road ran underneath him, Walter knew that there was something way bigger guiding him.

The Eyes of the

Wicked and the Good

Chapter 35

Bradford walked down the sidewalk on Shelton Street. It was filled with cigarette butts and trash littered yards. There were broken beer bottles and shotgun houses lined the street. He finally approached a yellow home with a screen door trimmed in green, chipped paint. There was a window air unit in the front window, dripping condensation on the porch. Adorning the porch, was a plastic lawn chair and a small table. A straw broom propped against the door frame seemed to hold the image together. Bradford opened the screen door and knocked several times on the door. A

242

voice echoed from inside, "Give me a second, for Christ's sake!" A short man with tiny eyes and a red nose looked him over quizzically. He smelled of liquor and cigar smoke.

"What is this? Are you a detective?" But before Bradford could answer him, he began again. "If you're lookin for that no good son of mine, I haven't seen him since he screwed his life up royally. So if he's done something illegal again, it's not any of my damn business." He eyed Bradford and looked him over. Then he smirked at him, revealing teeth that were tobacco stained with several just missing. He took a puff of the cigar he was holding and began to cough.

Bradford took a step back and felt sick at his stomach. This was the man who had raised his son? He couldn't believe what he was seeing and he couldn't believe how heartless and utterly disgusting this man was. "You are Larry Stewart, correct?"

"Yes, and what the hell do you want with the likes of me?"

Bradford turned back to the repulsive little man named Larry and asked him if he knew where his son was living or where he worked.

"Last thing I heard, was Ben had a year of volunteer work at that school for blind children." Larry cleared his sinuses and spit a large chunk of phlegm over into the bushes. "What's he done now? Hell, there's no tellin with Ben. That piece of crap was always getting into trouble."

"Larry, is your wife home, maybe I could speak to her for a minute?" Bradford was hoping that there was someone who had been in his son's life that was caring and loving. He just couldn't imagine what life had been like for him and had never pictured a family like this wanting to adopt. Things had changed now and to adopt these days would cost you quite a bit of money and require background checks. Maybe Larry had been different before? He always pictured his son growing up in a nice modest home with a dog or cat and a basketball hoop. He never once thought in a million years that he would be staring into the blood shot eyes of Larry Stewart, or that someone like this was the only role model his son had for a father. "Maybe your wife could help me, sir" he asked again.

244

"She's dead, asshole," and with that Larry tried to shut the door, but Bradford stuck his foot in the way. Bradford felt like he was in some kind of movie and this wasn't really happening.

"What are you trying to make me for, a fool?"

Bradford thought he'd nailed it on the head, when he said fool. He looked at Larry's thin white T-shirt and his scrawny, little arms and legs, he had cheap scotch on his breath and yellow stained fingers. "Larry I'm your son's real father. I just …just wanted to try to meet him." Bradford was speaking through clenched teeth now.

Larry looked Bradford over and wondered if he could possibly get any money out of him. He noticed his nice clothes and saw money written all over this character. "Who would have thought my Benjamin would have a father like you? Well, well what do we have here, a real professional, ah? So, what do you want to know exactly? I mean if there was something in it for me, maybe we could work something out." Larry smirked again and studied Bradford.

Bradford was shocked that he had allowed his own flesh and blood to be brought up with such filth. He felt sick at his stomach as if someone had punched him in the gut so hard they'd taken his breath. Before Bradford could think straight, he had doubled up his fist and knocked the hell out of Larry Stewart. It had all happened so fast, his adrenalin was pumping and he was shaking all over. He had never hit a man before. "Are you okay?" he said before thinking how insane that sounded.

"I think you broke my nose," Larry said, as blood ran out of his nostrils and over his lips. He gripped the door frame and wobbled back and forth coughing up blood.

Bradford was stunned, he had completely lost control and this was unfamiliar territory. He tried to shake it off and began to walk down the sidewalk, hearing Larry Stewart moaning and cussing with every step he took. His heart was pounding in his ear drums and he knew if he didn't turn around and leave right then, he'd be in danger of going to jail. He opened the Jeep door and hopped in and spun the tires leaving. All the way back to the office he replayed the whole scenario. He pulled into the parking garage and began to sob, he threw his fist in the air and he cursed God. "Why did you allow my son to be raised by such a sorry son of a bitch? Why God? Why? How could you let this happen?"

He thought about all the times he was out eating filet and lobster, impressing clients and all the vacations he'd taken and his luxury home that could house ten people and all the while his own flesh and blood was living in trash. His own son was being verbally and no doubt physically abused and he was sitting back and enjoying his life, without a care in the world. How could he? He wiped his nose on his jacket and tried to steady his breathing. What would he tell Desiree? What would he tell his parents?

He banged on the steering wheel and he swore that if it was the last thing he did, he was going to make up for all the hell his son had been through. Knowing he was in no shape to work now, he drove out of the parking garage and headed towards the school for the blind. His mind was filled with Larry and he kept replaying the scene over and over again, his fist smashing into Larry's face. He looked at his knuckles and they were red and swollen. Was it from him beating the steering wheel, or was it from Larry's face? He didn't know but his whole entire body felt numb.

He wondered what his son could have done to be in such trouble with the law. He had tried to do a background check, but apparently he was a juvenile at the time, and those files were sealed, unless a judge ordered them to be opened.

He pulled into the parking lot and walked up the steps into the school for the blind. The receptionist had a pleasant appearance and golden blonde hair, she looked to be pushing fifty and she smiled up at Bradford with teeth that looked a little too white, porcelain Bradford thought.

"Hello, I'm Bradford Stiltz and I was wondering if you could help me? I'm looking for a young man who is doing community service here at your school, his name is Stewart, Benjamin Stewart."

"Let's see," she said placing her bifocals up to the bridge of her nose, she thumbed through the clipboard in front of her. "Well, it looks like Mr. Stewart is no longer with us, he's completed his service here."

"Do you happen to know where I might be able to find him?"

"Sir, that's confidential," she said smiling at him. "But I do know that he was employed at Frank's Steak House on 4th Street while he was here." She winked and her eyes seemed to twinkle.

"Thank you, Miss?' He raised his eyebrows and waited for her to tell him her name.

"Mrs. Green, Alma's my first name, and you are most welcome."

Bradford smiled, thinking about how some women get lovelier with age. Alma's champagne colored hair and polished teeth, perfectly matched the fine lines that adorned her eyes. He thought about Desiree and how beautiful he thought she would look at fifty. He hurried down the steps and typed in the address on his GPS for directions.

The Truth Shall Set You Free

Chapter 36

Daniel decided he was taking Sandra and the twins to her mother's house for the evening. He felt like it was time to explain to Brenda his circumstances and the reason for his lack of support during their mother's slow, yet deadly decline. After talking to her on the phone, he knew it was hurting their relationship and that communication was the only way to get past the family difficulties. He was sure that had been the main problem between him and his father and he knew if he stayed home tonight he would just pace the floors and look out the window at the patrol car circling the subdivision. "Good ole Dad," he thought, "I wonder what you've got yourself into, Pops." He sure missed him and Mom. Life had radically changed in a little over a year. He missed Brenda and he needed her right now more than he ever had.

This was just what he needed to do to restore respect from Burt and explain things to his sister. Burt had been giving him the cold shoulder too long, he was aware that they all thought she wore the pants in the family and had him on a short rope.

He pulled in Brenda's driveway and spotted the patrol car that had followed him there, as well as the one circling Brenda's street. Knocking on the door, he was greeted by Sam with a hearty bark.

"Well, look who it is," Brenda said, while motioning for the dog to get back. "Come on in bro," she said smiling.

Daniel hugged his sister, anxious for the truth to come out. "You're lookin good, Brenda." He smiled and looked into her eyes searching for any trace of bitterness. "Is Burt still home, or has he already left for work?"

"Oh, he's here, called in too, it gave him an excuse to keep me company." She winked, knowing full well he was her rock. "The better question is where my darling niece and nephew are this evening?"

"Sandra had to stop by her mother's for something," he said half lying. They walked into the kitchen and sat down, making small talk for several minutes. Burt had never even come in to greet him. "Brenda the reason I came over isn't really about dad. There is something that has been eating away at me and I really need to get this off my chest. Do you think you could get Burt to come in here? I need to tell him too." His eyes were pleading and Brenda's mind was already in overdrive.

Was he getting a divorce, had she been cheating on him? Or maybe he had been having an affair? Well, it would serve Sandra right the way she's controlled him. What if he knows where dad is? Yes, that's it, she thought, he's been hiding him the whole time her mind continued to churn until Burt walked in the kitchen, eyed Daniel curtly and joined them at the table.

Daniel knew Burt was disappointed in him, if not angered. He could feel the vibes of uneasiness when he walked into the room. "Hey Burt, how's it goin man," he said, trying to lighten up the mood. Before Daniel knew it he had two faces staring at him. "Okay, well, I don't know exactly where to start. So, I guess I'll start with mom and my lack of support and help when you both needed me the most." He cleared his throat searching for the right words and picked up a salt shaker with a large red S on it and began to play with it nervously. "It all seemed to happen so swiftly and yet so slowly I didn't notice it at first. It steamed in full force, like a train you couldn't stop. Sandra, well, Sandra."

Brenda kept looking at him like, spit it out already. "My wife, Sandra was diagnosed with Multiple Sclerosis during Mom's last months with us." He began to choke up, and he fought back tears. He remembered the first time he had heard those words, those words that had changed his life forever. "Sandra was actually in the hospital for several days on steroids during some of mother's worst days and I'm so sorry. She became numb from the waist down and lost the ability to walk at one point." He looked up at Brenda who had placed her hand over her mouth in shock and then turned towards Burt. "I am really sorry I wasn't there for you guys. It was so hard to pick and choose. I had to choose my wife, but I know you all went through hell."

"It's okay Dan, we understand now. We just wish you would have opened up to us sooner," Burt said looking compassionately at Daniel. "Why didn't you tell us? We would have understood."

Brenda felt sick inside. She felt like the worst sinner in the world. All this time she had been condemning Sandra, judging her and even calling her an unfit mother and her so sick.

"I would have confided in you both sooner, but Sandra made me promise not to. She said that, well, she thought Brenda, that you just had so much on your plate already and she knew you would break your back trying to care for the twins and Mom. She has always respected you so much and prays all the time that you and Burt will be able to have children." He looked down and felt bad that he had brought it up. "She always says it's unfair that we have two and she's not even able to take care of them all the time, and here you both have energy. Well, you know what I mean. Now, we have all these problems arising with Dad, seems like it never ends."

Brenda looked at her brother and saw a tiredness in him she'd never seen before.

"How is she now, Dan?" Burt asked, remembering the last time he'd seen her at the funeral she had looked fine.

Brenda chimed in, "Yes Daniel, how is she," with a look of concern on her face. She knew MS was a serious illness, but she really didn't know that much about it.

"She's better I think, truth is I never know from day to day. She has a lot of balance problems and while Mom was so bad, Sandra's legs would just buckle under her. She has so many neurological difficulties, bladder issues, and cognitive issues and severe pain, you name it. I had to hire a housekeeper and put the twins in daycare while I'm at work, because we never know when she's going to have a bad day."

He felt like he was living in a nightmare, in somebody else's world. He tried not to think about how energetic Sandra used to be, hell, she had enough energy for the both of them. The saddest part of this disease was Sandra still looked the same. You really couldn't tell much was wrong with her unless you lived with her and witnessed the slurring and the fatigue.

"What can we do Daniel, how can we help?" They both looked at him with such compassion, it was breaking him. He had been strong for so long, but now he was just tired. He didn't know how anyone could help him save a miracle healing from God, or a magic wand.

"I'm fine now and Sandra started treatment, she's getting her shots and trying to adjust to this new life. I just wanted to explain my actions and get this off my chest." He sat the salt shaker down feeling a little awkward now.

"You know I'm here if you need me, Daniel? You know for that matter, Burt and I are both here and we are going to get through this. We are going to get through all of this," she said as she eyed the patrol car pulling down a side street. "Well, whatta ya say we go in the living room and sit and chat in front of the fire. I'll make some coffee and you and Burt can talk."

The men headed to the living room, Brenda opened the coffee container and began to measure out grounds. She felt so ashamed of herself for the way she had acted towards Sandra at the funeral. She was probably in excruciating pain the whole time she was there.

Brenda walked into the living room, sat down next to Daniel and she patted him on the leg. She looked up at her big brother and in a rather serious tone, said, "What are we going to do about Dad?" She had been horribly wrong about Sandra, what if she was wrong about her father? And then far in the distance she heard a voice. 'Collect call from Walter Kendal, will you accept the charges?' and then a vision of her finger pushing the 'end' button.

Reminiscing

Chapter 37

Desiree had tried to call Bradford when she got out of class, but only got his voice-mail. She hoped he had found his son's adopted family and was able to set up a meeting. She just couldn't imagine the emotional strain he must be under. She creased her brow and said an unspoken prayer that everything would work out.

The children had been remarkably well behaved of late. Jackie had been a great addition she thought, as the bird sat on the living room rug with his short stout legs and gray plumage. Even though she knew Jackie was only a bird, she could tell she was rather fond of Josh and had even begun climbing on top of his tennis shoes. Tabitha found it terribly funny and would roll on the floor holding her stomach. She had gotten used to cleaning up the bird poo and had begun to time how long Jackie could stay out of her cage without making a mess.

Josh would try and stand up and take a few steps without Jackie falling off, but his feet were not as big as Walters. Josh smiled to himself when he thought of Walter, but in a sad sort of way.

Desiree had decided to take care of some unfinished business. Since she was almost finished with the semester, and her life seemed to be falling into place. It was finally time to remove the painful reminders of the past. She went to the garage and grabbed a stack of empty boxes that she had kept just for this moment. She drug them through the hallway into the bedroom and went right to work. She went to the mirrored closet and pulled open John's side of the door. "It's time," she said aloud and sighed, feeling guilt begin to rise up in her stomach. She wasn't even sure which one she felt like she was cheating on, Bradford or John? But if she was going to do this, she knew she needed to do this fast. Even if nothing came of the relationship with Bradford, Desiree realized she had to get on with her life. She began to take each article of clothing off the hanger, fold them robotically and place them in the boxes.

Each shirt carried a memory, an occasion, a date, or a perfect ball game. She decided to make this a cheat night. As bad as she hated drunk drivers and irresponsible parents, she needed a drink. Of course, she would never get behind the wheel of a car and she just needed something to help her heavy heart.

Desiree walked down the hall and peeked in on Tabitha and Josh in the TV room. Josh and Tabitha were watching cartoons, lying on their bellies with knees bent and feet waving. One petite homing pigeon was sitting on top of Josh's back, like it was the most natural thing in the world to do. Desiree smiled and went to the china cabinet, she reached in the back cabinet and pulled out a bottle of cabernet sauvignon and a wine key. She poured a hefty glass, took a rather large sip and headed back to the bedroom. She remembered when she and John had started dating, she had loved her wine. That was before the children were born and she had to give up her cigarettes too. She thought she'd drive John mad before the baby ever came, hiding them in places no one would find. Sometimes she hid them so well, she forgot herself. There was the top of the medicine cabinet, pocket of any given coat hanging on the rack, but her favorite place was in John's tackle box. He'd smell it on her and say, "I know you're smoking Des, and I know it's not good for the baby, so fess up sweetheart." She told him every secret hiding place except that one, she figured one smoke a day wouldn't kill her. She knew she shouldn't, but she knew women that smoked the whole entire time and their babies were big as a horse. She heard footsteps coming down the hall and then Josh was standing at the door watching her. "Whatcha doing with all Daddy's stuff, Mommy?"

Desiree frowned, thinking that maybe she should have waited until the children were in bed or at her grandmom's house. "I'm putting Dad's things away," she said in a voice that was broken.

"But why Mommy, where are you taking them?"

"Well, Josh, Mommy's going to give some things to poor people who need clothes."

"Oh, you mean like Walter, right Mommy?" His eyes looked so concerned when he said it. She had so many mixed feelings about Walter. A part of her thought he might have been just a helpless old man, but another part of her thought he may be a dangerous criminal. She was keeping with the case and checking in with the detective. They felt sure he would go back home. "Right, Mommy?"

"Sure Josh, like Walter."

"Did you put the bird up?"

"Yes, Mommy!"

"Can I help, Mommy?"

"No, Josh, I think I've got this, but if you want, you can empty Daddy's sock drawer." Josh hopped like a rabbit over to the chest of drawers and began to place the socks in a box. Desiree was finished with the closet and had started on the top drawers of the chest. "You are such a big helper tonight Josh, I am really proud of what a nice young man you are becoming lately." Desiree reached over and took another sip of her wine and then grabbed Josh and started tickling him under his arms. "You have been so, so good for Mommy," she said, rubbing the top of his head.

"I have to be good," Josh said. "The angel wants me to obey you." He looked down and then continued to talk. "She said that I am very important and she has a very special assignment for me." His eyes lit up so bright and his facial expression had taken on the excitement of Christmas Eve.

Desiree's mind instantly thought about Josh and his history of tall tales. He'd been telling them since he learned to talk. But then Walter had been the truth and she had not believed him. "An angel, huh? Well does this angel of yours have a name?" She stopped putting the clothes away and looked at Josh, who had made his way to the bottom of John's closet and was pulling all the shoes out.

"Her name is Belinda and she is beautiful Mommy." His eyes were very large, as he spread the length of his arms out. "She's ten foot tall, as tall as a building," he said animatedly. He quickly grabbed his hands and put them over his mouth. He did not want to mess up his mission.

Desiree looked puzzled, but for whatever reason in her heart she felt like Josh really had seen something. She snapped out of her daze and went to check on Tabitha, who had crawled up on the sofa and was fast asleep.

"Josh, help me drag these boxes out to the garage, please." Josh pulled on his, but it was too heavy and Desiree had to point to a lighter box in the corner. She had gone back once more, this time alone and began to stack the boxes in a corner. Gazing around the garage at the rest of John's things, she sighed even louder, wishing she'd brought her wine glass with her. There were so many tools, big red shiny tool boxes that took up whole walls. There were motorized airplanes, model car kits and a canoe was hanging above her head.

"I miss you, John," she said in the silence. Then she came across a shelf filled with mixed matched items and objects that needed repairs. There was a jewelry box, solid cherry and hand carved by John. Desiree loved the box, but it had gotten knocked off her vanity table and the glass mirror inside had shattered, along with a secret compartment designed to hide her valuable rings. She remembered when John had given it to her and the witty remark he had made. "That's for the huge stones I will buy you one day." She smiled crookedly at the memory.

Then she picked it up and examined the outside, it was perfect. She didn't remember John fixing it and if he did why didn't he bring it in to her. Perhaps a surprise, she thought as she opened the box to find the compartment completely intact and instead of the mirror that had been there, now there was a carving of flowers. They looked like daisies and were so lovely, the workmanship was impeccable. She opened the compartment to see if there were any more surprises and found a folded note. "Oh, John, you can't do this to me!" She said it rather loudly and her eyes began to well up. Then she turned and walked back inside and grabbed another glass of wine.

"Well Bradford, I guess you are not the only one on an expedition tonight." She held up her wine glass and said 'cheers' in the silence. Her heart was pounding and she could not believe that this had been in there the whole time, and that she was digging up pieces of her heart that had healed. Maybe I should save this for Tabitha and one day pass it to her she thought. "No, this will drive me nuts, I have to read it!"

She took another swig of wine and felt a little woozy, but not drunk. Picking up the box, her fingers delicately traced the flowers and the small drawer that held the note and she sat down on the step. She took out the note, took another swig of wine for good measure and then told herself to breathe. As she unfolded the note once and then once again, what she saw made no sense. It was a check list. Desiree was confused at first. There was a list of grocery items and a list with a heading that said 'water' that had a list of numbers underneath. The second roll had a list that was labeled 'Payments'. Desiree read the first item and wasn't sure what to make of it:

1. Fixed sagging gutter – $10.00

2. Unclogged sink $20.00

3. glued rocking chair $5.00

Desiree's heart sank, this was not a letter from John, but a letter from that man, Walter, who had apparently tried to repay her. He was the secret angel, she thought. She just couldn't believe what she was reading. Had he really fixed her gutters? She sprung forward a little too fast and felt her head spin. Then she walked carefully out back to the patio and looked at the gutter that now stood proudly. Glancing back down at the note, she then flipped it over.

Dear Desiree,

My name is Walter and if you are reading this, there is a chance you know about me. I am so sorry for what I have done. I promise to pay you back if I can. I have never stolen anything from you except water and some eggs and toast and juice. I have kept track and even tried to repay you by helping out around here. I only stayed a couple hours a day to get out of the elements.

I lost my wife and I know you lost your husband. I wish I could escape the pain that fills my heart.

Please forgive me?

Sincerely, Walter

Desiree sighed again loudly, slowly letting the air escape her lungs. She knew she had to make things right, but how? She walked back inside the house with the jewelry box in hand and sat it down on her vanity table, slipping the note back inside the compartment.

"Mommy?" She heard Josh's voice, but she didn't see him until he peeped his head from around the closet door. There was a pile of John's shoes strung from one end of the room to the other. "Close your eyes, Mommy."

"Okay Josh," she said, thinking this was not a night that needed any more surprises.

"Are they shut tight?"

"Yes, Josh."

"Okay open your eyes Mommy, open your eyes!" Desiree looked up to see Josh standing with his feet planted inside John's leather, Justin cowboy boots. They were western style and so big on him they swallowed his legs, clear up to his thighs. He had taken off his pants and was only clad in red spider man underwear and the boots. Desiree couldn't help but giggle at him. His ruffled hair and big brilliant eyes only made Desiree admire him more. "Mommy, can I keep these?"

"Sure, Josh."

"One day Mommy, I am going to get bigger and walk around in my daddy's shoes!"

Desiree's glee went to tears in an instant. She quickly photographed the image to store forever in her memory bank. A perfect picture of her little boy, growing someday into a man like John, she hoped.

Blood is thicker than Water

Chapter 38

Bradford was on a mission and now that he had gotten this far, he thought why not go all the way. He had just left the school for the blind and was less than eight miles from Frank's. Boy did he feel like having a drink! He had no idea what to say to his son. For years he had rehearsed it over and over in his mind and he had thought of everything he would tell him. How he would explain Patti and the decision, how he wanted to keep him, he had replayed his words like a tape recorder, but now after meeting the scum he had allowed to raise his son, he was silenced. No words could ever make everything right. He always hated the words 'I'm sorry', they seemed like such a cop out to him. But he knew that he would say them because no matter how

269

hard he tried to come up with something better, he just couldn't. How could any words describe the sorrow he felt?

He parked and made his way to the entrance. The sky had grown dark and it had begun to rain. Bradford wished it could wash away his pain. There was a heavy oak door with a brass handle, above was an etched glass with the word 'Frank's'. He walked in and made his way down to the bar area and wondered if the bartender who greeted him was his own flesh and blood. He peered into his eyes and then read the name tag attached to his black shirt that said 'Scott'.

Bradford sighed heavily and thought about the day he'd had and how thankful he was now, that Desiree had not been able to come along for the journey. He knew how she felt about drinking and he knew that tonight, more than any night, he needed a drink.

"What can I get for you, sir?"

"I think I'll have a shot of Makers and a tall draft, what do you have on tap?" Scott gave him the run down and he ordered an Amber bock.

"Rough day at the office?" Scott smiled as he sat his hefty pour of whiskey down and Bradford downed it quickly.

"You could say that."

"I'll have another shot, please."

Bradford began to unwind and study the male servers that were coming in and out of the dining room. "So Scott, do you happen to know a guy named Benjamin that works here?"

"Yep, sure do, he's cooking tonight. Would you like me to go get him for you?"

Bradford didn't know what to say. He didn't want to stun him during work. It looked pretty busy in there and he knew this was not something you just did on a whim. 'Hello Ben, I'm your real father, nice to meet you.' Hell, what was he thinking anyway? Maybe he just needed to walk away. Maybe he would regret this more than he did meeting Larry. Now he knew why people didn't go looking for their children they'd given up.

"Well, I don't want to bother him now while it's busy, do you happen to know what time he gets off?'

"Yeah, he should be off by nine or nine thirty. He came in first and so he should be the first cut. Would you like a menu, sir?"

Bradford wasn't hungry, but he knew he couldn't sit here and drink for two or three hours with nothing on his stomach, so he agreed to look at one. There was a glass thick wall separating the line cooks and chefs from the dining room, but with a good eye you could faintly make out their chef hats and blurred images. Bradford looked around the bar at the faces. He wanted to relax but he just kept trying to get the words to come.

"Hello Benjamin, I have been trying to find you for some time now." "Hello Ben, my name is Bradford and I just learned recently that you are my son." No, he thought, that's no good. What if he acted as if Patti had just let him know he had a son? That might work he thought and then he decided that he needed to start this relationship with truth. About the time he had given up and his head had begun to swirl, a pretty young girl sat down next to him and his life would never be the same.

"Hey Scott, how you doin tonight? Is Benjamin still getting off early?"

Bradford was impressed to say the least. Wow, she was a looker; long blonde hair that looked like silk half way down her back and beautiful eyes, with a nice figure to boot. She wore glasses that made her look intelligent and strong.

Scott, nodded his head and smiled. "Hello Marcie! I'm alright, seems Ben's pretty popular tonight, he's got you and the gentleman next to you waiting for him to make an appearance."

Marcie turned and studied Bradford. "You're waiting for Benjamin?"

Bradford was caught off guard. No turning back he thought. I can lie and leave or act like it was a mistake, but with each thought, he knew he couldn't turn back. He knew he probably should, but he had wanted to find his son his whole life, and now he was going to do it. "Yes, my name is Bradford, and you are?"

"I'm Marcie, Benjamin's girlfriend." She was really curious about this guy, he was handsome and didn't look like the type to be affiliated with Benjamin. "You're friends with Benjamin?" Marcie crinkled up her brow waiting for his response.

"Not yet Marcie, but I sure hope to be."

Marcie frowned and looked confused, but before she could ask more difficult questions Bradford offered to buy her a drink. "Scott bring over a cosmo for the lady and whatever appetizers she would like." He pushed the bar menu over towards Marcie and smiled, anxious to get to know this young lady who was so close to the son he had never met. "So Marcie, tell me about you and Benjamin, have you been dating long? Where did you two meet" Bradford folded his hands and smiled at Marcie who wasn't sure how to take him.

"Hold up, easy now! What is this, twenty questions?"

Bradford realized he was a little intense and tried to relax. "Sorry Marcie, didn't mean to pry like that." Marcie decided to give him the short version.

"Well, let's see, we met at the School for the Blind, we both were doing community service work. I guess, we've been dating for a little while. I haven't really kept track." She lifted her martini glass and took a sip of her drink.

"So, how do you know Benjamin?" She asked.

Bradford didn't know how to start. He thought if he started from the beginning that maybe she could tell his son and he would listen. "Well Marcie, this is hard, this is the hardest day of my life. You see, I was engaged to a lady named Patti over nineteen years ago and she became pregnant. She didn't want to keep the baby and I did, but she and her family decided to give it up for adoption. And that baby just so happens to be Benjamin." His hands were trembling and he was scared to look into her eyes.

Marcie's eyes grew huge and her face was without expression, it was as if she were frozen. "You're Benjamin's real father? You're Benjamin's real father? Shut the door!" She kept repeating it over and over. "Oh my God, Oh my God, he is never going to believe this!" Her eyes were still very large as she looked intently at Bradford and tried to see the resemblance. "Oh God, it's true, you look a whole lot like him, except he's thin, painfully thin actually." She smiled and then laughed, her emotions going up and down. "Does he know you are here?"

"No Marcie, and I am petrified. I really don't know what to say. I had the opportunity to meet Benjamin's father who adopted him today and words can't describe how horrible I feel and how badly I wish I could go back in time and change things. Marcie, do you think you could talk to Benjamin for me and try to explain. Do you think he'll forgive me?"

Marcie was so excited about this, she was just sure Benjamin would understand. He needed family, he needed some good stable things in his life and Marcie thought this could be just what she needed to get Benjamin to open up.

"I would love to talk to him for you," she said, adjusting her glasses and pulling down her skirt that had travelled up her thigh. "He should be off soon and I'll take him outside or you could go outside, or?" She didn't know how to go about this. "Maybe you should go outside and wait until he's had a drink and then I'll bring him outside?"

Bradford didn't know what to do. Nothing seemed right and he was biting the sides of his thumb, something he rarely did. "How about I get a table in the back and then you can bring him over?"

Marcie smiled, she liked this idea best since it was raining and she didn't want Benjamin to leave abruptly. She looked up and saw Benjamin coming out of the kitchen. He had a towel in his hand and a plate of fried zucchini she had ordered as an appetizer. "Hello lovely," he said, sitting down the plate of food and kissing her on the cheek.

Bradford for the first time in his life looked into the eyes of his son. He couldn't take his eyes off of him, he couldn't breathe. He looked intently into his face studying every feature and he was forever changed. Before he knew it, Benjamin was headed back behind the thick glass wall to cook. Bradford headed to the men's room. He could no longer hold back the tears.

Homeward Bound

Chapter 39

Walter looked out the window of the cab at the olive hills that were becoming mountainous. His surroundings were becoming more and more familiar. It was as if he'd never left home and yet, it almost seemed as if he'd never lived there. He thought about all the lives a person lives. I must be a cat he thought to himself and chuckled. "Buddy, what time is it, it's lookin' dark?"

"It's a little after seven Clay, I mean Walter. Will I ever see you again, Walt?" Buddy looked at the old man he had become attached to and smiled.

"I sure hope so Buddy, I might want to take a long journey with you one day. What's the furthest away you been?"

Buddy smiled and began to sing the hit song, "I've Been Everywhere". Then he grabbed his beard and gave a smirk at the song he'd sung out of key. "Walt, I have seen just about all the United States, only problem is, it's all one big blur. You drive through one town and then before you know it, they all look the same. Shoot, I couldn't even really enjoy a vacation with my wife because I'd seen it all." He threw his hands up in the air to make his point and then placed them back on the steering wheel. "Mount Rushmore, the grand canyon, orange groves, corn fields and wheat fields, and frankly after driving as many years as I have, when you get home you just want to stay home!"

"I can only imagine Buddy, I can only imagine."

Walter looked out the window and realized he was about to climb out of Buddy's rig and he had no idea what the next chapter of his life would hold. He wasn't sure if his future held bars or freedom, forgiveness or animosity. He wasn't sure if his grandchildren would get to know him or if he would be a wandering vagabond.

When the children were small and he would come across a problem, whether it be with work or family or friends, he'd just go and ask Ruthie. She always gave him good advice and she always made him put himself in the other person's shoes. He wondered what she would tell him to do this very moment. He closed his eyes and pictured her, her hair a golden silver and her eyes as blue as the sea. And as he began to reminisce, suddenly it was all too real, Ruthie was right there beside him.

"Now Walter, you must not rush and be hasty, that is what's gotten you into all this trouble you're in today." Yes, he thought, she is so right. If I hadn't ran off this would have never happened. If I would have only told the children what I was feeling. Oh God, if I, you could say 'If I' forever and it never changed a thing. She smiled at him and patted his knee. "Calm down. Walter, the children are fine, they are probably drawing closer together because of all this."

Drawing closer? Yes, he hated to admit it, but she was right again. He kept his eyes closed and waited. The children were worried he knew that, but they had each other and they loved each other. Walter knew deep down, that even though he'd abandoned them they loved him.

280

He peered into her eyes and touched her hand. She seemed so real, so palpable. "But Ruthie where shall I go? Should I turn myself in to the police? I have really messed up this time Ruthie." He looked again at the eyes that held his heart for too many years. They were eyes that locked his spirit and captured him.

"You haven't messed up a thing, Walter Kendal! Now, listen here." She pointed her long finger at him and shook it real good. "It's not over, till He says it's over" and she pointed up to the sky. "And He ain't said its over, do you understand me, Walter Kendal?"

"Yes, yes, Ruthie!"

"You alright over there, Walt?"

Walter felt a tug on his sweatshirt and realized he'd drifted off to sleep. Or was that real? Boy it seemed real, like a movie screen. "Yeah Buddy, just talking to myself."

Buddy was feeling bad for Walter and worried as to what would become of the old man. He knew he was innocent, and he knew Walter Kendal was a good man. "You know Walt, if you aint ready to get out of this cab, I'll take you clear to Georgia with me and drop you off on the way back.

Hell, I ain't had no company in quite a spell and this road keeps getting longer. I swear I think it stretches through my dreams." Buddy had a habit of pulling on his beard when he spoke and a tendency of smiling kind of crooked after each comment. His eye teeth reminded Walter of a vampire and it struck Walter funny that this had crossed his mind.

Walter liked his mannerisms and his friendship. He'd spent so much time alone in the past year he was in due need of companionship, a man to talk to who understood loss. Walter rewinded the vision and heard her sweet stern voice, "You must not rush and be hasty!" Ruthie was always right. He had hated this about her, but finally came to terms with it after much stubbornness and much embarrassment.

The best thing about Ruthie though, was the fact that she never said, "I told you so, or see I was right." No, Ruthie sat back quietly and never said a word. Once she'd said, "When are you going to start listening to me?" That was the only time Walter could remember her being snide. He, of course, was right about a lot of issues that arose, but when it came to dealing with people she had it covered. It was almost as if she'd memorized the whole entire book "How to win Friends and influence People". It was as if she could crawl into a person's brain and read their thoughts, such a brilliant woman, too brilliant to lose her mind to such a horrible disease. Sometimes Walter thought that's why she lost her memory, because it was too crisp, too sharp. He shook his head at the image of her lost and wandering unknowing to even the most familiar of faces, Walters.

Walter didn't know how to reply to Buddy's invitation. He stared at his large belly, bouncing with the road and his dash ornament, a Hawaiian dancer whose hips shook with each bump as well. Her plastic face smiled up at Walter and her lei was a bright coral pink that matched her lips.

"Walter, I have been thinking about how boring my days would have been if I'd never picked you up that morning. I swear, I have picked up some characters in my day. Once in Chicago, I picked up a lady that I think used to be a man, you know, one of them transvestites. I didn't even know it, till we got to Indiana and the sun came up. Heck, she, he, had more facial hair than a dog in heat and hands as big as a lumberjack!" Buddy was shaking his head back and forth, all the while laughing. "I thought I'd never get rid of her...uh him? Real nice fellow though."

Walter was laughing too and it was nice to not think about all his pain for a minute. Boy, did Buddy have some stories to tell. He hated to put Buddy out and if he got into trouble on his account he'd never forgive himself and he already had a lot of that to deal with. He prayed a silent prayer, "God, you've led me to Buddy and he's kept me fed and dry and out of danger. I don't know where to turn or what to do. I need a specific answer Lord, so I am praying a specific prayer. If Buddy asks me to stay one more time, then that's your way of telling me to stay. But if he wishes me well, then I will get out of this cab and start walking"

Then a funny thing happened, Buddy turned to him and said, "Hot sand, I missed your exit and I gotta go weigh in. I guess you're just stuck with me awhile longer." He grabbed his beard and winked at Walter, his eye tooth shining in the darkness.

Pressing Forward

Chapter 40

Bradford motioned for the hostess to come over. He was more nervous than he'd ever been in his entire life. He couldn't even think of a time when he felt this tense. "Hello dear, I was wondering if I could get a table in the back, say for four?"

"Of course, sir, right away. We have a couple leaving as we speak, I'll get someone to clean it and we'll have it ready in no time."

She was all of twenty and part Asian, her long dark hair swayed as she walked. He watched her motion the busboy, who only used a tray to stack his dishes on. The table was perfect, but Bradford's stomach was nauseous and he was terrified about how the night would unfold. He thought he had already won the heart of Marcie, but his son could prove to be harder. The pretty hostess came back and escorted him to the table. He had paid his tab with Scott and was waiting for Marcie.

"Do you want me to tell Benjamin that you are his father, or do you want to tell him yourself?" She looked nervous.

"What do you think Marcie? I guess there's no easy way to say what I need to say."

Marcie pushed a strand of hair behind her ear and chewed on her finger nail. "Well, I think I'll let you tell him then."

"Okay Marcie, it is my responsibility at this point, but just in case things go sour, it was a pleasure to meet you."

"Same here Bradford, and don't worry, it will all work out sooner or later." She glanced at her watch and looked up at the bar area. "I'll go see how long until he's off." Marcie smiled nervously and made her way back to the bar.

Bradford watched her sit back down and motion Scott over, who then headed to the back to get Benjamin. "This is really happening," he said under his breath. He realized his life would never be the same, whether his son wanted to get to know him or not. He watched Benjamin come from the kitchen and take his chef hat off his head. He pulled the stool out next to Marcie and Bradford eyed them as they made conversation. Marcie's hands were fluttering and her mouth was running rapidly. He wished he knew what she was saying, but she was a smart girl and he thought she had liked him. He then saw Benjamin turn around and scan the room until his eyes were resting on Bradford. A chill went straight through Bradford. His heart accelerated and he became aware suddenly that he was soaking wet with perspiration and his eardrums were ready to burst from the pounding.

Benjamin threw his hands up in the air and walked back to the kitchen. Marcie turned, looked at Bradford and made a gesture as to say, 'I don't know what to do'. She eased out of her seat and walked back to the table. "He's not coming over, he's scared he's in trouble with the law or that you're an informant. He says he's not coming over."

Bradford pulled out his cell phone and asked Marcie if she knew the number to the restaurant. She gave it to him and he entered it into his phone.

"Do you have a smoke I could bum?" Bradford normally didn't smoke, he hadn't smoked since high school. They had smoked cigars at his frat parties in college, but that's as far as he took it. Tonight he thought he might need more than a cigarette to calm his nerves. He took a drink of his beer and put the cigarette behind his ear. Marcie looked up and smiled. Benjamin had a habit of tucking his that very same way. "I'm going outside for a bit Marcie, if you're a praying girl I need all the help I can get." He winked at her and then asked her to keep an eye on his table.

She watched him walk, so poised and handsome and she reflected on what a strong man she believed he was. "No problem Bradford, and good luck," she yelled as he made his way through the lobby and outside.

He lit the Camel and stared up at the street light that was casting a blush of illumination over the sitting area outside. The rain had stopped and the air smelled fresh. He knew this was going to be hard, but deep down inside he thought it was worth it. He hit send on his cell phone and listened to the ringing sound. "Too late now", his heart hammering with each ring, letting him know it would never be the same.

"Hello, thank you for calling Frank's Steak House, this is Alisha speaking, how may I help you?"

"Yes, Alisha, I need to talk to one of your employee's please, Benjamin Stewart."

"Sure sir, one moment."

He heard a clicking sound and then music playing softly, 'Tiny Bubbles in the Wine.' And then he heard a voice that would transform him, "Hello, this is Benjamin."

"Benjamin, hello," his voice was cracking and he was trying to stay strong. "I am the man who was waiting for you in the restaurant, the man at the table. I am not out to get you and this has nothing to do with any trouble you've been in, you have to believe me. Benjamin, I am your father."

Benjamin didn't know how to react. He had always said if he ever met his real father, he'd kick his ass for leaving him with Larry Stewart.

"Hello? I know this must be a shock for you Benjamin." Bradford waited for what seemed like minutes to hear a response.

"What do you want with me?" His voice was cool, hard and unemotional.

"Benjamin, I know this must be very difficult for you, as it is for me, but I really want to be a part of your life. I never wanted to give you up. You have to believe me."

"Yeah, well you didn't want to be a part of my life when my Dad, Larry was beatin the crap outta me, did ya?"

Bradford felt horrible, he didn't know what to say. "Benjamin, I can only imagine how hard life was for you. I met Larry today and he's the first man I've ever gotten into a physical fight with, think I broke his nose, actually."

There was another long pause. "Well, it's a little too late DAD..." He said the words sarcastically, but wondered if the guy had really punched Larry.

"Benjamin, I want to know you. I'm late, but I was hoping not too late."

"Oh, you want to know me, poor pitiful Benjamin. Get over yourself mister, you're nobody to me."

"Come on Ben, let's just give this a go. I met your girlfriend, Marcie. She's a lovely girl, very articulate and charming. I want to try and make up for the pain and heartache I've caused you. I want to make things right, won't you give me a chance?"

"What chance did you give me, DAD?" His voice was heated now.

"Okay, okay, I know, I made mistakes but your mother was the one carrying you and it was her, not me that wanted to put you up for adoption. I tried to marry her and she kept saying she wasn't ready for a family. You have to trust me on this one, Benjamin. Please, I'm begging you!"

Benjamin wondered if this was true and he wished he could just say okay and walk out there and look in the eyes of his real father, but how could he? He felt like such a jerk now and he had never thought that his mother was the one who didn't want him, but now he didn't know what to believe. "What's in it for you? Do you need a kidney or something?" Benjamin laughed halfheartedly.

"Benjamin, I think we can have a good life getting to know each other. I think I can help you. I want to pay for your college and I'm an attorney, I can help you with any problems you've gotten yourself into, as long as you promise to get help if you need it. Whatta ya say man? We got one go at this and I don't want to miss another moment without you in mine. You're my son and I love you, I have never stopped thinking about you. I have looked in the eyes of a million faces searching for my son. Don't throw this chance away when it's so close."

Benjamin heard something in his voice that sounded real, more real than anyone he'd ever heard a promise from. He guessed since he was here he'd take a look at him. He had always been curious what his real father looked like. He'd always felt like he didn't belong, and he had always felt invisible, maybe Bradford was the missing piece to his new life. This could help him work out his issues with Marcie. Maybe he could actually come clean and tell her the truth. "You still at the restaurant?"

"Yes, Benjamin, I'm outside having a smoke." Bradford was trying to get on his level, make him relate somehow.

"Okay, I'll be out in a second."

Bradford started to say thanks, but then he heard the dial tone. Benjamin had hung up. He didn't know whether to go back to the table or wait outside. He decided to wait outside.

Somehow it didn't seem so cold, he had sweated so much. The breeze was hitting his sweat and cooling him off. "Thank you, God," he said out loud and raised his hands up to the sky. "Give me the right words to speak." He sat down in an iron chair and wished he'd brought his drink. The door swung open and he practically jumped out of his seat, to look directly into the eyes of his son. He wanted to hug him so badly, but he was unsure of how Benjamin would take it. It hurt so bad to not put his arms around his son and give him all the love he had saved up inside all these years.

Benjamin looked in his eyes and then looked him up and down. His eyes shifted back and forth and then he stuck out his hand and said, "Hello, I'm Benjamin."

"I'm Bradford," Bradford could smell the scent of grilled steaks and pleasing aromas that came from his son's clothing. He went to reach for his hand and couldn't contain himself, he grabbed Benjamin and embraced him tightly. "I've been waiting for this moment my whole life!" Bradford said those words in between choking sounds and moans that couldn't be stopped.

Benjamin felt an emotion and a stirring inside himself that he could never remember feeling before. He stood back

293

and looked at his father. "We have the same chin," he said rubbing the cleft in his and smiling crooked.

"We sure do," said Bradford, wrapping his arm around his shoulder. "How bout I buy us some dinner and we catch up on our past."

Benjamin felt uncomfortable in his presence, and yet he was eager to get to know him. If Bradford really was an attorney, maybe he could help him, at least he had money. Benjamin could see that and he could always use some cash. But Benjamin noticed another thing about Bradford, he was genuinely crying over their embrace. He thought maybe that's what real love feels like, but then real love would have never given him up for adoption. He followed Bradford through the double doors, wondering what the night would bring.

They came in and sat at the table together. Marcie ran over and congratulated them both. She told Ben she was going to have one more drink and call it a night. She didn't want to interrupt their time together. Marcie winked at Bradford and came around the table to give him a hug. "So very nice to meet you, Bradford." He stood up and pushed his chair back and patted her on the back.

"Any friend of my son's, is a friend of mine."

"Woe, you ain't met all my friends," Benjamin said, his eyes a little too huge. It kinda perturbed him that he was already referring to him as 'son'. I mean, come on, the guy just showed himself and all the sudden he was acting like they were best buds. Benjamin was trying to figure out how to play this.

They both watched Marcie walk off and nervously eyed one another. Bradford picked up his menu and said, "So, Benjamin what do they have good to eat here?"

"Well, what do you like? I mean it is Frank's Steak House, hence the word steak."

"Ahh ha, gotta sarcastic one here," said Bradford, smiling from ear to ear. "I can't believe I am sitting here with my son, I cannot believe this is real, somebody wake me up!"

Benjamin nodded, "Yeah, it is pretty crazy!" He still didn't know what to make of Bradford.

"So Benjamin, tell me what's been going on in your life, I'm guessing you like to cook?"

"It's pretty cool I guess, I haven't thought about it much."

"So, do you have a career you're interested in pursuing?"

"Like I said, I haven't really thought on it lately."

"Well, what have you always dreamed of doing?"

Benjamin lowered his head and thought about how he had only dreamed of survival. "I don't know, not much I guess," he shrugged his shoulders. The conversation was making him really uncomfortable. "You met Larry, my pops today, huh?" He chuckled and looked up knowingly.

Bradford shook his head. It felt like somebody had stabbed him with a knife. "Yes, Benjamin, I did and I'm sorry that you had to be raised by him. I never dreamed your life was going like that, you have to believe me."

Benjamin studied his face and he seemed sincere, but that didn't erase all the pain. He couldn't just walk in here and say, 'sorry' and think that everything was just grand all the sudden. There was a few minutes of awkward silence and then Bradford tried to bring the focus again to his son.

"So, back to a career, what do you enjoy doing in your spare time?"

Get a load of this crap thought Benjamin, spare time? What kind of world was he living in? Only rich lawyers had spare time and the only spare time he had was when he was sitting in a jail cell rotting. "I don't know, can't say I really ever had too many hobbies or dreams about my life."

"Well, that's all going to change. Now think back to when you were real small and you just started school, did you ever want to be a policeman or a dentist, doctor?"

Benjamin thought back, but he couldn't remember anyone asking him this. His friend Clark had always wanted to be a scientist, but Benjamin never thought about it seriously. Of course, like most teenagers he wanted to become a rock star and play guitar, but that was different. He remembered writing a fiction piece in his English class, the teacher said it was really good, even said he had potential. He remembered how it made him feel first-class.

"I dunno, maybe a writer?"

"A writer, that's incredible. My son the writer, the next Hemingway, the next Capote!" Bradford beamed with pride and Benjamin was so caught off guard, he didn't know how to react.

Benjamin had never read any Hemingway novels, in fact he hadn't picked up a book since he was in jail and then it was mostly science fiction or murder mysteries. But he could see that his father actually wanted good for him, no strings attached and this scared the hell out of Benjamin. He could handle the Marcie lust slash love thing, but a real person who was interested in him and his future? This was more than he could imagine. And yet why would he allow him to help now? Part of him wanted to make him pay miserably for leaving him in the clutches of Larry. Why did everything always have a dark side? Why did all his anger seem to want to erupt at that moment on a man he had only met, a man who made a mistake when he was young? Yes, he had been that mistake. A mistake was all he'd ever been.

Bradford kept talking and Benjamin tried to listen, his thoughts racing. "I know this is all a shock Benjamin, but I want to pay for you to go to college. How does that sound? And you don't even have to work while you're in school unless you want to? And I want to help you get a car and even an apartment if you need one. You probably have an apartment?" Bradford looked at Benjamin, who seemed dumbfounded and decided he needed to slow down a bit.

"Ah yeah, I got a place. It's just a small loft, but I'm trying to get a nicer place."

"Does Marcie live with you?" Bradford knew that most the college kids today just lived together instead of marriage.

"Nah, we only been dating awhile, I don't want to be too quick you know?" Not wanting to, he smiled at his father and studied his facial features. The resemblance was uncanny. The only difference was Benjamin wasn't muscular, he was thin and Benjamin had long hair. Apparently he had his mother to thank for his small teeth, because his father had a mouth full of normal size teeth.

"So, you married Bradford? Any brothers or sisters I need to know about?"

"No, son you're it."

That seemed too good to be true thought Benjamin. 'Too good to be true', he said again to himself. Benjamin looked up at the bar to see Marcie and Clark sitting and talking together. She must have felt his eyes on her and she turned around and smiled. "So you're an attorney at a big law firm, huh?"

"Well, it's not the biggest, but yes. Benjamin I am. When you feel like confiding in me as to what happen, just know I'm here for you. I know you had to do community service work, but that's about it."

Benjamin lowered his head and wished he never had to tell him, but he guessed this is one relationship he should start out with honesty. God knows he hadn't been with anyone else. At this point he figured, why not? Maybe if Bradford knew he was a murderer, he'd know for sure if he was the real deal.

They ordered steaks, loaded baked potatoes and Caesar salads to start off. Bradford had suddenly worked up an appetite. The night seemed to be improving and before they knew it, they were both more at ease smiling and joking back and forth. Bradford thought Benjamin was still holding back and sizing him up, but every now and then he seemed to want to open up. "What do you have planned for tomorrow, Benjamin?"

Benjamin knew he was hinting that he wanted to spend more time with him, but he wasn't sure he wanted to jump in so quickly. Then there was another part of him that wanted to make this man, who sat across from him, pay for every rotten thing that had come into his life. "I don't have any plans and as a matter of fact I'm off work too, what are you thinking about?"

"Well Ben, I met a lovely lady who has become a big part of my life and I thought maybe you and Marcie, the four of us, could go out, say to one of my favorite restaurants and then maybe a blues bar? What do you say?" Bradford punched him lightly on the shoulder.

"I'm not sure we can get in a blues bar at our age."

"Well, I know a place that's like a pizza pub and you can be under age because they serve so much food. I assumed Marcie was twenty-one by the drinks she ordered." Benjamin looked funny and shrugged his shoulders. "So you on?"

"Yeah, I may be able to swing it. I'll ask Marcie, we'll kick it around a bit, see what happens."

"Well, I meant what I said Benjamin, I want to spend the rest of my life getting to know you and spending time with you. I hope you believe that," he stopped eating and looked Benjamin in the eye.

Benjamin wanted to scream, 'Then why the hell weren't you there for me! Look at the mess you left me to deal with.' He wanted to shake him and yet, he so needed a father and it was such a good feeling inside to know he didn't come from Larry Stewart's blood. He might have been raised by that jerk, but he wasn't a part of him. No, his father was an attorney, his father had made something of his life and Benjamin knew that even though he had been told since before he could walk that he was useless, garbage, good for nothing a worthless piece of crap, deep down, he knew he was more. He was somebody! He looked at his father and wondered what his real name was.

"What's your last name, Bradford?"

"It's Stiltz, Benjamin, Bradford Stiltz."

He was somebody, he was Bradford Stiltz son!

Copper Top

Chapter 41

It was four days before the anniversary of Ruthie's death and Brenda and Daniel wanted to go to the cemetery and place flowers on their mother's grave. They decided to go to the home place and see if there were any signs that Walter had been around. Daniel had picked up Brenda that morning and after breakfast they set out to investigate. The house had become somewhat of a nuisance and had kept both Burt and Daniel busy on their off days. They took turns mowing the lawn and mulching the leaves, but neither had been over there in quite some time now. The electricity had been turned off by choice, but they had decided to keep the water on because it was so cheap and they never knew when their father might turn up again.

They had boxed up their mother's clothing, but had left her keepsakes and trinket boxes out. She loved things that Brenda always said just sat and served no purpose, except to collect dust. She missed her mother terribly though. She missed her kind spirit and the fact that she never met a stranger. She missed her soft voice and her capability to listen without interrupting you, really listen. Brenda knew their lives would never be the same without Mom. Sometimes she snuck over to the house and went through old photo albums of her and Daniel when they were small. She looked out the window at her mother's iris gardens that were overgrown and dead from the cold. It saddened her that something she took so much pride in was left to choke with the weeds. Brenda had tried to get over there and prune shrubs and weed the gardens, but it had become more difficult as time went on. She plopped down on the couch and grabbed a photo book. Leaving Daniel to his snooping, she was digging into memories that had escaped her.

The photo album was bright blue and green with a cushion cover, there were raised gold letters that said, 'Photo album'. She opened the cover and peered into the eyes of a little red headed girl wearing a toboggan and a striped scarf, her cheeks kissed from the cold, standing next to their beagle puppy, Willie. Her brother Daniel, was pulling their sled up the hill in the park. She wondered where time had gone and who that little girl really was and who she had become. She turned the page and was instantly taken back by a black and white photo that didn't seem to fit in with the rest of the colored pictures. It was her mother and father, her father was wearing a sports coat and his hair was greased back, in the typical fifties duck tail. His shirt was high collared and his smile was just as high. Her mother was wearing a long pencil skirt, her hair was swept up and her eyes were sparkling for the camera, but her father's eyes were mesmerizing, like a kaleidoscope into Ruthie's. Brenda could tell he was all but oblivious that anyone else was even in the room. Brenda knew that she and Burt had a good relationship, she knew he loved her and vice versa, but she never knew a man more lovesick than Walter.

She remembered once when her father had just hired a new secretary who was young and quite attractive, he had taken to working longer hours during the summer months. Her mother had grown suspicious that her father may have been falling for this young lady. She was so bent on catching him she snuck into the office, crept past the waiting area and spied on them at his desk, going over mortgage insurance. She was so sure she had trapped him and then she held her ear as close as she could without getting caught. That evening she overheard the sweetest words ever, "My wife, Ruthie, is just the most beautiful woman in the world. I hate working these long hours, but I am saving to get her a diamond wedding ring. She's been wearing a simple gold band for too long, and she deserves so much more."

The young secretary had commented on how thoughtful he was and her mother had tiptoed as quietly out as she had come in. Years later she had confided secretly about her snooping. She loved that ring more than anything and she had acted so surprised when she opened the case, maybe too surprised.

"Ahhh Daddy, what have you done? Have you become senile?" She was talking out loud now and feeling rather guilty about the night Jackie had shown up there. That was right after the funeral and she had already paid the private investigator. She knew her father was running away, but she was so angry that he had left her to fend for herself. They had all left her.

Just the sight of Jackie brought a flood of memories. She was only around seven years old when her father had taken her to a feed store down the road. The man's name was Russell and he took them to the back of the store where he had three baby pigeons in a nest crying. They were called white homers. Their beaks were opening and closing and the sound was like a cry to her heart. "Can we get them Daddy? Please, please, please Daddy! They're so cute and I will take care of them."

Her father kept talking to Russell about the birds. Finally, they were able to bring them home. She remembered feeding the babies herself. She took a syringe and put the milk like formula in it. Their little beaks were opening and closing and they were crying like an infant. Brenda had loved those birds. She remembered the sturdy loft cages her father had built and how they would release them each day and let them fly around the land. She had been the one that cleaned their cages and removed the waste. Feathers and dander filled the air and her mother made her tie one of her father's handkerchiefs over her mouth and nose. But Jackie, she was a special bird and Walter knew when he took her, that anywhere he went, if he released her she'd come home.

Brenda was so angry when she read his note, she just went berserk not even thinking it through. The note was so 'poor pitiful me' and it just didn't cut it. I mean how he could think 'sorry' could fix everything he'd done was beyond reasoning. She had stormed in the house looking for an ink pen. She passed through the hall on the way to his office and there was the family portrait hanging on the wall. She stopped and looked him in the eye, "Oh yeah, Dad, you're sorry, well big deal!" She took the picture down off the hanger and held it where she could look him in the eye. "You left me and you left my mother and if you would have loved her as much as you put on, YOU would have stayed till the bitter end and YOU would have wiped her butt and YOU would have held her head as she vomited and YOU would have listened to her fanatical talking and YOU would have listened to her choke on her saliva and YOU would have been there when she forgot how to breathe and still her eyes didn't know me!" She grabbed the photo and threw it against the wall, "Sorry, oh you're sorry are you, and you are pleading for forgiveness well YOU ARE UNFORGIVEN!" She had screamed at what was left of his reflection in the shattered glass. She had grabbed a bright red marker out of the drawer and wrote in all caps 'Unforgiven'. She remembered rolling the paper up tightly and placing it in Jackie's holder and lifting the bird back up into the sky, the whooshing wind whipping in her wings, was the only sound she could hear. She knew her father was close by. He would come for his bird, but why couldn't he have come for her mother?

Brenda began to cry at the emotions that flooded back along with the painful vision of what her mother went through, and how much she had to carry for the whole family. She was sobbing uncontrollably and she hadn't heard Daniel walk in from outside.

"Brenda, are you okay?" He sat down and let his eyes hunt for a Kleenex box, but found nothing. He walked to the bathroom and grabbed a roll of toilet tissue and handed her a roll.

"Thank you," she said blowing her nose into the paper.

"What's going on, hun?" He reached and put his arm around her and began rubbing her back. "It's okay Brenda, we're going to get through this. I'm here now, Sandra's much better and I'm going to deal with whatever Dad hands us."

She wanted to believe him, but she wasn't sure and plus he didn't understand. He knew nothing about the note or the phone call. She was going to have to forgive her father somehow.

"I know you're angry with Dad. I understand, I do, I mean what he did was wrong."

She knew what the next word would be, 'But', she didn't want to hear an excuse, she wanted to hear a legitimate reason.

"Brenda our father was a good father. He worked hard, paid for our educations and he was always faithful to our mother. He was kind, caring and he never drank, never even cursed that I know of. He took us on vacations and he took us to church and he taught us how to love. Are you going to hold this against him forever?"

Brenda knew it was eating away at her and it was probably the reason she hadn't been able to conceive. She realized her father was a good man, she thought that was what made it worse. If he would have been a verbally or physically abusive father, perhaps a drunk who couldn't keep a job, she might have been more prepared for this. She just couldn't get over the betrayal of him leaving her to fend for herself. She closed her eyes and envisioned the little girl in the photo. Her father had placed her on the bright red sled, but she was so frightened.

"No Daddy, I don't want to!" She whined and crumpled up her forehead, "Please don't make me, Daddy!"

"It's okay baby, Daddy's got ya." He had crawled in behind her and held her close to him. His arms were large and she felt as if she had been tucked inside her knapsack. He lowered his head and peeked around at her, "You ready girl?" Before she could answer he had pushed off. He smelled like pine cones and pipe smoke and everything good daddies smelled of at that age. She had tried to keep her eyes closed, but it was all much too exciting for her. The trees were whipping past her and the chilly air was moving ever so fast or was it them? She heard her father laughing and holding her close to him. "See, I told you I wouldn't let anything happen to my best girl." The sled came to an abrupt halt and her hat had fallen off from the wind. Her father picked it up and shook off the snow, then bent down and brushed her hair back before placing it on and tying it around her chin, "You're my copper top princess," he said winking at her in the snow. He always called her his copper top. She suddenly missed him more than she knew.

Comparing Tales

Chapter 42

Benjamin was stretched out on his bed with his arms folded behind his head. He was lost in thought and his eyes were creating pictures out of the water stains on the ceiling. He kept replaying the evening and he kept envisioning the face of his father, his real father. Marcie was being her whimsical self and chatting away about the evenings events.

"So what did you think of your father? He sure is distinguished looking isn't he?"

"I'm not sure Marcie, I mean this is all really sudden and I am still shocked. It's all rather surreal."

"But you liked him, right?" She licked her thin lips and took her glasses off.

"Yeah, I liked him and he seems genuine enough, but where was the bastard when I needed him? I'm not in his league and he has all these great expectations for me and all. 'What do aspire to be Benjamin?'" He mocked Bradford's words sarcastically. He looked at Marcie, who was studying him and sighed. "I mean, I don't have the greatest track record, you know."

"Ben, this is not something you should even be thinking about. This man wanted to find you. He seems very sorry that he was not a part of your life. Your past is your past Ben, this is your future."

Benjamin knew she hadn't a clue about his past. He knew the best thing to do was just tell him, come clean at the beginning. Then, thought Benjamin, if he walks away I won't be attached or feel guilty for allowing him to help me. He turned over and peered into Marcie's eyes. He needed to come clean with everyone but how? If he told Marcie the truth now, she'd know he had been deceiving her all along.

"Didn't he say he'd pay for college?"

"Yeah, he did and he said I wouldn't even have to work."

"Well, that's so awesome Ben. I think this is really going to change your life."

Benjamin lit up a joint and thought about how he would have to change all his habits and become this clean cut Joe Shmoe. No more pot and no more drinking, the straight and narrow. He wasn't college material and he wasn't going to be able to stand up to his father's standards. Why get excited about it? He took a long toke off the joint and passed it to Marcie.

"You don't seem too thrilled about meeting your father," she said looking into his eyes.

"It's not that Marcie, it's just I'm not going to be anything but a letdown to him. Plus it kinda ticks me off that he can just walk in there after 20 years with his nice easy life and expect me to be so forgiving. I'm not going to do anything but bring him down."

"Why do you think that, Benjamin? I mean you are a really super guy, you've just had some bad knocks. I mean he met Larry, he knows you are bound to have issues."

Benjamin wished he could just forget all of what went on before. He wished his horrendous past could be erased from his memory, but it haunted him daily. "He wants us to meet him and his lady friend tomorrow for dinner. Do you want to go?"

"Of course, Benjamin, it sounds terrific."

He looked at her pretty facial features and her wonderful smile and wished he could just escape. He knew he was playing with fire. Before long all the excitement and love he was feeling would disappear. He would blow out the candles on his cake and be left in the darkness alone. Nevertheless, he thought that was a safe, familiar place and one where he wouldn't have to worry about hurting someone or being hurt in return. Plus, his father could have looked for him before now. Why did he wait so long? If Bradford would have come earlier he probably would not have killed John Levite. He probably would not have done a lot of the foolish things he did. Why should he get to come around now and just act as if he was always there?

"You know Ben, I think you are really looking at this situation wrong. I mean he went searching for you, and he claims he never wanted to give you up for adoption. I think he's legit. You need to stop worrying about how to impress him and just let him help you out. I mean he's got money and he doesn't have any more children." She took a drag off the joint and held it in her lungs a little too long and began to cough.

"Easy killer," he smiled as she composed herself. He thought about what she said and realized that she was right. Only she wasn't aware that he had taken a man's life, a father's life and he didn't deserve to have a father now. There were two children tucked in bed right now who would never see their father again because of him. He wondered why he couldn't hit and kill someone who was like his father Larry, some drunken bum nobody would miss? Instead, he had to kill John Levite, loving husband and father of two, Boy Scout leader and softball coach. He probably took his children to cool places like Disney World and Yellowstone Park and probably would have taught his son to fish and play football. He didn't deserve love and he didn't deserve having a real father. Was this some kind of cruel joke God was playing on him to riddle him with more guilt than he already felt?

"What time is dinner?" Marcie asked, snapping him back to reality.

"It's around seven, some pizza place with live music, I dunno, never heard of it. He's supposed to call and give me the details."

"I'll pick you up Ben, and we can meet them there, but let's get there early and sneak in a drink or two."

For sure, thought Benjamin, he was going to need a couple to get through the evening. He wasn't good at impressing people that was all Marcie, she was the pro at it.

Marcie pulled her long blonde hair around to one side of her neck and looked out the window. "My father's a real piece of work. Maybe you'll have the pleasure of meeting him one day."

"Sounds fun," said Benjamin, smiling at her wit. "How about I tell you some stories about my father, Larry. We'll compare childhood horror stories and see who can top who?" He looked at her with a glint of devilish charm. She had heard a few Larry stories and she knew her childhood could not compare. It was horrible, but in a different way.

"Let's see how about the time he took me to a bar on 7th street and told me to sit in the booth and if any fights broke out to hide under the table till it was over. He knew the owner real well and they'd let me in while mom was at work. I would sit at the table alone with a comic book and a coke, while he sat at the bar getting hammered. One night this big guy came in and he was all tattooed up, real rough looking character. He had dark eyes and an unshaven face. He grabbed this one guy by the throat and they started going at it. I was only around seven or eight at the time and I remember the beer bottles crashing into the walls. They pulled over tables and threw punches. Then the big guy pulled out a carpet knife. He looked around the room, his eyes darted and fell on mine a little too long and then passed. He grabbed the guy and stuck that carpet knife right in his gut. I ducked under the table and watched him cut him from one side to the other, just like he was gutting a deer. Talk about scared. I peed myself. I remember I was more scared Larry would find out that I'd peed myself, than I was of the dead man lying on the floor. Isn't that jacked up?"

Marcie's eyes had grown huge and her mouth was agape. "God Ben, I never knew it was that awful." She couldn't even begin to tell him one of her stories none would even compare.

Benjamin lit the joint back up and took a few more hits. "It's pretty disgusting, huh? Meanwhile, Bradford was probably shore side, sipping drinks in Cancun." Benjamin realized that if he ever told Marcie the whole truth, she would never believe all the truths he had told her before, like the one that had just escaped him. He was sure she would just consider the whole relationship one big fat lie.

Marcie sighed and looked at Ben, not knowing what to say after such a ghastly story.

"Oh Marcie, it's over now, builds character and anyway, I always had the best stories in school." He chuckled, smiling and showing his small white teeth, but Marcie could see behind the smile. She could recognize the pain. It was like looking in a mirror.

"Did you get in many fights in high school?" she asked.

"Most of the people I hung out with were scared of me, just because of Larry's reputation and so I never really had to fight. Plus, I wore black every day and didn't talk much, so people thought I was really strange."

"Well, I think it's disgusting that he would even take you to a bar at that age. My father sounds like a saint compared to yours, but he's still a jerk," she said smiling.

"Come here you," he pulled her head to his chest and smelled the apricot shampoo she always used and thought about how well she fit snuggled up to him. Was there anyone else in the world carrying such a huge secret? I can't think about this anymore tonight he thought. His life seemed like a deck of cards and in the midst of all those two's and three's someone had thrown him an Ace and a King, but they were still different suits. He didn't know what to discard or what to keep, and he was scared to death to lay them down.

Unfolded Smiles

Chapter 43

Desiree picked up the phone in mid ring and walked back out to the garage. She had just poured another glass of wine and was putting the rest of John's shoes in a box. "Hello?"

"Hello Desiree, its Bradford."

"Brad, I'd almost given up on you."

"Oh Desiree, my son is so wonderful! I am without words right now. I have been driving around for an hour looking at the stars and replaying the whole evening. I never thought this day would come and it has finally arrived and I have you to thank for it, you and Josh and Tabitha!"

"Wow Brad, that's so amazing, you finally met your son! I can't even imagine!"

"I know, I keep feeling like it was all a dream and I'm going to wake up, but it's real. I can't even begin to tell you how much my life has changed since I met you. You have helped me so much. I feel like heaven is smiling down on me and its entire angelic host! I really don't deserve a second chance with my son, but I pray that I will get it. Oh, if you could have seen how he was raised Desiree, it was appalling to say the least. I never imagined that they could allow people like this to adopt a child, but that was almost twenty years ago. I just never knew nor expected to see the things I saw today but I am going to try and make it up to him. I am just glad that the initial awkward meeting period is over and I can start trying to form a relationship of trust and making memories. I wish I'd done this years ago. But I just have this feeling that everything is going to work out and were going to bond. You know what I mean?"

"I do, Bradford, I do. I think it's incredible that this is all coming together for you. I know if he is anything like his father, then he's a great young man!"

"So, what has been going on with you this evening? How are your little man Josh and his bird doing?"

"Oh Bradford, that bird acts like Josh is her mother, she gets on his back and sits while he watches cartoons. She hops on top his tennis shoe and lets him walk around with her. Tabitha thinks it's hilarious. I am rather pleased we kept Jackie, she really has a lot of character for a bird. Other than that I have had a very busy day myself. I found an interesting letter, Bradford. The homeless man, Walter left it here for me."

"Really, well what did it say?"

"Oh Bradford, It's not important, tell me more about your son, what is his name?"

"No, you go on. It is important and I want to hear every detail of the letter."

Desiree took another swig of her wine and walked back to the bedroom. She picked up the jewelry box and opened the compartment door.

"Well?"

"Well, he just said basically that he was sorry for entering my home and he made a list of repair jobs he'd done to try and repay me. Remember when I told you my sink had been clogged and I had come home and it was fine?"

"Yes, you mean that was him?"

"Yes Bradford, and not only that, he fixed my gutters in the back that were sagging and even glued Tabitha's rocker back together! He also wrote something about his wife dying and about John's death and how he just couldn't go on and would I please forgive him? I feel so terrible now, Brad."

"It's okay Desiree, you couldn't have known he was harmless. It's not your fault and besides, they'll find him and maybe we can be of assistance to him?" He heard sniffling in the background and knew she was crying. "Honey, it's alright, calm down."

"I know Brad, it's just this poor, sick elderly man with nowhere to go and now the police are going to throw him in prison and all the while he was just lonesome and heartbroken." She was slurring her words and not making sense at this point.

"Have you been drinking, Miss Desiree?" He said rather comically.

"Just a little wine, can you tell? Is it that obvious?"

"Well, you are slurring a tad bit. So, does that mean now would be a good time for me to come over there and take advantage of you?"

"Bradford Stiltz, what are you implying? On second thought how fast can you get here?" They both laughed and Desiree wiped her nose on a tissue.

"I missed you tonight, Des."

"I know, I missed you as well. I'm just so glad that this is all behind you and now you can spend the rest of your life getting to know your son. And I can't wait to meet him. Does he look like you?"

"Oh, you'll get your chance to meet him tomorrow night. I have already set the whole thing up. Even called grandmom and she has agreed to watch the children."

"You have got to be kidding me! You called grandmom?"

"Yep, sure did, she says 'hello'." He smiled knowing that would get her going.

"Bradford, what did grandmom say when you called?"

"She said, 'It's about time you took that granddaughter of mine out on a date'.

"She did not?" Desiree blushed, "What did she really say?"

"That is what she really said, oh and to tell Josh and Tabitha she looked forward to seeing them."

"Gosh Brad, you are something else."

"I try. Anyway, I'll pick you up at seven or you can meet me there."

"What are your plans for the evening, Bradford?"

"Well, I am going to take them to dinner at Christy's, where we met for lunch the first time and then over to Ray's Pizza Pub, they're having a blues band."

"Wow, sounds fun, I can't wait to meet him. Do you think maybe I should just meet you there, in case you two want to spend some time alone afterwards? I mean, you never know?"

"Desiree, I hope you know... I'm not pushing you aside now that I have met my son.

Please know that I want to spend time with both of you. Unfortunately I can't ask him to tag along with us everywhere or vice versa. You do realize don't you? I feel like we are just starting to connect."

"Of course Bradford, and I'm going to step aside and let the two of you bond."

"I don't want you to step aside Desiree, I care about you." Bradford's heart was pounding in his chest so hard he could feel it pulsating in his eardrums. He never thought he'd feel so much for her in such a short time.

Desiree was touched. "I care about you, too. Have a great night, Bradford."

"Sweet dreams, Des." She hung up the phone and stood in her bedroom shocked and stunned that a man as brilliant and handsome and charming could care for her. She looked into the mirror of her vanity and said, "He really likes me?"

She looked at her reflection and wondered how he saw her. What he envisioned when he looked at her? Then she thought about John and… "Oh John, I'm so sorry, I do miss you." She stared at the jewelry box with its hand carved design and pictures of him began to flood her from her past. They were bitter sweet, but how could she get past the guilt and move on without any fault? She had to, she knew in order to start a new life for her and the children she would have to move on. She pulled the comforter back and stared at the empty closet space where John's clothes once hung and felt relief to not see them there. She couldn't explain why it was liberating, but it was. She crawled in bed and propped the pillows up behind her head and wrapped her arms around herself as if she were being embraced. She closed her eyes and tried to shut down her brain.

Left Hand Pocket

Chapter 44

Buddy pulled onto the side road next to a motel with a flashing red sign that said, 'Valley View Motel'. Underneath was a smaller sign that said 'Vacancy'. There wasn't really a view and the pool out front was closed for the season. He walked inside and told Walter to wait there while he paid for a room. A few minutes later he came out holding a large plastic key with room number 225 on it. They walked past the pool to the far right hand side and up a flight of stairs. Then Buddy opened the door to their room. The walls were painted a soothing taupe color. The window was covered with floor length green drapes and each double bed was adorned with a green and tan plaid bedspread. There was a small table and two chairs that sat in front of the window area and a dresser with a television and cable box. The heater was blowing and Walter was thinking it had been long ago since he and Jackie had spent months in a motel similar to this one.

"Walt, it ain't much but it's clean and warm."

"I am just thankful, Buddy. I'll never be able to repay you."

"Actually, I was wondering if you play pool. They got a nice little pub with the best cheeseburgers and hot wings in town and a couple tables in the back. Whatta ya say we play a game or two, have a little fun?"

"I'm all for it, Buddy, you lead the way."

"Well, let's get cleaned up first and head on over there."

Walter walked to the bathroom and turned on the shower. The water pressure wasn't the greatest, but it was clean. There were the regular small wrapped bars of soap and plenty of snow white bath towels. Walter could not help but think back to the last shower he'd taken at Desiree's house. He couldn't stop replaying the whole scene in his mind. He missed his bird something awful and he hoped the situation with Josh was faring well. He undressed and stepped in under the warm spray of water. Before he could help himself he was singing:

"Fallen leaves that lie scattered on the ground.
The birds and flowers that were here, now can't be found.
All his friends that he once knew are not around.
They are scattered like the leaves upon the ground.

Lord let my eyes see every need of every man.
Make me stop and always lend a helping hand.
Then when I'm laid beneath that little grassy mound,
there'll be more friends around than leaves upon the
ground."

He thought about the words and about Ruthie, who was now laid beneath a grassy mound and how he had not even gone to the graveyard to be with her. His tears just streamed under the warm water and ran mingled with the shower water down the drain.

He was going to have to shake this off and get it together so he and Buddy could have a fine evening, because he didn't know how many more he'd see. He turned the shower off and stepped out to dry off, sure that before too long he would have to turn himself in. You could never continue to run from your problems, because they would eventually catch you and overtake you. It was kind of like lying, if you told one you had to tell another and another. Walter knew you had to meet it head on. With two days left until the anniversary of Ruthie's death, he decided that he would be at the graveyard to spend it with her and then turn himself in.

Maybe Desiree would find the note he had left. Maybe Josh would tell her he was harmless. Maybe as Ruthie had said in his dream, "It ain't over, till the good Lord says it's over". Walter knew that God had always been a part of his life and although many no longer believed in Him or His power, he was sure that He had been with him every step of the way. He never blamed God for Ruthie's death or her disease. He believed God was good and sometimes bad things happen to good people and in the end it would all make sense.

He opened the K-mart bag and looked at the items Buddy had purchased for him. There were brand new underwear and socks, a pair of jeans and even a belt in case they were too big. What a blessing he has been, thought Walter. He dressed and brushed his teeth and walked out of the bathroom to find Buddy sound asleep on one of the double beds. Buddy jolted with a snore and a startled look.

"You want to just stay here, Buddy?"

"No Walt, I'm gonna get ready, just getting a little shut eye."

"Well Buddy, I was able to get a lot of sleep, but you were driving and I know you just dropped off a load in Salt Lake City before you picked me up."

"I'm good Walter, just give me a second to get ready. I just hope you saved me some hot water." He smiled at Walter, grabbed his clothes off the chair and headed to the bathroom.

Twenty minutes later they were sitting in a pub with a basket of chicken wings and a pitcher of beer. Walter couldn't drink much, but he enjoyed a cold beer on occasion. He'd have a couple and then switch to a soda. The wings were tasty and the jukebox was playing an old Merle Haggard tune. The bar area was completely full and at least half the tables. "You ready to play a game?" Buddy asked looking at Walter with that eye toothy smile.

"Ready as I'll ever be." They headed over to the tables and Buddy racked up the balls. "I sure am glad you picked me up, Buddy. God only knows where I'd be right now."

"It's okay Walt, truth is I've been pretty lonely and pretty depressed. You have helped me get my thoughts straight and as soon as I drop off this load I'm going home and take care of some things I have needed to do for a long time. I have a daughter Walter, and she needs a father. I haven't been around much because her mother hurt me pretty bad. I been thinking about how it sure wasn't Emily's fault and I haven't done right by her. You know, I was always proud of the fact that I always paid my child support, but that's only one part of being a father. I really want to get to know her and spend quality time with her. You made me think about how important it is to spend time with the ones you love, because you never know when you might lose them and there is more than one way to lose them."

Walter chalked up his stick and hit a red striped ball in the right hand pocket like it was the easiest thing in the world. He walked around the table studied it for a minute and then hit the yellow striped ball in the left hand pocket. He began to whistle a tune to Merle Haggard and study his next shot. Buddy laughed and shook his head.

"You didn't tell me this was going to be like 'The Color of Money', shoot we should hustle some of these boys up and make a penny or two." Walter looked up and smiled.

"I guess I should have warned ya, Buddy." Just then the sound of another ball going in and a hearty laugh that Buddy had yet to hear out of Walter. "I play a pretty mean game of pool," Walter said with a smile that was downright contagious.

Door Ajar

Chapter 45

Marcie sat at her make-up table and plucked at a few unruly eyebrow hairs. She put dark black eyeliner on and thick mascara. Then she removed her glasses and put in her contacts, something she rarely did. Marcie loved meeting new people and going to eat at new restaurants. Christy's was new to her and she was just as excited about the pizza pub with the live band. She loved music and getting dressed up. Benjamin had called Clark and invited him to the pizza place to meet his father and hang out for a bit. Marcie wasn't sure how she felt about that, because he tended to annoy her on some level. He was always sizing her up and smiling a smile that was more than just a friendly greeting. Her new black velvet pants and boots, would look great with her new purple cashmere sweater. Pulling her long blonde hair up, she made sure that every detail in her appearance was perfect so that every eye would be on her tonight. The attention always gave her a rush. A half an hour later she was pulling into Benjamin's apartment. They had planned on meeting there and having a few beers first. They weren't legally old enough to drink, although they both had fake ID's, they both didn't want to drink around Ben's father. Marcie knocked on the door with a six pack in her hand and a look that made Benjamin suck in air. "Hello there you," Benjamin said, while eyeing her up and down seductively.

"Hey Benjamin, are you about ready, because I...." She got no further than that when he had grabbed her and kissed her with such passion that she almost dropped the beer. It was very unexpected although it was nice, it wasn't what she was used to getting from him. The Benjamin that wouldn't come clean, the Benjamin that stood her up on Saturday night or forgot to call was the one she was attracted to. It was the chase or the game that really kept her there. She knew it was a sickness but she couldn't help it and thought somehow it stemmed from her father or lack of one.

"Well, what a nice greeting, Ben!"

"You look smoking hot, I don't even care about going to meet them, we could just call it off and stay here." He smiled at her, knowing she wouldn't go for that. He was wearing a dark grey silky shirt and a black pair of jeans, something about him was different but she couldn't pin it down. After careful consideration she noticed he had shaved.

"So Benjamin, you're not ready to go through with this, are you?" She could see it in his eyes. He had those sad puppy dog eyes, even when he was cheerful they appeared sullen. Marcie could get lost in those big puppy eyes, if she wasn't careful. "So are you?"

"I guess as ready as I'm ever going to be," he said a little sarcastically.

"Are you chickening out, or what?"

"No Marcie, it's just not something I'm good at and why should I just let him get over?"

"What do you mean, get over?" Marcie grabbed a beer and uncapped it.

"Why should he just get away with leaving me with Larry Stewart for a father? Come on Marcie, my life was hell and he was probably on a ski lift in the Alps or tanning in the Bahamas!" Marcie handed the beer to Benjamin and grabbed one for herself. She walked to the ugly green refrigerator and placed the carton on the shelf.

"Benjamin, are you ever going to forgive him? I mean he's trying here. He already told you it wasn't his choice, it is your mother that you should have this anger towards! She's the one who gave you up, not him." Marcie took a swig of beer and began to pack down her cigarette pack.

"Yeah, well, so he says. I dunno Marcie, I just hate putting on an act for him and his girlfriend. I mean you know me, I'd rather go in there high and drink a few pints of beer and be myself, but I can't do that and I don't even know what to talk about."

"I know, Benjamin, but you can't let this man out of your life, you can't push him away. I mean you saw how much he loves you."

"I did? And when was that Marcie?"

"Remember how he hugged you and how his eyes were so bright when he saw you?"

Benjamin thought back to that night and how good it felt to finally look into the eyes of his real father, but part of him still had so much anger towards him.

"I heard more excitement in his voice, than I have heard from my own father in my entire life!"

"Okay, okay, I'll try, but I can't make any promises." Why does she even care, he thought, is it because then I could be at her level with a father who's a big shot like hers. He felt sick inside.

"Clark's meeting us at the pub when we leave Christy's, is that okay?" He needed Clark there so that if things went sour he could just disappear. Anyway, a guy friend was always better than a girl, they stuck by you no matter what.

Marcie loathed the idea of Clark, but she nodded in agreement. She pulled out a compact mirror and applied some lip gloss and pulled a couple strands of hair down around her neck. "What time is it, Benjamin? We have to be there at seven and I don't want to be late."

"Well, I don't want to be early. I want them to already have the table ready and be seated."

Marcie lit a cigarette and inhaled deeply. Hanging out with Benjamin sober, was new. They were always high or drunk and this was all new to her. She wasn't even sure if she knew what she wanted anymore and for some reason the whole evening seemed like a drag all the sudden.

Benjamin grabbed two more beers and looked at the clock in the kitchen, it was six forty-five. They had fifteen minutes to get there if they wanted to be prompt, but he wasn't about to do that, no he was going to make an entrance. "That rich bastard can wait." He smiled to himself and remembered that he held the cards now, he called the shots. Come to think of it he had everyone in his clutches, including Marcie. He pulled a pipe out of his jacket pocket and lit it.

"I thought you weren't going to show up high, Benjamin." All the sudden she was sounding like his mom and he didn't like that.

"I thought you weren't going to show up high, Benjamin..." he mocked her in a whiney tone and took a toke off the end.

All the sudden Marcie was feeling uncomfortable, but also a little more into the game. This was the Ben that kept her interested. He passed the pipe to her and she felt a rush from knowing that this was going to put them both out of control for the evening. "We still have one more beer to drink a piece before we leave and I'm not showing up before seven thirty."

"Come on Benjamin, that's rude."

"I don't care, I had to wait twenty years for that jerk, he can wait for me!" He took a few more hits off the pipe and passed it to Marcie. He was starting to feel calm and suddenly, he didn't care what his father thought of him.

Marcie was getting high and wondering how the night would end. She knew deep down she didn't want to act like an idiot in front of Bradford or his girlfriend for that matter, but she was so addicted to Benjamin she couldn't stop herself. He scooted over next to her on the sofa and ran a finger across her lips. "My, my, my, how did I ever get you? You look so gorgeous tonight." Then he pulled her face to him and began to kiss her softly and slowly and suddenly she was hooked again. They continued to smoke until they were both giggling and had not a care in the world.

Marcie took another swig of beer and decided not to have anymore because she had to drive and she was tired of always having to be the designated driver. It would be nice, she thought if she could get wasted and let him drive her around for a change. "So, when do you think you'll be able to drive again, Benjamin?"

"Never, why are you askin'?"

"I just thought, I mean it's been awhile since the accident and well…"

"Well, what? You don't know what that was like. You have no idea what I been through. And if you're tired of driving me around just say so, I'll call Clark!"

Marcie was really starting to get agitated with the whole scene. "If you want to call Clark, go right ahead!"

"Maybe I will, maybe you don't have to do another thing for me."

"Come on, Benjamin, I know you're stressed over this meeting with your father, but do you really have to treat me like this?"

Benjamin sat there flipping the channels with the remote. His face showed no emotion and his eyes were glazed over from the weed he'd smoked. Marcie sat in silence, not really knowing what to say. She knew she probably should not have brought up the accident and could only imagine what that was like for him. Thinking about how she would feel if she had a wreck and killed Benjamin made her decide to finish her beer after all. She could tell that Benjamin really didn't want her there now and that made her nervous. "So Benjamin, are you bout ready to go?"

He sat there with a smirk and that glazed look. "You go ahead, I'll catch up with you later."

Marcie took another drink and lit another cigarette. She knew if she left it would be even harder to come back to Benjamin. Why did he have to play these games with her heart? "Are you really going to call, Clark? I mean, after all, I am here and I am ready and I do want to meet your father and his friend." She looked at Benjamin until he met her eyes.

"Na, I don't think I'm gonna go now, you go ahead."

Marcie felt so uncomfortable. She hated men, why did she always go for jerks. "I'm not going without you that is the dumbest thing I've ever heard. Why would I want to go meet your father and his girlfriend, when you are who he is expecting? If you don't show up you're an idiot!" She picked up her purse, chugged the rest of her beer, sat the beer bottle down on the coffee table a little too hard and crushed her cigarette out in the ashtray.

She walked out the door and left it fully open, deciding not to slam it but make him get up instead. That made her smile for some sorry reason and she couldn't wait to get out of his sight. Her heart hurt, but she was used to it. And what better way to treat a hurting heart then another drink and another guy, she was going to head to Frank's. It was perfect, all his friends thought she was hot and they'd let her drink all she wanted. She took her aggression out on the clutch of her beetle bug, and squealed tires leaving the parking lot. For some reason it made her smile. "Good bye Benjamin, have a wonderful time!" She said under her breath as she sped off.

Anticipation

Chapter 46

Desiree was excited about the evening, but a little uncomfortable too. People didn't like change, she supposed and she was leery about meeting Bradford's son and what he would bring to their relationship. She was happy for Bradford and knew that this journey was something he needed. His son was going to be of extreme importance in his life, an added blessing. He would be a whole new discovery and chapter, she just hoped she didn't get left behind in the excitement.

Desiree had already gotten the children ready and the bird situated. Josh was busy talking to Jackie about his secret. He had been on eggshells with excitement over this, chatting all week to Jackie in whispers and speaking of Belinda his angelic friend. Desiree was not sure what to make of it all, but she knew Jackie had been a great pet for both the children and her. Jackie had a personality that was very special. Desiree had even grown fond of watching her interact with both Tabitha and Josh and on occasion she'd lightly fly by her head to say hello.

She had dressed quickly and was now trying to apply makeup over the makeup she had put on that morning. Getting a manicure and washing her hair was out of the question at this point, but she spritzed her hair with water and added some gel, then blew it completely dry. After a quick spray of perfume and a pair of dangling hoop earrings, she studied herself through the glass and whispered, 'Bradford, don't forget about me'. She was certain she was being silly, but what if his son had extreme issues or better yet none and they spent each weekend at football games and movie theatres?

She phoned her grandmom to let her know they were leaving. The local florist was on the way home from work and she had stopped in to pick up some flowers. She chose an arrangement of purple lilacs and babies breathe. She missed Grandmom and hoped the fresh cut flowers would brighten her day.

Bradford had phoned and they had agreed to drive separately and he had promised to spend Sunday with her and the children. He was already at the restaurant when Desiree arrived. Somehow, he had managed to get an amazing table in the back in a comfy corner. When she walked in, he was immediately up to greet her. "Hello Des, you look incredible as usual. How's my favorite grandmom?"

"Oh, she is wonderful, Bradford. I picked up a bouquet of flowers for her and spent a little time there. Any sign of your son?"

"No, he hasn't gotten here yet? I'm so nervous, my palms are sweaty." He laughed a little uncomfortably and ran his fingers through his hair.

"It's going to be fine Bradford, you are getting nervous over nothing." She adored the childlike look of anticipation and hoped that the evening would be magical.

"Well, he is a little behind schedule...I called his cell phone a minute ago and he didn't answer." Bradford looked up at her with eyes that seemed to plead.

"He's probably stuck in traffic or didn't hear the phone ring. You know how these young people are today and it's Saturday, calm down." She patted his arm and looked down at his glass of wine and wondered if he intended to drink and drive. He knew how much it bothered her for anyone to drink and drive. She'd just have to make sure he was safe, she was sure he was just nervous.

"I know, I know, Desiree, it's just what if he's had a change of heart? What if he has decided not to go through with this?"

"Then Bradford, we will just keep pursuing him and loving him, until he is able to trust us. Why don't you try and call him again, it won't hurt anything." Bradford's eyes were skimming the room and he was searching the doorway and not even looking at Desiree as she spoke, but instead nervously shifted in his seat. "Go Bradford, call him."

"Okay, I'm going to walk outside where it's quieter and call." He looked at her with an anxious grin and walked towards the atrium. It was a side porch, enclosed with open windows, which wrapped around the side of the building. There were potted plants and beautiful pieces of art hanging at eye level. He nervously pulled out his cell and hit redial, listening to the rings and his heart drumming in his ear drums. "Hello."

"Hey Benjamin, its Bradford, are you still coming to dinner. I was getting a little worried about you."

"Hey, ah, yeah, I was just getting ready to call you. Marcie and I had a spat so to speak and I lost my ride."

"Oh, I see, well, I can come get you or send a cab, there's a taxi sitting right out front of Christy's."

"Yeah, sure Bradford, I'll take a taxi." Bradford's voice was elated as he wrote down the address to give to the cab driver.

"Alright buddy, well, I'll be waiting out front for you, okay?"

"Sure, Bradford, see you in a minute."

Bradford heard the phone click and he headed to the driver out front, handed him the directions and a twenty, and then nervously bummed a cigarette. He stuck it behind his ear and pulled his sweater down, it was green wool and matched his striking eyes. He opened the door to the Atrium and walked back down the steps and to the back where Desiree sat eating dinner bread with pineapple butter.

She could tell by the bounce in his step and the light hearted grin that he had succeeded in getting his son on the phone. "Oh, he's coming isn't he?" She grinned, already knowing him too well.

"Yes dear, it seems he had a small argument with his girlfriend and was delayed. I've sent a taxi to pick him up."

"He doesn't drive?" Desiree asked with a peculiar frown.

"No, Hun, I haven't gotten that far yet, but I'm going to finish my wine and then head out front and wait for him to get here. You don't mind do you, Des?" He spread a hefty amount of butter onto a slice of crispy French bread and looked up at her.

"Of course not! You go wait for your son, you've been waiting for a lifetime. Anyway, then you can both make a grand entrance and I can see if he resembles you." She smiled at his precariousness, it was so nice to see him so excited and so alive. He raised the wine glass and took a hearty sip and then patted Desiree on the leg. He looked in her eyes and said, "I'm so glad you are a becoming a part of my life. I can't imagine it without you." Their eyes met and then suddenly they were interrupted by the waiter as their lips met.

"Give us just a minute please, there is one more guest coming." The waiter nodded at Bradford nervously, took his drink tray and scurried to another table. Bradford rose up out of his chair and headed to the front door. "I'll be right back and don't you go anywhere, I can't wait for you to meet him." He winked at her and it made her heart flutter, she was falling and bad.

Desiree called after Brad, "Hey, what's his name?" But, he was too far away to hear her.

Bradford stepped outside into the chilly air and lit his cigarette. It was already growing dark and the valets were pacing for the next car to park for tip money. Bradford sat down on a wooden bench and inhaled the tasty treat, he knew he shouldn't but some cravings never went away. Blowing smoke, he thought about how drastically life had changed for him in just a short time and he knew he had Desiree to thank for that. Now his son would be a part of it too. He finished his wine and sat the glass on the side of the seat. The cigarette was nearly gone, when the lights of a taxi pulled into the front circle drive. Bradford rose up quickly, anxious to make this relationship work. The door opened and out stepped Benjamin and he nearly ran to meet him.

"How you doing kid?" Before he could answer Bradford put his arm around him, just before punching him lightly in the shoulder. Benjamin smiled and wondered if this was going to work. He was still kicking himself in the butt over Marcie, but he could get her back whenever he wanted, he knew that. "You ready to go in and meet my lovely lady and order some food? I'm getting hungry, how about you?"

"Sounds good Bradford, sound's good." His eyes were still glazed over and he was feeling no pain.

"You don't have to call me Bradford. Benjamin, you can call me dad, well, when you feel comfortable." And with that they opened the front doors and began walking towards the back booth. Desiree sat waiting patiently, not knowing that her life was once again going to change.

<u>*Liars and Fires*</u>

<u>*Chapter 47*</u>

Marcie flung the door open to Frank's and walked with a strut, knowing that every eye in the room was glued to her tight black velvet pants and high heeled boots. With her hair pulled up and her low cut cashmere sweater, she knew she was causing disturbances even with the married couples, as husbands and dates stared a little too long at her curvy figure. Marcie smiled to herself and flashed her bright eyes adorned with the dark shadow and mascara. She wiggled her way down the steps to the bar area and waited for Scott to come over and get her drink order. Adrenalin rushed to her head as she looked around the bar and tried to decide which man she wanted to get to know for the night.

"Hey hottie, where are you going tonight?" Scott whistled and fed her ego a little more.

"I dunno, that might depend on where you plan on taking me?" She winked and began the start of one of her favorite games. 'Daddy, you have taught me so well,' she thought. She flashed her sexiest smile and watched out of the corner of her eye as an older business man strained his ear to catch her every word. "I'll have a martini, Scott, and make it dirty, with extra olives."

Scott grabbed a bottle of Absolut and started pouring her drink into the shaker, just as Clark came around the corner. "Well, look at you girl!" Clark let out a whistle and smiled. "Where's Benjamin at?"

"Benjamin who?" She said, taking a drink of her martini.

"Oh, it's like that now is it?" Clark shook his head and looked her over more than once.

"Yeah Clark, it's like that." She always found Clark a little untrustworthy, but he might be just what she needed to get back at Benjamin. She smiled at the idea of all his coworkers watching her snuggle up to Clark.

"Well Marcie, if he let you get out of his sight tonight, he ain't real bright." Clark's eyes were fixed on her cleavage. "I'm going to have to have a talk with that boy. Man...."

"Well, have you talked to him tonight?" Marcie already knew Benjamin had invited Clark to the pizza pub to watch the band. He was supposed to meet them there after they had dinner at Christy's.

"Yeah, he called, said a taxi was picking him up and he'd see me at the pizza joint later on, like around nine or ten. What's up? I thought you both were getting along good and this was supposed to be an exciting night, meeting the dad and all?"

"Yeah, me too Clark, but I guess I'm not as fun as his dead fiancée. I'm tired of trying to compete with a dead person!" Marcie picked up her martini glass and took a gulp, while pulling an olive off a spear and seductively putting in her mouth. She turned and smiled at the business man who hadn't taken his eyes off her since she'd arrived.

"Fiancée? What are you talking about? Benjamin's never been engaged before?"

Marcie looked confused, she pulled out a cigarette and instantly had two lighters in front of her. "You know Clark, his fiancée Debbie, the one who died in a car wreck."

"Oh man, whoa, whoa, back up, who told you this? Marcie, I've known Benjamin since we were little kids and he did date a girl named Debbie, but they weren't engaged and she is alive and well. She left him for an older man, lives over in the Cambridge apartments."

All the color drained out of Marcie's face. All the life went out of her body. Why did she always pick men who were sorry pieces of crap? "All men are liars," she said, liars and she was naive and stupid enough to believe their schemes. "So, they were never engaged and she didn't die in a car wreck?"

"No baby, she is very much alive and living with some old dude."

"But Benjamin said that's why he walks everywhere and why he can't drive anymore." Her brow was crumpled up and she was in shock, she didn't know what to say or do.

"Scott, bring her another martini and put it on my tab," Clark said in a stern voice.

"Baby, Benjamin doesn't drive, because Benjamin got a DUI and some other things happened. Somebody died alright, but it sure wasn't anyone he knew. That's why he walks everywhere. I'm sorry Marcie, really I am, but Benjamin's not good for you. You deserve better," he said, as he rubbed her shoulder.

Marcie was so confused and so stunned she didn't even feel like flirting anymore. She just felt empty and so betrayed. All she wanted to do now was drink till the ache left her.

"I'm gonna go change clothes. I'll be right back, okay?"

"Okay Clark," she said, as she inhaled her cigarette a little too hard and motioned for Scott. "Hey, I think I want to do a shot, you know how to make a purple hooter? Ahh skip it, just give me a shot of tequila, with lime and salt."

"Marcie, mixing vodka and tequila might not be such a good idea." Scott gave her a face that reminded her of her father's. She wanted to just punch Scott and jump over the bar and take the whole entire bottle.

"Scott, I'm a big girl, I'll decide what's good and what's not, okay?" She smiled a smile that said jerk wad, just do what I say already. All of the sudden, she wanted to take every business man at the bar to the nearest hotel and take their wallets and their clothes and then call their wives on the way out. She felt very vindictive at the moment and very determined to make Benjamin pay and what better way she thought than with his best friend Clark.

Clark came out of the back wearing some tight, faded jeans with a rip in the left knee, a white button down shirt and a pair of cowboy boots. He sat next to her and ordered a Guinness on tap, the dark thick beer always made Marcie sick, but he seems to relish it. "What are you going to do now, Marcie?"

"Oh, I'm going to the pizza pub, you can count on that." She turned the shot glass up and sucked on the lime, then licked the salt off her hand. She wanted answers, she wanted the truth and she wanted to hear it out of Benjamin's mouth.

She pulled out another smoke, just as Scott sat down another shot of tequila, "Compliments of the gentleman to your left."

Marcie turned and eyed the business man. He had thick, black, curly hair and a tan that was much too dark for the winter. He had a shot in his hand and was lifting it towards her. Marcie scooted her bar stool over and held hers up to him with a grin. She did a count and they both took the shot in unison. "Thanks," she said, licking her thin lips, which were unnoticeable due to her large striking eyes. "I'm Marcie, and you are?"

"Hello, lovely lady, I'm Steve and I was just admiring your beauty." He smiled and nodded his head.

Clark turned and gave the older man a look that said back off and grabbed Marcie's hand. "Now look, there's no need for you to go looking for Benjamin tonight. You can come over to my place and drink all you want and I'll make sure you're alright. You can have my bed and I'll take the couch."

Marcie was starting to feel better, another drink and she wouldn't even care. All of a sudden Clark seemed to be more handsome than she had remembered and not nearly as untrustworthy. After all, they are all liars and cheats she thought to herself, what does it really matter? She might as well get even or get hers. "But I need to confront him. I need to tell him I know what a rotten fink he is. Either you are driving me or you're not." She turned back towards the business man and pulled her sweater down a little more. 'Men they're all snakes,' she thought to herself. I just need 'fresh meat' stamped on my forehead.

Clark was trying to figure out how to get her home with him. He knew Benjamin and he were best friends, but he had dated his ex, Sherry right after they broke it off and fresh game is fresh game. 'Ben shouldn't have let this one get away,' he thought to himself. If he took her to his place, knowing her, she'd just complain about Benjamin all night, but if he took her to see Benjamin, she might become so enraged she would sleep with him. Clark couldn't remember the last time he had sex. He eyed her tight, firm little body as she did a wiggle to the ladies room and decided to just do whatever she wanted. Steve was eyeing him and Scott was chatting with some servers who kept looking at Clark to see what he would do.

Marcie came out of the restroom and plopped down next to Steve. "Hello there Steve, are you about ready for another shot of tequila?" She smiled and licked her freshly painted lips. Clark had not seen this coming and was wondering what to do now.

"I am, if you are." Steve's eyes lit up and a twinkle seemed to glow in them. "You sure are a tiny little thing to be slamming back those shots little girl." She liked the way he called her little girl and decided to sit next to him for a while. Scott came over and brought two more shots. Marcie picked up her shot and asked Steve with the too dark tan and even darker eyes, where he was from.

"I'm from Virginia, just here on business, staying over at the Hampton." He smiled and lifted his shot and asked her if she was ready. As she salted up her wrist and just as they downed it, he reached for her wrist and licked the salt off seductively. His gold Rolex shined under the bar lamp, along with his shiny diamond ring. Marcie hadn't even noticed Clark on his cell phone chatting frantically, nor did she notice when he exited Frank's…she was much too busy figuring out how to take Steve back to his hotel room and steal his precious possessions. She hated men and just like her father, this one loved his image. The Hampton was in walking distance and Marcie, although she was tipsy could handle her alcohol with the best of men. She reached under the bar and placed her hand on Steve's thigh and began rubbing it, all the while her eyes rested on his Rolex.

Darkness to Light

Chapter 48

Desiree had gotten lost in the ambience and the appetizer, it was fried calamari with a chili pepper dipping sauce. The dish was perfectly prepared and she was enjoying the peace and quiet of the restaurant. The lighting was dim and the artwork was simply amazing, she had also become distracted by the soothing décor of taupe and deep rustic textures. The staff dressed in dark wine sports coats, black slacks and bow ties, were busily scurrying throughout the dining area with bottles of champagne and trays filled with entrées. She wasn't even looking up as Benjamin and Bradford approached the table. Abruptly, there he was. She was looking into his eyes, the man who had murdered John, the man who had taken her life and her children's lives. Bradford's voice sounded as if it were in a tunnel far, far away. His eyes were peering, spinning, penetrating into hers. She began to have flashbacks of Benjamin in the orange jump suit, shackled, yet he had a smirk on his face. The calamari in her mouth turned to cotton and she couldn't seem to force it down her throat. There must be some kind of mistake, why was he here? Her mind was flashing like a strobe light. The coroner, the sheet. The body. It was a maze of memories and heartache and right in front of her was the man who caused it. She felt hatred you could taste, smell and feel in the air. And still she was frozen. "Desiree...Desiree, this is my son, Benjamin." Bradford had said it once already, but now he wasn't sure what was going on, something wasn't right. Her eyes were piercingly evil and there was a scowl of rage on her face. So, Bradford had repeated her name a little louder, bringing her out of her shock.

Benjamin spoke first, "What the hell is this? What kind of charade is this? You plotted this the whole time. Wow, I have to admit, you had me going Bradford!"

"What are you talking about, Benjamin?" Bradford wasn't sure what was taking place between Desiree and Benjamin, but he could tell something was wrong, something was dreadfully wrong.

Benjamin was dumb struck by what was happening, it was surreal, like a bad movie. "What a flipping dark, twisted joke? You're not even my father," he said shaking.

"Of course, I'm your father Benjamin, why would you say that? I'm your father, you have to believe me." Bradford was feeling strange and the evening he had hoped for was crumbling right before him.

Benjamin's eyes glared from Bradford to Desiree. He ran his fingers through his long hair nervously. "I should have known better," he pulled a smoke out of his jacket pocket and began to search anxiously for his lighter. Why did they want him to meet them here? His mind couldn't comprehend what was taking place. He suddenly thought about Larry, and how he could be so brainless to think his real father was even out there or would even care about him. "You son of a bitch, you're sick," he said looking Bradford in the eye.

"But Benjamin, I am your father. I swear to you."

Benjamin mocked him in a sarcastic high pitched voice. "I am your father. You both are sick." Benjamin shook his head and then turned from the table, but not quickly enough because Desiree was already behind him grabbing his shirt and spinning him around. He had his cigarette in between his lips and a twisted grin on his face.

"I'll tell you who's sick, you are, you filthy bastard! You don't deserve a father, my children don't have one anymore, remember? You left him in the street, in a pool of blood or have you forgotten?" Her hands were trembling and so was her voice. The adrenalin that was pumping through her had put her in a manic state. "You walk the streets free and my husband is six foot under, you slimy piece of crap, you don't deserve to live! You are a monster!" And then she shoved him as hard as she could. "You drunken murderer, words can't even describe how revolting and nauseous you make me feel." Her voice was rising with each adjective she was using to describe him and people were starting to gawk. "Thanks to you, nightmares grip my children and they are FATHERLESS!" Her words spewed from clenched teeth. "You took the love of my life, you took my soul." She grabbed him by the shirt in the front of his chest and with her teeth gritted and her face snarled she spat on him.

At this point Bradford was speechless. He was standing in between the two most important people in his life, not knowing how this could have happened.

Desiree looked at Bradford and said, "Bradford if this is your son... I can't stay here, I can't look at him, he repulses me."

Benjamin shoved past her and started towards the door. He turned and mouthed, "Don't bother lady, I'm going!" He walked past them both. Desiree's reflexes got the best of her and she grabbed Benjamin by the arm, swung him around and with an open palm started to slap him. Bradford grabbed her in the nick of time and spun her around to him.

"Desiree, get a hold of yourself!" The manager and a few of the staff had gathered around them.

"Your son is the man who murdered my husband, John." Her whole body was shaking with rage. She peered into Bradford's eyes looking for something, compassion, empathy? Her own eyes held so much pain and her heart felt so heavy and so full of grief and hatred, she wanted to erupt, she wanted to run. She didn't know what Bradford was thinking, but what she saw disturbed her. He wasn't even listening! Didn't he hear her say that Benjamin killed her husband? His eyes were gazing right past hers as if he were weighing which one to try to keep in his life.

Benjamin was already walking towards the foyer, making his way to the exit. Bradford let out a yell, causing an even more abrupt scene in the restaurant. "Benjamin wait, don't go, Ben." His words held a plea that even Desiree could sense was heartfelt.

Desiree stood in shock. He was choosing his son, a young man he only met once, and a killer at that. What about her? He might be his son, but he was still a murderer! 'Blood is always thicker than water', as they say and she guessed the quote was right. She grabbed her coat and glanced at Bradford's wine glass and thought about how ignorant she had been. The staff and the managers were trying to hush everyone, not only that, but they were getting ready to phone the police.

The manager had grabbed Bradford's coat and was literally pushing him out the door. Bradford was set on catching Benjamin and still he was turning to try and console Desiree. His heart was shattered. What was happening to the night he had envisioned? What could he do to make amends? "Desiree, I didn't know, I had no idea. You have to believe me." He peered into her eyes and he wasn't sure what to say. But she wasn't listening anymore, she was walking away.

Desiree was glad she had driven. She was at the boiling point, and was racked with anger, hurt and rage. Just seeing him that close and listening to him run his mouth had made her blood pressure soar. Bradford had turned and was headed towards Benjamin and she was headed to the parking lot. She reached the van and seen the two of them in a confrontation in front of the building. Just their shadows made her feel so betrayed and so alone with her fears.

Bradford had finally caught up with Benjamin and he was trying to hold back tears. "You have to believe me son, I had no idea." He was looking intently into Benjamin's eyes and pleading with him. "Please don't let this steal our future together, I've just found you."

Benjamin was looking into Bradford's eyes and he could see the similarities and he could feel his passion and he was lost. How could it ever work now? How could they ever have a relationship with Desiree in the picture? Why wasn't anything in his life easy? And how could he ever make the almost too perfect father in front of him respect him after this?

"You would have been better off never finding me Bradford, I'm a real loser! My life has been screwed up since the day I was born. You'd be better off to go after her and us part ways." He lowered his head and tried to forget what he had seen in Bradford's eyes, and what he had heard in his voice. He turned the corner and started walking down the cobble walkway with Bradford on his heels.

"Look son, I have thought about you every day since the day I knew you were in your mother's womb. I never wanted her to give you up. I begged for her to keep you, but there was nothing I could do. Please give us a chance. I need you and you need me." He grabbed Benjamin by his arm and spun him around. He was looking directly at Benjamin now and his emotions were insufferable. "Every time I saw a baby my heart sank, every time I saw a little boy my eyes would search so intently for you, for any part of me, for any part of your mother. I thought you were being raised by a loving family. I never dreamed it was someone like Larry. Had I known all the heartache you were going through, I would have searched for you sooner, but I didn't want to confuse you. I didn't want to disrupt your home life. I thought you were in a good place with two parents who loved you. Desiree, is not worth me losing you. Oh Benjamin, please don't leave us like this." He held open his arms and stood there waiting, his heart was pounding in his chest and his heart was begging for him to accept his invitation. Then slowly almost methodically Benjamin began to step closer, unsure of what he was doing, he allowed the man who stood before him to embrace him. Suddenly, he felt something welling up in his eyes, something that hadn't happened since he was a very small boy. He had learned how to become numb and he had taken every drug and every drink there was to make sure he never had to hurt again. He had pushed every ounce of emotion down to a place of no return. But at this moment, Benjamin felt something stirring inside him that scared the living hell out of him. As a tear slid silently down his cheek, he asked himself a question, 'Is this what emotions feel like?' Was his frozen heart beginning to unthaw?

Back on the Road

Chapter 49

Walter awoke to the sound of the heater blowing from the window. The warmth of the soft cotton blanket and plaid bedspread felt so good, he did not want to leave the comfort of the bed. He glanced over at Buddy who was propped up with some pillows behind his back, sipping coffee from a hot, steamy cup.

"Mornin' Walt, how are you feeling this morning? "

"Couldn't be better."

Buddy smiled and walked over towards the dresser where he had made a pot of coffee with the complimentary packages the motel had provided. The pot was small and it held four cups, but Buddy could tell he'd be lucky to get two out of it. "Let me get you some coffee. Cream? Sugar?"

"I got it, Buddy." Walter eased out of the warm bed and added a little cream to his styrofoam cup before pouring and then sat down at the table by the window.

"So, you feel like going to Georgia with me Ole timer? If you want to go, it's going to be at least a day before I can get you home."

Walter continued to sip his coffee and stare out the window in deep thought. He knew he could have a good time traveling with Buddy and playing pool and eating in truck stops, but when would it end? Plus he felt like a leach. He enjoyed Buddy's company and at times he had almost completely forgotten about his trouble with the law, almost… but not really.

"Yeah Buddy, if you don't mind, I think I'll run that load with you and wait till Sunday to head home."

"We should be back by Sunday afternoon, evening the latest, Walt." Buddy ran his hand through his beard as he had a habit of doing and picked up his coffee cup, stood and looked out the window. There was a maid pushing a cart

374

along the balcony and a number of people putting suitcases and laundry into their vehicles. It was almost check out time and Buddy wasn't ready to get in that rig again, but he guessed it had become a part of him. He looked over at Walter who was clearly in deep thought and tried to snap him out of it. "You alright, Walter?"

Walter looked up at Buddy and nodded slowly. "I am just thinking too much, that's all. Sunday is the anniversary of Ruthie's death and I was hoping you could drop me off at the cemetery. I have yet to go there and talk to her. I want to sit with her for a spell before I turn myself in to the police. I really just want to go be with her, Buddy." Walter looked up at Buddy, his dark brown eyes looked like a sad puppy and they held him with their plea. It was as if they were begging to be closed and no longer a part of this earth. "I really can't think of anything I'd rather do than go be with her. I don't hear many a man talk about their wives too good these days and times have changed, I'll give you that, but she was my world. We had a mutual respect. It was as if she were a reflection of my own soul. We were always finishing each other's sentences and we had laughter, gut wrenching laughter. When I close my eyes at night, she is the last thing

I think about and when I open my eyes in the morning she is the first picture that I see, a reflection of her beautiful smile."

Buddy had tears he was choking back, just listening to this man talk had changed his life. He was going to secretly do whatever he could to help him with an attorney or bail or whatever he needed. He just knew he could not watch this friend he had become so close to, rot away in a prison.

"Walter, that sounds like a great marriage. I hope one day to meet someone that will make me feel special. I love hearing about Ruthie and the love you shared, it gives me hope. We seem to never understand death or life after death. When you talk about Ruthie you talk as if she is still alive waiting for you. I guess you could say you have made me think about my faith. I mean you act as if you have no doubt that heaven exists and that you intend to spend eternity with Ruthie. I guess Walt, not only have you made me think about how important family is, you've made me think about my future. You even have me thinking about God, yet, you never really have brought him up. Funny how a lot of religious people talk about God and His Son and even angels, but they just don't seem to have much love, sometimes they make you feel worse about yourself and even hopeless. Yet you, you Walt, have given me hope and a hunger to rekindle my relationship with my daughter and I believe yes, even God. Does that sound strange?" Buddy cracked his knuckles in nervousness, not really knowing what had come over him.

"No Buddy, it don't sound strange at all. I took my children to church for years and even was an usher at the First Baptist Church. I memorized scriptures and even paid my tithes, but it took me years to get the Father's love in my heart, not just my head. I think God wants us to be lights that shine in a dark world. He wants us to bind up the hurting and hold the broken and be his messengers, but too many of us walk out of our homes every morning with one thing on our mind and that's ourselves. It's when we see other people's needs and reach out, that he heals us."

The two of them sat in silence for a few minutes, wondering what the future held for both of them.

"You bout ready, Ole Timer?"

Walter nodded with a half grin, "About as ready as I'll ever be, I guess."

Holding the Pain

Chapter 50

Desiree was sitting in the parking lot, she could see Bradford and Benjamin talking down the walkway under the street light. She was still feeling so much hurt, so much rage. She watched as they embraced and couldn't contain herself. Bradford was patting Benjamin on the back in a manly fashion. The two were deep in conversation and here she sat all alone. "Don't you know what he did to me? Oh Bradford he took my children's father away. Can't you see?" She was talking aloud in the front seat of her van, knowing that no one could hear her. Then she heard another voice in her head say, "Desiree, that is his son, he can't help it. He loves his son." She began to answer the voice in her head. "Yes, he can! He can help it, he can at least see my side too!"

She started the van and drove off screeching her tires. Finally, when she reached the expressway she had started to take deep breaths and exhale. Benjamin would never know what he had put her through. "Oh, he could never repay, he could never repay," she repeated aloud. For him to even be able to breathe, was a crime in itself.

Her children could never get their father back. Josh's face flashed before her, and then memories of him and John throwing a ball in the backyard. John had been such a great father. She could hear him cheering Josh on, "Catch it Josh, you can do it! That's my boy!" Josh's eyes were squinted in the sunlight, but his grin was as wide as the catcher's mitt he had on. She had memories of her daughter with her delicate features and angelic face resting in John's arms, her head lying upon his sturdy shoulder, hidden in the security of a father's strength. But Tabitha's chance to know her father had been snatched from her. The little patter of feet running to greet him, "Daddy, Daddy," had been silenced. He would never walk her down the aisle. Her father would never teach her how to swim or ride a bike with no training wheels. Her father would never see her or Josh graduate from high school, or college. He would never see Tabitha in a prom dress. He would never see her become the beautiful woman she would one day and he would never see his grandchildren. He would never be able to teach Josh how to drive a car or become the young man he intended.

Desiree began to talk aloud, "What are the odds? Come on God, why is this happening to me? Why can't anything good happen in my life? Why do you hate me so much? I was just getting over John and beginning to live again? Why? Oh, it's no use, I hate you, I hate you God! Do you hear me? You never give me good gifts. How are you love? You're not love, if this is how you show love, I don't want to know you."

All she wanted to do was go get drunk. If Benjamin could, why couldn't she? Oh, but she wouldn't drive drunk, no, she wasn't that stupid or selfish! She pulled into the wine shop and bought a bottle of Beringer and a pack of Salem lights.

The man behind the counter double bagged her bottle in brown paper and smiled up at her greasily. His beady eyes rested on her chest and then arose. "Good evening," he said smiling. She snarled her lip and peered at him with eyes that said, mister, don't even think about it. Without even saying 'Thank you,' she grabbed the bag waited for her receipt and left.

"Scum, they're all scum." She stepped into the van and tried to breathe for the first time since the episode. She kept replaying each scene in her mind. The smirk on Benjamin's face, the concern Bradford had for his son, save none for her.

She was going home alone, and she was going to get lit. The children would have to wait. Tomorrow she would go back to being Desiree Levite, faithful mother and good upstanding citizen. I'm turning into him, she thought as she packed the cigarette case and un-wrapped the cellophane paper. Desiree lit the smoke and took a deep breath, it didn't take too many drags for her to feel dizzy. Feeling guilty for doing it, she called her grandmom and told her that she wouldn't be able to pick up the kids until morning, even though she really should. She pulled into the driveway of her home and sat there unable to even get out of the van. There was no one else whose life compared to hers and she just wanted to escape, just one night of forgetting. Dwight Yoakam sang in a high twangy voice from the radio.

She wrapped her arms around herself and she began to sob. Holding herself because there was no one to hold her. No, it was just her now, her against the world and as she felt her hands rubbing her shoulders, trying to ease her own pain, it became too much for her. "John, oh how I wish you were here!" In the darkness, she began to weep until she thought there could possibly be no more tears left inside her. Then she picked up the bottle of wine and made her way inside. She was going to drink until the bottle was as empty as she felt.

Angelic Covering

Chapter 51

Daniel was thankful that things were coming together. He felt closure and a sense deep down, that everything would be fine. Sandra had been sleeping a lot, but she was regaining her strength and not having as many bladder issues. He noticed she was very off balance and as bad as she loathed her cane, she needed it now to get around safely. The twins wore her out and to lift them was beyond her strength. She had tried on one occasion and after almost dropping one, she decided it was best to not attempt it. Nevertheless, she seemed more positive lately and eager to face this monster they'd met, named Multiple sclerosis. He too, was adjusting to this new wife who was often lethargic and depressed. They were beginning to find new things to do as a couple, slower things, like old movies and nights around the fire sipping tea and reading to the twins. Going out on the town or playing tennis together were foreign now and he had come to terms with his lack of sex life now. It was something they did less often due to her fatigue, but it seemed to have more meaning, more of a genuine sweetness and more bent on love. He didn't know what the future held and at times he became frightened by Sandra's illness, he thought this was partially due to his mother's suffering. He was thankful now for the support he was getting from his sister and Burt. Just telling them felt as if he had untied a huge load he'd been carrying.

Spending the day with Brenda had given him hope that Sunday would be a pleasant time. They had reminisced over past photos and memories of their childhood. And they had bonded over the cares and struggles they had both dealt with that year. They were going to the cemetery and spend the day with their mother. He was getting a vase of artificial yellow roses and the twins would be laying real ones down. They were taking bread to feed the ducks at the lake that was just past the Memorial gardens. He was so thankful that the tension between him and Brenda had subsided, and the truth was finally out about Sandra.

They were going to take a picnic lunch to a nearby park after visiting with their mother. The cemetery was more of a haven filled with sculptures, plants and gardens with sitting areas. A huge pond filled with ducks and swans in the distance were watched over by a guardian angel whose marble features were indescribable. Her hair was long and wave after wave held her arched neck and out stretched wings. Her eyes were pools of desire and she wore the sweetest expression, as if she were greeting each member and taking them up to Saint Peter himself. Daniel had been thrilled about the spot and knew his mother would be content there, with the beautiful flower gardens that she had loved so much while here. Soon he would have to come to terms with his father. He knew his father had been dying silently for so long watching his mother deteriorate, and that his father needed him and he hoped that they could be a family again and that the twins would one day get to know their grandfather. Yes, he had a strange feeling that everything would be alright. For some reason he felt as if closure and answers were coming. He felt a peace that he had longed for and a knowing that good things were on their way. Daniel folded the blanket and placed it by the bags he'd gotten together for Sunday. The phone rang and startled him as he was in deep thought. "Hello."

"Hey Daniel, its Brenda, you ready for Sunday?"

He detected a joy in her voice, an almost giddiness. "Yeah, just packing up some things for the twins and getting ready to make lunch for Sandra, you?"

"Yes, and so is Burt. We're taking Sam and letting him run around a bit. I haven't heard from the police in a while, how about you?"

"No, no news is good news, right?"

"Yes and no, I would sure like to know where Dad is though. It would be good to have this all out in the open and know what truly happened and how his mental state is."

"Yeah, I know Brenda," Daniel said with a sigh, "It sure would be a big relief."

"Speaking of good news, I have grand good news!"

"Oh, well do share, I am ready to hear."

"Oh, no, no, no…you must wait until we meet on Sunday, when Sandra, Burt and the twins are there. I want to tell everyone!"

"Well, I can't wait till then, you know me, give it up already!"

"But Burt doesn't even know yet!"

"So, you can tell him when you tell everyone else and I'll act surprised."

"Daniel, I just went to the doctor yesterday and I'm PREGNANT!" She screamed in the back ground, excited at her own words.

"Oh, I am so happy for the two of you, I know it's something you have both longed for and now it's finally here. How far along are you?"

"Just a couple months, but I can't even believe it's real. I keep rubbing my belly and talking to this little life force that's just waiting to come out and bring me more joy than I have ever felt."

"Brenda, that's truly wonderful and I promise I will act more surprised than anyone there!"

"Well, I gotta run, Daniel. I'll see ya Sunday."

"With bells on, sis." He hung up the phone and smiled to himself, "Yes, I feel it in my spirit, everything is going to be alright!"

Rivers are Damp

Chapter 52

Marcie stumbled across the walkway with her arm cupped around the arm of Steve. He was the older gentleman with the dark tan who she had met earlier at Frank's. He was leading her to his hotel room that was adjacent to the Steak House. Steve was old enough to be her father and worse than that, he reminded her of him. He only cared about his material possessions and what little trophy girl he could get to dangle from his arm. They passed his Corvette and he pointed out to Marcie how good she would look in the front seat next to him. Marcie in her drunken state was still able to notice his empty ring finger, where a permanent indent showed ample evidence that his wedding ring had been removed. Marcie hated men. She wished she could just escape, or better still just end it all. What kept her here? Her mother was worthless and weak and her father was cruel and selfish, merely caught up in his wealth and prestige. What was the point of living? She had no job and no true friends and college was just a place to go so everyone in her family could say she was a graduate. Life sucked and she was tired of the whole thing, not to have to wake up in the morning and struggle through it would be a relief. She doubted anyone would notice she was gone and then Benjamin would have a real story to tell. Yes, he would have a real woman that was a part of his life that died, not some fictitious story he had fabricated in his mind.

"You like champagne?" Steve said bringing her back to her inebriated state. "I can have some brought to the room." Steve was smiling wickedly, while soaking in her body and thinking about all the things he wanted to do to her. Marcie was indeed repulsed by him, but she had drunk way too much for her one hundred and twenty pound body to handle and she was off balance at this point. She really just wanted to lie down and sleep it off. Marcie half stumbled, half fell onto the bed.

"Yes, that's it get comfy," Steve said while rubbing her back.

She kept drifting in and out of an unconscious state until Steve quickly jolted her into reality, she could feel him tugging on her. What was he doing? Marcie tried to open her eyes and focus, but the room was spinning a bit and she wasn't feeling so well. He yanked her boots off and she felt more comfortable and he had even gotten a pillow for her head. She was just about to doze off again when she realized that Steve was trying to pull her black velvet pants off and he did not seem to care if she was impaired. Marcie tried to kick Steve, but she was so wasted it was a futile attempt. He just didn't seem to want to give up. His hands were like octopus tentacles and he was not going to let her get away it seemed. Then Marcie decided to try and scare him. "You know I'm only seventeen, right Steve?" She was slurring but still had her wits about her. "Maybe you know my father, he's president and CEO of Stewart Enterprise? I gots a fake ID Sheve," she said through slurred lips.

"Darlin, there's no way you are seventeen. I wasn't born last night and I really don't care who your daddy is, because he isn't around at the moment now is he? So, come on pretty lady let an older man show you what a little girl really needs. You've been hanging around little boys too long, that's your problem. Shhh now, don't you worry about a thing, I'm gonna take mighty good care of you" He began to unclasp her hair and push it back out of her eyes and then he began kissing her forehead and down her neck line.

Marcie was so tired she just wanted to close her eyes and go to sleep and never wake up again. "God, why do I keep waking up?" she slurred into the darkness. Steve finally after multiple massages and kind whispers succeeded at his attempt to remove her pants and she succeeded at passing out and coming to, not really even aware of the motions.

She didn't care about herself anymore. He might as well use me, she thought, and go on his way, every other man has and now she felt like trash anyway. No respectable man would want her and so she laid there and waited for him to finish using her, as more silent tears slid across her cheeks. Marcie seemed almost certain now that killing herself was the right thing to do. "Please God, help me never wake up again," she said aloud, as she felt him roll off of her and onto his side. She had an empty place inside her soul and an ache inside her heart that felt too large to ever heal properly. She thought of the many different ways she could kill herself, each one reminding her of something or someone she knew.

Sylvia Plath had stuck her head in the oven while her children took a nap. She didn't think she was that far gone, but who knew? If she had children then maybe she'd have something to live for, but she didn't. She had no one now. She once had a good friend in high school who had hung himself by the lake. No one found him for days and she remembered how disturbed his parents were over it. Her own parents, she thought would be relieved. She thought about taking a handful of pills, that could be the easiest way to go and then as she pondered it all, she thought of a poem she had memorized in high school by Dorothy Parker:

> Razors pain you;
> Rivers are damp;
> Acids stain you;
> And drugs cause cramp.
> Guns aren't lawful;
> Nooses give;
> Gas smells awful;
> You might as well live.

For some reason the poem made her smile. Maybe it was because someone besides her had been thinking about all the ways to die and decided to live. But Marcie couldn't think of one reason to live, not one tiny itty bitty one! She drifted in and out of unconscious sleep, until she was aware of her surroundings and the sunlight that was trying to peep in from behind the heavy drapery. Marcie then slipped quietly out of bed and went to the washroom and began soaking a wash cloth and rubbing the small square of soap into it and she started scrubbing the mascara that had ran down her cheeks with her tears. She washed under her arms and then she got the hottest water she could and tried to scrub the places Steve had invaded, but she knew she could never scrub that filth off of her, no, no matter how much soap and water she used, she would always be dirty.

She dressed quickly never letting her eyes land on Steve. She thought if she looked at him he might feel her eyes and she'd never get out of there. She picked up his dress slacks out of the floor and pulled the fat black leather wallet out of his back pocket, then she walked to the nightstand next to the bed and picked up the shiny Rolex and the keys to his even shinier Corvette. She grabbed her purse and her boots and gently opened the door, turning the lock back silently, she slipped down the sidewalk and pushed the unlock button on the Corvette's key chain and eased herself behind the wheel.

'Been hanging around little boys too long huh Steve?' So you think that's my problem? I just needed a real man to teach me, is that it? Well, I'll teach YOU STEVE! And with that she squealed tires and burned rubber out of the parking lot. Marcie reached into the side pocket of her purse and lit a cigarette, she inhaled deeply and blew out a perfect line of smoke. Then she screamed into the sunlight that was just breaking through the clouds, "GOD, WHY DO I KEEP WAKING UP?"

Conversations

Chapter 53

Desiree had drank an entire bottle of wine and smoked one cigarette after another, all the while crying and sobbing uncontrollably over her horrible existence. "God, how could you have been so cruel to me? Why did you let John die? Why is this happening to me?"

Desiree thought about all the Sunday School lessons she had learned and all the prayers her grandmom had prayed and she was sure that if God could part the red sea, then he could prevent John's accident from happening! She hated this life. Every time it seemed things were looking up, something like this would happen. Bradford seemed perfect and what were the odds that his son, who he put up for adoption would be the same person who killed her husband? You couldn't write this stuff!

Oh, she was angry and heartbroken and she had grown sour, a bitter root seemed to be taking over her body. "YOU could have stopped this whole thing! YOU could have stopped John's death and YOU could have stopped my children from suffering, O, but You watched from your throne room up there in the clouds, you watched as my little boy stood by a casket and my heart was smashed into a million pieces of nothing! You could have at least prevented me from falling in love with Bradford Stiltz! You're cruel, You're not a God of love, no You're a God filled with evil!" She was screaming into the darkness. "I HATE YOU!"

Yet, deep inside she knew she didn't hate God. Deep inside of her was a place that had become so dead, it had snuffed out all the light that she had. God was no longer the friend He'd been. No, He had got lost along the way and replaced with a sickness that was taking over her mind, spirit, and body.

She was feeling so many emotions and a rage that seemed to be erupting out of her. She was actually pacing now, with her wine glass in one hand and her cigarette in the other, all the while screaming at God. After repeating over and over how hurt she was, she started feeling like her words were just bouncing off the walls. After the way she had yelled and cursed God she figured He certainly would not hear her now. Of course He doesn't hear, she thought to herself, it's obvious he doesn't hear me or I wouldn't be going through all this!

She'd been through hell for years. First, she lost her husband to a drunk driver and then she lost the business they'd worked so hard to establish, her hair started falling out in handfuls and the children's disruptions over losing their father. She replayed every horrible scene from the casket being lowered to finding an old man on her couch. She had let her steep brick walls fall to Bradford, only now to rebuild them even higher!

She wrestled with her emotions till it was almost daybreak and then she drifted off to sleep. That night Desiree dreamed a dream so incredibly real, it left her panting for air and caused her to break out in a sweat. Each time she drifted back into sleep, she would be jolted from her fitful sleep and back into reality. At first in her dream, she was back in the restaurant, she was grabbing Benjamin by the arm and jerking him around to face her. Then doubling up her fist she swung around roughly, hitting him in the jaw as hard as she could. As her fist struck his jaw bone it seemed to jar his whole head. Then something crazy happened, it was no longer Benjamin looking intently into her eyes, but it was Jesus. His eyes looked so sad and there was a pleading look in them that seemed to say, don't do this, you are wounding me. Then she had another vision and this time she was slapping Benjamin across the upper cheek and spitting in his face. She had felt so powerful slapping the man who had murdered her husband, but Jesus looked so hurt by her actions, it was difficult for her to look into those humble eyes and yet he wiped her spit away gently and just stood staring at her. His eyes seemed to hold no hate.

Desiree couldn't handle it anymore, she was tossing and groaning in her disrupted state of sleep. Then Desiree cried out from her dream and said, "No, Jesus I would never do this to you. I would never hurt you Jesus, you died for me! This is not about you, it's about Benjamin, he's the murderer!" Jesus eyes simply looked at her with such disappointment. Then Desiree heard an audible voice that shook her very spirit to the core, it simply said, "If you've done this to the least of these, you've done it unto me. I want you to forgive Benjamin." And she awoke covered in sweat and breathing as if she had run a marathon. She lay there upon her dampened pillowcase with her wet hair stuck to her neck and tried to steady her breathing. For some reason though, she could not get the images out of her head and she could not get the voice out of her spirit. The words kept ringing in her ear drums, "If you've done this to the least of these you've done it unto me." Then there were more images of Benjamin morphing into Jesus.

She knew she had to shower and go to her grandmom's to pick up Josh and Tabitha, but her head was pounding from the wine she had finished just hours before. She made a pot of coffee and rehashed the previous night's events. Wondering how long it would take for Bradford to try and contact her and whether she would even be able to talk to him without crying. Was it the wine or was it possible that the creator of heaven and earth wanted to talk with her? She walked to her book shelf and took out her King James Bible and opened it up randomly. Her eyes fell on a scripture that seemed to stab her through the heart.

"For if ye forgive men their trespasses, your heavenly father will also forgive you: but if ye forgive not men their trespasses, neither will your father forgive your trespasses (Matthew 6:14-15)."

Desiree was feeling too many emotions and she decided to take a quick shower and go talk to her grandmom about all of it. If anyone had the answers it was her she thought. Desiree walked to the bookshelf and placed the Bible back on the shelf but suddenly felt sadness wash over her as if Jesus himself didn't want her to put His book up. Then a small journal caught her eye. She had purchased it for Josh after John had died, it was for him to write his thoughts in. He had colored some pictures inside the pages, but Desiree really had not paid much attention to it. She remembered how she had taken both Tabitha and Josh to the park with three helium balloons that she had tied notes to. Each note was addressed to John or Daddy and each balloon was released from their small delicate hands. They all had intently watched as the red, yellow and blue colored balloons drifted out of sight. She had told both the children that the balloons would travel straight to heaven and reach their father, who would untie each note and read them with joy. Their father then would wait with patience until the day they could all be joined together again. Tabitha had no idea what was going on, but

Josh had really taken to the idea that his father would indeed receive the note in heaven.

Desiree opened the book and studied the hand colored picture of Josh holding a balloon. His stick figure drawing was colorful and he had even added all three balloons, as well as the park setting. He had written in black crayon on the bottom of the page, 'Hi Daddy'. Tears welled up in Desiree's eyes as she turned the pages filled with pictures drawn from hurting little hands that only wanted to be near his father. She placed the journal on the couch by her purse and shuffled off to the bathroom to shower, but not until she had swallowed four Tylenol for her head that was pounding uncontrollably!

Forgiven Forest

Chapter 54

Bradford awoke with the previous evenings memories. Benjamin was all he could think of, he remembered his smile, his eyes, and his laughter. He also could see his hurts and his insecurities. He had ached for this relationship with his son his whole life, it was something that was constantly on his mind. Every time he saw a father and son or was introduced to his co-workers children, it haunted him.

"You have a child somewhere, Bradford." A voice would echo through his mind. It had been so bitter sweet, the evening spent with his son. And now he had to come to grips with the fact that Benjamin had been irresponsible and that had led to the death of a man, Desiree's husband. He was overwhelmed with guilt and remorse for allowing Patti to give up their child.

"None of this would be happening if Larry Stewart hadn't been in the picture!" He kept thinking out loud and contemplating what to do, now that Desiree wasn't speaking to him. He had waited a lifetime to find his son but he had also been waiting for companionship and she was everything he had been looking for. She was beautiful, intelligent, a wonderful mother and just plain fun to be with. He knew in his heart he had cared for her, he had even been excited about their future but now what? He felt torn apart and displaced. How could he ever work this out? This was a problem much too large for Bradford Stiltz and yet he was in the problem fixing business. At least he tried to make things less difficult for people who were going through divorce, child custody battles and of course other difficult cases. But even he couldn't make order out of such chaos, but he sure wasn't going to give up without a fight!

He decided to call Desiree and try and explain his side. There would have to be some kind of closure. There would have to be some kind of conversation, they worked together and she was just too important to him. He picked up his cell phone and let it ring until all he heard was the answering machine. He wasn't really prepared for what to say and feeling heartsick he hung up. "What a coward," he thought to himself, he decided to phone Benjamin instead and see how he was faring.

"Hey Benjamin, how are you doing?"

"Umm I'm good, how are things with you?"

"Fine, just fine, I wanted to call and tell you that I'm sorry about last night. I mean, I didn't know the history between the two of you and well, who would have thought? I really would like to get together again sometime soon, if you're up for it, that is?"

"Yeah, okay Bradford, we can do that." Bradford wished his son felt comfortable calling him Dad but he guessed it felt awkward and he hadn't been a father at all up until now. "So, did I cause you to lose your girlfriend? Cause I can always step back out of the picture. I have been out of it until now anyhow."

"No, don't be ridiculous Benjamin, we work together, but that's really it."

"I thought you said she was your girlfriend?"

"Not really Benjamin, she is a friend, but you are my son and I'm not going to let anything come between us. So, what happened that night Benjamin? I mean do you feel like talking about it? I know it must be horrible for you to deal with."

"Not really much to tell, Bradford. I got drunk, I hit a car and the next thing I know, I'm looking at a mangled body and then iron bars."

Bradford could cut the tension with a knife and now he wasn't sure what to say. "Benjamin, I know just from meeting Larry, that your life was anything but pleasant. I can't imagine the hell he must have put you through and I know that you did not intentionally get into your car that night bent on taking another human beings life. I know that, son. So, listen son, I am not here to badger you, okay?"

Benjamin felt nervous and he wasn't sure how to answer or even how to respond to Bradford. On one hand, he was his father, but on the other hand, he was just some guy he'd met and all these deep conversations were not what Benjamin was used to. He was missing Marcie and wondering how he was going to get back into her good graces. "So, you never answered the question did I or didn't I, cost you your lady friend last night?"

"Benjamin, you haven't cost me anything, but I see that by my absence, I have cost you everything."

There was a silence and again Benjamin wasn't used to this sort of communication from a guy. He was more used to men like Larry who would cuss you and slap you upside the head, all in the name of love. "Okay Pops, you with her or not?"

"Would it make a difference in our relationship Benjamin, or is our relationship separate?"

"You attorneys are good at never giving a straight answer and dancing around the question aren't ya? It's almost comical waiting for you to respond. Is it true that all attorneys are liars?" His voice sounded sarcastic, but Bradford could also detect humor.

"Okay, you got me Ben, but as far as Desiree goes I haven't talked to her yet and no we're not all liars, some of us are good guys believe it or not. Now as far as she goes, I believe she needs to forgive you or it's going to destroy her life. And you, Benjamin, are going to have to forgive yourself."

Benjamin heard wisdom in his father voice, he knew he was right on, but how does one forgive himself when they took an innocent life? "That's insane, Bradford! I know she will never forgive me and truth is I don't blame her, I can't forgive myself. I still have nightmares that haunt my sleep and images that flash through my brain of her husband sprawled out on the pavement, looking like hamburger helper. God Bradford, why would she ever want to forgive me? I hate me!"

Bradford thought for a minute at his question and he thought about how much his son had gone through. He had been through more travail in his short life time, than Bradford could ever dream of. "For her own self, and for her children," he blurted out.

Faith rose up inside of Bradford and he sensed that everything would be alright. All the sudden, he knew that when he presented it to her that way, she would have to understand how sick she was making herself and her children. Desiree had been caught in her own trellis of tentacles that were choking her. She was hurting herself by holding on to this bitter, bitter root. It had grown so fast and spread so deep, she couldn't even see it was destroying her. He hoped she would see the cause and effect it was having on her life.

Benjamin was lost again for words and in awe of how very different this father was from his previous one. "Well, if it makes you feel any better I'm in the dog house too, with Marcie."

"Say, maybe we can have a contest and see who can get back into good graces the fastest?" Said Bradford.

Benjamin was quite sure he could win this contest hands down, all he needed to do was find Marcie. He also was certain that if his new father went back to Desiree, their relationship would be very difficult, and how was he supposed to try and get a girl back who he'd lied to about everything important in his life and on top of all that, treated like crap. If his father was going to try and woo the woman whose husband he had killed one night while driving drunk, the whole thing was sure to explode in his face. "Good graces, is something farfetched in my case," said Benjamin.

"Well son, I am going to go, you've got my number, don't hesitate to call and I'll be back in Frank's to see you real soon."

"Okay Bradford, later," he said rather cool, as if he really didn't need this strong man in his life. Benjamin hung up the phone and wondered for the first time in years what it would feel like to live, or to even want to. "Forgive myself," he said out loud. How am I ever going to do that?

Rolex Road Rage

Chapter 55

Marcie had spent the morning driving around town squealing tires and going down back streets and alleyways. The adrenaline rush from knowing that this was her biggest heist yet made her giddy. Then she noticed the gas gage was almost on empty, pulled into a quick mart and pulled the black wallet out of her purse. "Hmm, let's see what we have here, Steve." She thumbed through the credit cards and pulled out a Visa. "This should do the trick," she said, as she lifted the lever for the gas pump. Even though it was clearly a no smoking zone, she lit a cigarette and inhaled deeply, she was nervous and unsure of where to go. Steve should be waking up about now, she thought to herself. Maybe I'll give him a wakeup call, she smiled to herself and dialed information on her phone.

"City and state please?"

"Lexington Kentucky, the Hampton Inn on Conner Street, please."

"Thank you, one moment."

Marcie heard the phone ring and then the pleasant operator. She pulled out the wallet and studied his driver's license, "Steve Watson's room please."

The phone began to ring and then a groggy voice said, "Hello."

"Mornin Steve, how you feeling this morning? I was just thinking about how right you were. I have been hanging around little boys too long. You were just what I needed, a man, a real man and I have to tell ya Steve, this Corvette purrs just like a fine tuned women. It's so easy to handle. I kinda borrowed your watch too, so I wouldn't lose track of time ya know. I didn't know if you had any appointments today or not?"

Marcie heard a loud object fall that she felt sure was the lamp by the bedside table. Suddenly, Steve seemed more awake than he'd ever been before. Curse words began to spew out of his mouth like a waterspout.

"Hey, where's my wallet? What is the meaning of this? You get back over here with my things or I'm calling the police and reporting them stolen! Do you understand me little girl?"

Marcie was laughing uncontrollably and she thought her sides would never stop hurting. All the while, Steve kept right on screaming in her ear, the louder he screamed the more hilariously funny she found it. She laughed so hard she thought she'd pee herself and then she said, "Steve, I'm just going to hang up until you can talk to me nicer."

"Wait Marcie, don't hang up, please just bring back my car Marcie, that's all I'm asking of you." She could hear the curtain being pulled back and picture the horror on his face as he stared at the empty parking spot. "Marcie, I'm calling the police!" He screamed. Marcie stopped laughing and got a hold of herself. The image of the night before and his octopus arms coming in every direction made her suddenly more vindictive than ever. She wanted every man to pay for what they'd done to her, from her father all the way down the line.

"Well Steve, I wouldn't call the police so soon if I were you. I happen to have your home address here on your business card and also a home phone number. I was just thinking about calling your wife. I was just thinking about telling her all those little things you did to me last night. Bet you didn't know I have a camera on my cell phone and you should see the pictures I got this morning of the two of us in bed together. Oh Steve, your mama would be proud, yes she would. I got one of me, just in those little red panties you liked so much laying on your chest, and then I got one that well, let's just say it truly speaks volumes." There was silence on the phone and then Marcie began to torment him more. She figured she couldn't torment Benjamin at the moment, so why shouldn't some other snake get it. There seemed to be a deafening silence on the phone and Marcie felt a surge of power in her voice.

"So Steve, I was thinking about doing a little shopping today, Macy's is having a huge sell and I was wondering if I could use the MasterCard or the American Express? Do you prefer to pay it all off at once, or let's see? Oh. You do have some cash in here. Should I just use that?"

"Marcie, this isn't funny. Now bring me back my car and my wallet. I'll buy you whatever you like, take the cash, but just bring me back my wallet and my car! Please," he was begging now and Marcie liked the sound of his pathetic pleas.

"All men are pigs," she said, "You're all pigs! Did you hear me Steve, pigs!" She hung up the phone and decided to drive over to Benjamin's, let him see her new boyfriend's car. Yeah, that will get him, she thought. She pulled out of the Quick Mart and continued laughing at the whole situation. For whatever reason, she didn't even care if he called the police. Her life felt so out of control already, she figured it couldn't really get any worse. Spinning around the corner, she began gaining speed flying through the gears. If it were summer, she would have put the top down. Her life was whirling out of control, and she had the urge to drive through the guardrail and over the cliff. She was so tired of this life, so very tired. The speedometer hit one hundred miles an hour as she shifted into fifth gear. Suddenly, she heard a siren. Marcie wasn't stunned by the flashing blue lights in the rear view mirror and she wasn't sorry she was being pulled over. Frankly, she was still in a state of shock at her own actions and the whole thing seemed surreal.

"Morning there," the officer tipped his hat and leaned down to Marcie's view. He was quite tall, a state trooper. "Can I see your license and registration, ma'am?"

Marcie fumbled through her purse and handed her license to the officer, while he was looking over it, she stuffed Steve's wallet under the seat. She reached over and opened the dash and pulled out the registration and insurance card and handed it to him.

"This car isn't registered in your name?"

"Uhh, it's a friend of mines, Steve Watson."

"I see, hold on a minute." He walked back to his car and sat down behind the wheel and began looking over her papers and talking on the phone.

Marcie lit another smoke and thought about how it was probably getting ready to be her last. "Oh Daddy, you'll be so proud of me." She said softly under her breath sarcastically.

The officer approached the car and told her to step out with such dramatization that Marcie began to pour on the tears. "The only reason I took the car was because he raped me last night...you have to believe me. I wasn't trying to steal it, I was just trying to get away from his hotel until I could figure out what to do. You have to believe me," she sobbed.

"Whoa, calm down Ms. Owens, are you saying you stole this man's car? I thought you said he was a friend of yours?"

"I swear officer, I will do anything just don't take me to jail. I drank too much last night and this married business man took, well I didn't know he was married, he just said he was on business from Virginia. Well, one thing led to another and then he ended up raping me."

The officer eyed her black velvet pants and her purple sweater that was revealing a little too much cleavage. "You know you're going to have a hard time proving that, don't you?"

Marcie didn't answer but sobbed all the louder. "I hate men, it's not fair just because I am attractive and curvy, everyone just will assume I wanted it. Well I didn't want to have sex with some dirty old man. Call his room if you don't believe me. Here I'll dial the number for you." She took out her cell phone and hit redial to the hotel. "Steve Watson's room, please."

"Marcie, is that you, bring my damn car back, do you hear me." Marcie had already put the phone up to the trooper's ear.

"Mr. Watson, this is Officer Tanner and you can pick up your car at any time, it's at the corner of Wicket and Barnet." He handed the phone back to Marcie and looked at her sternly. "Ms. Owens, you been in trouble with the law before, I really shouldn't even be having a conversation with you. I should be putting cuffs on you and placing you in the back of that patrol car. But I tell you what I'm gonna do."

Marcie looked up, her eyes were swollen and her face was red, if it wasn't for the stone cold heart that was incapable of feeling, you'd have never known it wasn't real. "I will personally drop you off at the emergency room and let them give you an examination and then we can fill out a report, or the other option is taking you downtown for grand theft auto. Understood?"

Marcie nodded and tried to control her sporadic breathing. She climbed into the patrol car and sat silently, wondering what the next episode of her life would bring. Suddenly feeling nauseous and on the verge of a mental breakdown and if she thought she could pull it off, she'd try and get them to keep her. If only there was a pill or drug strong enough to make her forget the pain forever, but they always wore off too quickly, leaving her feeling more empty and hollow than before. She shut her eyes and began to hum a song that she always could relate to. "Addiction keeps her up at night. Yeah, it steals her sunny days. She'll tell you she was adopted if you ever meet her family. She wears mascara too thick now and her eyes bleed black tears but she'll give you a smile through the pain , yeah the pain helps her feel...She says she can hear Jesus calling her , he calls out in her dreams.."

Letters

Chapter 56

Desiree sat on the couch across from her grandmom and looked into the soft, blue eyes that held such wisdom. She felt close to having a major melt down, but she knew she couldn't. Needing advice and desperate for answers, she began to pour out her heart.

"Grandmom, I had horrible nightmares last night, I barely slept at all. I have so much to tell you, I don't even know where to begin and I have so many questions for God. I can't seem to figure out why my life is so drastically different from everyone else's. Everyone I work with has a husband or at least an ex-husband to take their kids. But mine has to be murdered on the way to the grocery store! My life is a complete disaster. I mean how many people do you know come home from work to find a crazy old man wearing their deceased husband's clothes, sitting on their sofa? Yeah, some stranger just sitting on the couch like it's the most ordinary thing in the world. To top it all off, I have a son whose best friend is an imaginary angel name Belinda," her voice was rising with each sentence. "And now, Bradford's long lost son happens to be Benjamin Stewart, the Benjamin Stewart that murdered my husband! Tell me grandmom what horrible wicked sin did I commit for all this to happen? Why is God punishing me so much?" Her face was beet red and her neck and chest were covered in hives, big red blotches. She wished she had a cigarette and began to chew her fingernails.

Grandmom sat there as peaceful as could be. Her eyes were calm and her expression had not changed. She looked down and picked up her Bible off the end table. "See this book Desiree, this book is filled with people's lives that have stories just like yours and God used them all and he will use you too. King David's own son tried to murder him. Joseph's own brothers threw him in a pit and sold him to slave traders. Daniel was thrown into a den of hungry lions and Naomi not only lost her husband like you, but both her sons died too. She said, 'don't call me Naomi call me Mara for God has made me bitter'. So you see Desiree, to blame this all on God or think that he is out to punish you is just not truth. God will take the pieces, the fragments of your life and he will put them together if you will give them to him. Now what is going on with Bradford?"

Desiree began to confide in her about the previous night's horrific display in the middle of the restaurant and then about the horrible dreams of Benjamin and Jesus. She was crying and couldn't seem to shake the vivid pictures from her dream.

"Do you really think you are hurting Benjamin by holding on to this hatred and rage or have you ever thought that you are truly hurting yourself and yes, even those children. Now Desiree, I'm going to be honest with you. Bradford has been the best thing that's happened to you in a long time. Why, it's been the first time I've seen you take an interest in your appearance and even see a hint of happiness in your eyes, in I don't know how long. He's a good man and he really cares about you. How can he help what his son did? He's just now found him. Forgiveness isn't something that just happens because we say we forgive them. It takes time and energy and prayer. If you are ever going to move on with your life and find true peace you are going to have to forgive him. You do not know what led up to his son getting drunk that night. We don't have all the information. You and Bradford may have come to a close in your relationship because of this, but to be angry and hold all this hatred, it will only keep you as dead as John. Give it to God, Desiree."

Desiree tried to soak in her words and listen. "I know grandmom, but it hurts, it hurts so badly."

"You are going to have to let this go and give it to God. This young man was a child. He made a huge mistake and he has paid for it every day, I am sure of that. Living with another man's blood on your hands at such an early age, well, I just can't imagine. Maybe if you knew more about this young man and tried to erase from your mind the images you have conjured up to be true, because I know you have, Des. I know that you picture this young teen out joy riding drunk without a care in the world, but I bet there's a story there. Everyone in this life has a story Desiree, just like the ones I told you about in this book."

Desiree gazed back down at the worn Bible and back up at her grandmom's gentle eyes. For the first time she tried to think about how Bradford must feel. She knew her grandmom was right, but she didn't understand the pain she had been through. How could she? How could anyone.

Hugging her grandmom, she got the children's things together. All she wanted to do was go to bed, she was hung over, tired and drained from all the emotions of the last few days. Tomorrow she had to work and she had no idea how to face Bradford. There wasn't much she did know anymore.

She drove home in a fog. Josh was talking up a storm and telling story after story about grandmom and everything they did. Desiree couldn't even hear him. Her mind was so full of anxiety and sorrow she just kept nodding her head and saying, "That's nice Josh."

They pulled into the driveway and Desiree pulled Tabitha out of her car seat and grabbed their overnight bag. She walked up the driveway feeling more and more sluggish with each step. Jackie was cooing and jumping at the sound of Josh and both children seemed happy to be at home. Desiree laid the keys on the table and sat down on the sofa. She noticed Josh's journal was still lying out on the sofa, picked it up and began to flip through the pages. Staring intently at the colorful drawing with the balloons, then turned the page.

Each page was filled with letters and every letter was addressed to Daddy. Desiree's heart sank in her chest as she read over each word scribbled with red crayon, all written in her little boy's handwriting.

"Goodbye Daddy. Daddy you are my best friend. You are my most wonderful friend and my best friend in the whole universe."

"I miss you Daddy, you're my bestest friend in the whole wide world and bester then all my friends and I miss you Daddy. You're so smart and I miss you."

"Tabitha is going to miss you playing in her sandbox. We went to Chuck E Cheese today. I wish you could have come. The sun was shining today. I hope it's sunny in heaven.

We're getting ready to watch Space Buddies. I love you. I'll write more tomorrow."

"Daddy, you're a good Dad and we been to your memorial and I love you and you're my bestest friend in the whole entire world out of all of my friends. I have a collection of buttons and I have a hockey medal. Bye. We'll miss you forever. We have a new neighbor named Walter and his wife Ruthie is in heaven with you, Daddy. I whittled

tonight on a stick. It rained here today. I'll write more later."

"Dear Daddy, I have a new friend named Belinda, she is an angel. I still miss you. I saw a baseball card that I really wanted to buy you. I'll write you again soon. Love Josh."

"Daddy, you will never believe I got a new bird named Jackie. She can play with you and she is nice. Her feathers are soft. We're going to do a field trip to the aquarium and I wish you could come too. We still really miss you."

"Dear Daddy, I played hide and go seek today. I met a man named Bradford and he took me to a doctor and she had playdo factory and I made really cool stuff. Tonight we're gonna watch a movie and have popcorn with it! I miss you and you're my best friend."

Desiree looked down at the scribbled pages and wept. Her heart was shattered. How did God expect her to deal with so much pain? She could not imagine how he could expect her to keep breathing. She felt so much ache and anguish for her son. "Oh God help me!" She cried out, just as Josh walked over to the couch.

"Do you like my letters to Daddy?"

Desiree wiped her eyes and shoved the lump down from her throat. "I sure do, Josh! They are the best letters I've ever read!"

"I have the bestest idea Mommy! I'm going to keep writing Daddy and then we can get more balloons like the ones with the notes we sent up to heaven. And we can tie my notebook and a pencil to it and then we can let it float up to Daddy. Then Daddy can write back to me, pop the balloon and send it back down!"

Desiree took Josh in her arms and held him. She held him like she had never held him before. She held him with all the love and comfort and emotion she could penetrate into his broken heart. Then when she could finally speak without her voice cracking she explained that Daddy couldn't send it back down, but that he could write a journal to him, and then we could pray that God would let Daddy see the words. Josh put his head down and thought about it for a moment and he seemed alright with her explanation. He picked up the journal and went and sat down by the television and began to look through the pages. He seemed to be studying each drawing and each letter very intently. Then he came bouncing back to the couch with his notebook in hand. He was smiling so proudly and his dimples were showing.

"Mommy, I know how I'm going to get my journal to Daddy! I'm going to write in it every day for as long as I live, and then when I die I'll put it in my hand in my coffee and take it to him myself!" His eyes lit up and Desiree's heart continued to bleed. She opened her arms and once again embraced her son until he squirmed free from her clutches.

Goodbyes

Chapter 57

Buddy was coming to terms with the realization that in a matter of minutes Walter Kendal would be stepping out of his rig and awaiting his destiny. He wondered what would become of this wise ole friend that had crossed his path. Buddy was never good with saying goodbye and it was going to be hard for him to let Walter leave and turn himself in. Although Buddy had met many different people throughout his travels, he had a feeling Walter was special. For some reason he felt like God was watching over Walter and that it was all going to work out fine no matter how bad the circumstance looked. He was almost certain they'd cross paths again. Yes, he was sure he'd meet up again with his ole friend in time.

"You're going to take a right up here at the light Buddy, and then follow the road down to the cemetery."

"Okay Walt, I see it." Buddy down shifted into third and then second to make the turn. His belly was jiggling and his seat was bouncing, keeping time with his Hawaiian hula dancer on the dash.

Walter turned and intently looked at Buddy. He would miss this man who had taken him to breakfast, dinner and even to play pool, but he knew it was time for him to part ways for a season. "I want to thank you, Buddy for all your help, all the meals and especially the company. I don't know where I would be right now if it wasn't for you." But before Buddy could reply, Walter chuckled and looked over at Buddy again and said, "Actually I do, behind bars more than likely!"

Buddy smiled, "Don't say that Walt, let's stay positive." Buddy studied his friend and chose his words carefully. "Walter, I know you are innocent. The police will figure out that you meant no harm to that boy. Now I'm going to be watching the news and I'll give you my number and we will get you an attorney, hear?"

Walter nodded his head, not wanting to think about a life behind bars. He gazed out at the statue of the angel that seemed to welcome everyone to the grounds. Her long carved hair draped around her breast and gave way to her flowing gown. Her perfectly chiseled eyes gazed forward like lipid pools. Her face seemed so serene and peaceful as she stood watch over the spirits that lay there. Arched wings hovered behind her with such glory and her graying marble didn't give justice to her craftsmanship. The trees seem to envelope her beauty, but not overshadow it.

Buddy eased the truck to the side of the road that led to the grounds. He stepped out of the rig and walked over to the cab door, just as Walter stepped down.

"Would you like to meet her?" Walter asked as he made his way towards the grassy mounds.

"It would be an honor!" Buddy exclaimed, as he followed Walter's footsteps. The sun was just coming up and the birds were giving song to the day. Walter knelt down next to the stone that held his beloved's name and began to pull up the grass that had grown up around it. It was a double tombstone and Walters name was next to hers. The tombstone listed his birth date and an empty space seemed to echo what Walter knew would one day be engraved with his death date.

"Well, here she is Buddy, the love of my life."

Buddy felt like he was interrupting a sacred moment, but reached out and patted Walters shoulder. He stood for a moment in silence, remembering all the wonderful stories he had heard about this lady name Ruthie, even felt like he knew her.

"Well, I best be going Walt." He turned and gave him a hug and another pat on the back. "Here's my number and a little something in case you get hungry."

Walter took the twenty that was folded in half and the scratch paper scribbled in ink and humbly put it in his pants pocket. He had lost all his independence and had come to grips with allowing Buddy to help him. "I don't know how I can ever thank you," he said, his brown eyes penetrating Buddy's.

"I don't know how I can ever thank you," Buddy said his voice cracking. Buddy was always a big teddy bear at heart and he often cried over a sappy movie when no one was watching. "Take care, my friend."

"You do the same, Buddy." Walter watched his friend walk back to his eighteen wheeler and get in. He studied the flames painted on the side until Buddy was out of sight and then knelt back down by his wife.

"Ruthie, I want more than anything to make things right and I'm sorry I let you down. I want to ask you to forgive me for not being there and for abandoning you. I just thought since you didn't know if I was there anyways, why did it matter? But now I know my actions have hurt our children and possibly another family as well. Oh Ruthie, I've made such a mess of things. Will you forgive me?" Tears were slowly easing down his cheeks and his heart ached. He waited as if he expected to hear her voice, and then began to speak again.

"I want to ask you to forgive me for leaving our children and not being there for them and especially our grandbabies. But Ruthie, I promise I am going to try and do everything I can to make it up to them. Will you trust me?"

Walter sat and looked up at the blue sky dusted with faint clouds. He knew she was not there, but in a better place. His heart ached for the life he used to have. Time and space could never erase her touch or her voice. He rose up and studied the area and made a mental note of the moment. He would have to make his way to the police department soon. There was no other choice except to keep running and Walter knew he had run long enough.

Jackie's Flight

Chapter 58

Josh sat in a daze. His ruffled hair was even more unruly that day and his almond eyes were heavy. He had just written a note to his father again in his book his mother had found that day. Picking bright red paper and he wrote each word as carefully as possible, he had to write small to fit everything on the small sheet of paper. He sure did miss his dad and remembered it all so clear, the day when they lowered his father's coffee into the ground and how he could hear his mommy crying in the night. He wanted to go get in bed with her and help her, but when he knocked on the door she always shooed him away. This made him angry because he needed her.

Josh wanted to forget it all but as hard as he tried, he couldn't get the nightmare out of his mind. And even though his mother thought he didn't know, he heard her crying in the shower too. If only my daddy was still here Josh thought. He coiled himself up in fetal position on the couch and watched Jackie light on the bird stand Bradford had bought for her. His eyes were so heavy he couldn't continue to keep them open. Josh was traveling and spinning into a dreamlike state. He was half awake and half asleep when the angel, Belinda appeared to him again.

"Josh, it's time." Her cherry scarlet hair glowed under the transparency of her white dress and her eyes looked deep within him. It was as if she could read his thoughts. Her face was mesmerizing and he was in awe of her presence. "You must complete your assignment."

Josh looked at her out stretched hand and he paused a moment, knowing the outcome. But suddenly Josh was taking her hand again and soaring above the tree tops. He loved the feeling of flying like a bird so freely. Belinda's golden purse was in the other hand and soon they had eased upon the ground ever so lightly. "You must release the bird now Josh, it is time." Belinda opened the purse where Jackie sat peacefully and lifted her out towards Josh.

"But I don't want to," Josh said his voice high-pitched, nasal and sad.

"Josh, you must. She will come back to you." Her voice tinkled like fine bone-china and her face glowed like the sun. "Go forward Josh, it is time."

Josh was scared, he didn't want to lose Jackie. He had already lost enough. "How can I be sure she will come back to me?"

"You must trust me, Josh."

Josh looked down at Jackie, he stroked her plumage and whispered soft words to her. "Please come back Jackie, I love you so much. I will be waiting for you to come back, okay Jackie?" Josh began to lift Jackie into the air, and then he gently raised her up into the sky. He pushed her towards heaven and the spacious sky that drew her away from him. He felt her wings brush softly across his face and then watched as she soared towards wide open spaces of blue. But as soon as she was gone, poor little Josh was heart sick. "I want her back," his lip quivered up at Belinda, who stared at him with such sadness.

"Once Jackie takes her flight, you will be rewarded." Belinda looked up towards Jackie, who now was a tiny speck in the clouds. "Don't you understand, Josh?" But before he could answer she took his hand and they began to soar through space and time and back to Josh's home.

Josh stirred out of his dream sleep to find Jackie jumping and squealing like crazy. She was flying into the windows and trying to go outside. Josh had a sick feeling in the pit of his stomach, but he knew he had to obey the angel. As bad as he didn't want to, deep inside he knew it had to happen, he had to release her. He shooed Jackie from the window and tried to calm her down for a bit. Then he decided to tear out his latest note he'd written to his daddy and roll it up and tuck it in the holding device on Jackie's leg. He glanced down at the note and carefully read it again before rolling it up. It had to be rolled up ever so tight in order for it to fit in the tube.

'Dear Daddy, you are the best daddy in the whole wide universe. Do you have birds there too? I met a friend named Walter, Daddy and his wife Ruthie is in heaven with you. Did you see her Daddy? He weally misses her too, Daddy and I miss you.

Love, Josh Levite'

Josh crinkled up his forehead and pushed the note into the tube. Who knew, maybe Jackie could carry his letter straight to Daddy in heaven and then they could communicate? Maybe that was the reward. "Yes, that must be it!" He put his fingers in his mouth and chewed a thumb nail nervously. But then he smiled thinking about how great it would be to get a note back from Daddy.

Josh walked outside and with Jackie in his arms and lifted his hands towards the sky, as Jackie took flight across the clear blue. Her wings fluttered and softly swept across his cheek just like in the dream. He wasn't sure, but he thought he heard Belinda's voice chiming in the distance, "Your obedience is recorded in the book. You have finished your mission. Well done, my son."

Josh walked back into the house, but his heart was hurting and as much as he knew he did the right thing. He wanted Jackie back, would she come back soon from heaven.

Revelation

Chapter 59

Brenda and Burt sat at the picnic table across from Sandra and Daniel. It was a gorgeous day and the children were tossing bread crumbs into the water and watching the ducks scurry to lap up each bite. They had just eaten turkey and ham sandwiches with pickles, chips and potato salad. Brenda and Daniel were laughing and talking about how much Mom would have enjoyed knowing they were celebrating her life. But the conversation quickly turned to Walter and emotions ran high as they discussed his mental state and where he could be hiding.

"I think he's really lost it now," Brenda said, shaking her head.

Daniel knew his sister had grown bitter towards their father, but he hoped in time, they could all have closure. "I know he took it hard when Mom lost her memory and motor skills. I think he died right then." Daniel continued to talk, hoping Brenda would listen. "And I have to admit it, I still miss him and truly hope he's safe."

Brenda looked at her brother and thought about how quick he was to forgive and forget. She wished she could be more like that, but she had a stubborn streak that matched her fiery red hair.

Sam, Brenda's German shepherd was running along beside the twins guarding them as the good protector he was. The signs of spring were all around, and the trees had begun to bud. The dogwood trees and the flowering cherry trees were in bloom, the wind was chilly but the sun was shining brightly.

"I'm starting to grow tired," Sandra whispered to Daniel under her breath. Daniel knew that sitting up at the hard picnic table and the day's events would take a toll on his wife, but he just longed for some normalcy.

"Okay dear, we'll head to the grave site and cut this short."

"You feeling okay, Sandra?" Brenda inquired.

"Yes, just tired and a little fatigued today."

"Well, I won't keep everyone waiting then, I have an announcement to make." Brenda patted Sandra's shoulder and Sandra fought the urge to yelp from the pain a mere pat had brought to her muscles. Sandra forced a smile and waited patiently for the celebration to be over so she could go lay down. Brenda stood up and cleared her throat teasingly. All eyes were on her and all ears, but Daniel's, were waiting for her news. Then she looked at Burt and glanced around the table. "I'm pregnant!" Her eyes lit up and her laughter brought a refreshing jovial feel to the moment.

Burt's jaw dropped and Sandra got up to congratulate her. Burt grabbed his wife and held back the tears. They had waited so long for this moment.

"Ahh Brenda, I'm so happy, that's wonderful news!"

Burt placed his hand on her stomach lovingly. "How long have you known, missy?" He smiled and held her for a few seconds, shocked at the great news.

Daniel had already been informed, but acted just as surprised as if he hadn't. "Hey Jessica, Jessie, you're going

442

to have a brand new baby cousin to play with! Aren't you excited?" Daniel blurted at his twins. The twins giggled and ran off chasing Sam. They weren't used to pets and he was something new to capture their attention.

Brenda thought about how she longed for her mother to be here when her baby arrived. She knew her mother would have been a terrific grandmother and it hurt her heart to know that she would never take part in the child's life. Burt's mother lived in Wisconsin and his father never was a part of his life. And her father, well, she didn't know how she felt about him coming back into the picture. Honestly, she felt like he wasn't even a part of her life anymore. She had silently divorced him and all his idiosyncrasies.

About that time a bird soared overhead its wings flapping restlessly. The bird kept making a circular motion above the site and there was something bright red attached to it. It was a homing pigeon. Brenda looked intently at the bird and realized it had a familiarity about it. Oh yes, she would have known that bird anywhere, it was Jackie and tucked inside her leg was a bright red sheet of paper rolled up. "Well, well Daddy, what will your note say this time?" Brenda's mind went back to the moment she took his note and wrote in ink as bright as the red paper, one word, 'unforgiven'. She stood

443

for a minute watching, before flagging Daniel over. "Hey Daniel, Daniel, come here! Do you recognize this bird?" Brenda pointed up above her, as Burt pulled Sam's leash back from the bird that was cooing and swooping downward.

"Well, if that's the bird that I think it is, Dad can't be very far from this site," Daniel said. The group instantly scanned the site for Walter. That bird should have traveled straight to its home, which was a good ten miles away from the cemetery; but Jackie had simply followed the wings of an angel with crimson red hair. "I bet I know where Dad is," said Daniel. "I bet he is visiting our mother right now as we speak."

"Oh my gosh, Daniel, what are we going to do?"

Everyone fell silent and then Jackie landed on the picnic table and began to hop about. Brenda bent down and pulled out the note tucked in the holding device and began to unroll it. The words were scribbled in black marker. She began to read aloud as everyone, including the twins gathered round to hear her.

'Dear Daddy,

You are the best daddy in the whole wide universe. Do you have birds there too? I met a friend named Walter, Daddy and his wife Ruthie is in heaven with you. Did you see her Daddy? He weally misses her too, Daddy and I miss you.

Love, Josh Levite'

Brenda and Daniel's eyes locked and there was a genuine sadness in them for what they had just read. "Isn't that the little boy on the news?" Daniel said.

"If it is, it all but proves he is innocent," said Burt.

Daniel nodded in agreement before speaking. "This is truly so sad. This little boy has lost his father and he is trying to send him a letter through Daddy's own beloved Jackie.

Brenda thought about the situation and began to realize her father was just making friends with a child and of course he would never hurt one. She felt sick at her stomach. All this time she had had such wicked thoughts toward her father and here this little boy could never see his own father again. She wanted to be a family again, she wanted things to be right. "Daddy, if I ever get the chance again to see you I'm going to make this right," she said under her breath, just as Jackie cooed from the table. "We've gotta go see if Daddy is at the grave site!" said Brenda.

"Yes, and we may need this note to show the police that Daddy didn't hurt this boy."

Brenda took Sam by his leash and quickly led him to their jeep. Daniel and Sandra loaded up the twins and they all made their way down to the cemetery. They each had different reasons for the many thoughts that were racing through their minds. There were thoughts about a small boy who wanted desperately to contact his father but couldn't because he was dead. And how they each wished they could see and touch their mother again, but even more than that, they ached for their own father. Was Walter still alive and safe? Could they all forgive and move forward? Brenda picked up Jackie and placed her in her lap as Burt pulled out of the park and quickly followed Daniel and Sandra to the cemetery.

Hot Tea

Chapter 60

Marcie eased out of the patrol car, her head was pounding and her legs were wobbly. She didn't want to go inside the hospital and notify them that she had been raped. They would just think it was her fault anyway, it was always the woman's fault if they looked and dressed like her. If only she hadn't drank so much. If only Benjamin hadn't hurt her so. She placed his gash next to the other scars that lined her heart, right next to the deep whelp her father had inflicted on her and all the other men she had ever let inside her world. She always loved too much, too strongly and much too carelessly. When she loved she gave every ounce in her. She told them every secret and every dream she'd ever

447

aspired to reach. She told them the story of when she was six and wet her pants the first day of school and how everyone laughed at her. She told them about how her virginity was stolen at 15 by a young Navy boy who promised to marry her when he came back from his 6 month float overseas. She waited and wrote letter after letter, but instead he had married another. She picked songs that reminded her of them and bought music that captured how they made her feel. And she sure as hell didn't have the energy to tell the world some creep named Steve had raped her!

Marci had taken a friend who was raped to the hospital once, she knew how humiliating it was for her friend and she sure didn't need any more torture. The nurse had taken her friend Whitney's underwear and then they had combed her down there and snipped hairs and probed her. And while the nurses were invading her private area, the cops interviewed her as if nothing was going on. Whitney was bleeding and crying and her face was bruised. She had been leaving the office and walked to the parking garage only to be grabbed from behind with a knife in her back and a monster whispering in her ear. No, Marci didn't need any more humiliation, she was capable of making herself feel like a whore without any help from the outside.

She walked in the door and waited for the police officer to watch her sign in and then he left. Going into the ladies room, she stood in front of the mirror. Her face was puffy and her breath was foul and she reeked of alcohol from every pore. Her sweater was soaked in sweat. Dabbing a paper towel in water she tried to wipe the black eyeliner and mascara that had smudged under her eyes. "Oh girl, when are you ever going to learn?" she said to herself. Her choices seemed bleak and she sure as hell didn't want to go back to her parents. Her car was at the hotel right next to Frank's and she was certain Benjamin or Clark had noticed that it had never moved. Marcie opened the door to the restroom and walked down the hall to the exit sign. She walked outside and decided to just keep walking, knowing she could call her mother or her father and make a scene, but for some reason she didn't have any energy to play a leading role in a film that day, so she continued to walk.

Lighting a cigarette, she tried to scrub the slime off her teeth with her tongue then dug her shades and cell phone out of her purse. She wanted to cry and had tried to make the tears come, just to cleanse herself, she felt so empty. She knew alcohol was a depressant, but it seemed to dull the ache and the guilt she felt.

Her fingers kept scrolling to Ben's number but she couldn't push the button. He had pushed her buttons and pushed her away and he continued to thrust her out of his life. Yet, she knew she would crawl to his apartment if she thought he'd give her the time of day. 'Where is my self-worth?' she thought to herself. There were a million men in the world and yet she only wanted the ones who didn't want her. She replayed the night's scene and Steve's filthy grin and the twinkling glitter of lust that filled his eyes and wanted to puke. 'I'm disgusting,' she thought. 'Who would want me now?'

For some reason she began to think about her grandmother, Lilly and her perfect tea set with the little sugar cubes with tongs and the delicate cream pitcher. Them sitting on the porch of her quaint cottage, enjoying the sunshine and the humming birds that were drinking from the feeders. She suddenly needed her grandmother and some kind of serenity, and longed to listen to her old stories of her grandfather and the war. She wanted to look at black and white photos and admire the latest quilt she'd pieced. Her grandmother always introduced her to new types of music and made her want to take a music class because she realized she had a great love for many different genres. One of Marcie's favorites was a song called, 'I Wish I Didn't Love You So' by Betty Hutton. Another one she liked was Nat Cole's "L-o-v-e-d". He spelled out all the ways he adored her by using all the letters.

Marcie decided to call a taxi, go fetch her car and then head to her grandmothers. She needed a break from the world, hot tea, scones and a hot bath sounded suddenly very inviting   indeed.

Heaven's Heart

Chapter 61

Desiree had just gotten the children home and fixed a pot of spaghetti, when Josh burst into the kitchen wild eyed and frantic. "It's happened Mommy, it's all really real!"

"What's really real, Josh?"

Josh was running back and forth through the kitchen and his face was covered in excitement. "The angel Belinda, Mommy. She weally showed up and I had to let Jackie fly to heaven! She's on her way right now!" He said elatedly.

Desiree walked into the living room and scoured the room for the pigeon that was suddenly missing. "Slow down Josh, what do you mean Jackie's in heaven?"

"Belinda, Mommy, remember the angel mommy? She told me to let Jackie go and that she would come back and that I had to and that I would get a reward Mommy!"

"Josh, what did you do with Jackie?" Desiree had heard all about his angel and how lovely she was but now she was a little put off by Josh and his stories. She then realized again that Walter had been real all along and she hadn't taken that one serious, so maybe she should just let him talk. "Okay Josh, have a seat and tell Mommy all about it."

Josh scooted into the kitchen chair and began to move his arms while he talked frantically. "Belinda is the angel Mommy, and she is bigger than the tallest most gigantic building in the whole world and she has red hair, Mommy and her gown is very white and she has big wings and can fly, Mommy." He just kept talking faster and faster without coming up for air. "She took me flying and we took Jackie and she said I have to let Jackie go. But then it was a dream Mommy, but when I woke up Jackie wanted to go so bad, that I just lifted her up to the sky and let her go to heaven."

"Slow down, Josh. Why was she going to heaven?" Desiree waited, knowing then that this had something to do with John.

"Because Jackie can take my letters to Daddy! Mommy, don't you see, we don't need any more balloons cause Jackie can fly them up to Daddy! But now I miss her and I hope she comes back soon." He stopped jumping around so much then and looked up at her, his eyes sad for just a second.

Desiree felt more tears welling up inside of her and she just didn't know how much more she could take.

"Mommy, how long does it take to fly to heaven?"

"Josh, I'm not sure, I don't think anyone knows." Desiree wasn't sure what to tell Josh, if Jackie didn't reappear in a few days, what would he do. She had just gotten attached to the stupid bird and had just bought it everything it needed. Bradford had even bought the fountain for her to splash in. "Josh, what if Jackie doesn't come back?"

"Mommy, I know she will because Belinda said so, and angels can't lie Mommy! Aren't you excited Mommy that we can talk to Daddy again?" His eyes were huge and he was grinning from ear to ear. Desiree just didn't have the heart to tell him that his wishes would never be.

"I don't know Josh, I'm afraid Jackie might not be able to find Daddy. You know heaven is a very big place. Or for that matter she might not want to come back here. I hear heaven is a spectacular place."

Josh wrinkled his forehead in thought and then smiled again. "I know Mommy, but the angel promised Jackie would come back." With that he threw his hands up in the air and raised his eyebrows and smiled at her. 'Oh, the faith of a child,' she thought, as he left Desiree with more to ponder.

Merely Existing

Chapter 62

Benjamin was getting ready for work and he had a lot on his mind. Marcie was just one of the things troubling him. He knew he had hurt her. It seemed he was good at hurting people. Come to think of it, Clark was really the only person he hadn't run off, but then again they had been together through more than most.

He wanted to try and get to know his father, but even that seemed difficult with Desiree in the picture and what were the odds of that happening? He didn't even want to try and calculate it. Once again, Benjamin was certain it had something to do with fate. There was always a reason. His mom always told him that nothing happens by chance.

Benjamin was a little nervous that Bradford wanted to come check out his place. He was embarrassed by the area of town and his furniture, which consisted of a collective display of thrift shop finds and dumpster relics. It was a tad of an eye sore. He could only imagine how Bradford lived, he probably had a big nice home with an iron gate. Benjamin on second thought, decided that maybe Bradford would feel bad for him and help him get a better place. But what if he wanted him to move in with him? He wouldn't be able to smoke his dope or drink until he blacked out. Benjamin buttoned his shirt and grabbed his hat and headed out the door. By the time he reached Frank's, he was already ten minutes late for work. "Hey, Clark."

"Hey Benjamin, man, you missed it last night."

"Whys that?"

"Just seen your girl, Marcie getting in her car to leave, you just missed her. She was at the hotel all night with some creepy salesman she met at the bar."

Benjamin's heart sunk. He knew he pushed her away, but he didn't want anyone else touching her. Didn't she know she belonged to him? "Oh well, she's a big girl. I guess she got what she was looking for."

"She was looking for you man, but then she started talking some crazy crap about you being engaged and having a wreck and killing your fiancé? I don't know where she got such crazy ideas? Whatever you were feeding her Benjamin, she believed it all. I told her it all was a crock of crap. Sorry dude, but I was caught off guard. Then she started ordering shots, one right after another. I didn't know what she was talking about or I would have played along and kept it cool, you know the story you fed her to cover your butt? But before I figured out what was up, I'd already told her the truth. Dude, she was so drunk, she was slurring."

Ben felt bad suddenly at how his pride and fear had caused him to destroy their relationship. If I would have told her the truth right off none of this would have ever happened, he thought. But it was too late now, she would never forgive him and he wasn't sure now if he could ever forgive her. He might have been a jerk and lied to her, but he didn't cheat on her.

One thing he hated was a woman who cheated. He could handle just about anything else. He once dated a chick addicted to cocaine. She stole all his money, which wasn't much, but he still forgave her. He knew a little about addiction. But once she got so bad she was willing to sell her body for a fix, Benjamin was out of there. He liked his weed, it kept him mellow and drinking was something that calmed his nerves, but he rarely messed with the other stuff.

He decided to dismiss Marcie and began his new life with Bradford. Possibly get a clean slate and maybe a fresh start. Benjamin knew that ever since the accident he had been merely existing. He tried to think back to a time in his life when he was living, but suddenly realized his whole life had been him trying to survive. Either trying to survive the verbal and physical abuse of his father that raised him, or trying to survive watching his mother deteriorate from cancer. The last survival attempt had left someone dead, and he had been dead since the day he took another man's life.

Purifying Water

Chapter 63

Desiree decided to call Bradford.   The situation was overwhelming, she wanted to share Josh's story, but first she needed to make things right. The guilt of how things had gone down at the restaurant was building and she wanted him to understand her shock and anger. There was no way to know how it would all end, but she needed closure. They had worked together for a long time now and they had always respected each other. She picked up the phone and dialed his number nervously.

"Hello."

"Hey Bradford, it's me."

"How are you doing today?"

"Hey, I'm okay, what about you, Des?"

She hated that he had used the nickname he'd given her, because it only made her miss him more. "I just wanted to call and say I'm sorry for my actions and the way I exploded last night. I was so shocked to see Benjamin there and everything was happening so quickly, I just blew up. Can you ever forgive me?"

There was silence for a moment and then Bradford said, "Desiree, the question is can you ever forgive my son?" Again a long pause and then Bradford continued. "Desiree, you've been holding this bitter unforgiveness inside for so long that it's making you sick and effecting your children. I don't think you're even aware of how much it controls you. Of course I forgive you, I care about you, no matter what you decide, but I think if you ever want to have any feeling of freedom, you're going to have to take a step towards forgiving him. Even if Benjamin wasn't my son and I had no feelings for him at all, I would still tell you what I'm telling you right now."

"I know you're right, Bradford. I know everything you and my grandmom are telling me is for my own benefit and I want to have freedom, but I don't know if I'm there yet."

"Can I take you for a drive this evening, I want to show you something?"

"Right now, Bradford?"

"If you can arrange it."

"Well, I just picked up the children from grandmom's and was making them dinner, but I could call a sitter."

"It's important to me and I think it might change how you see things."

Desiree knew in her heart that she just really wanted to be with him. She had just let down a mountain of walls and was starting to like herself again and had just started thinking that she was worthy of a good man like Bradford and now what? Being in the same room as his son was something she wasn't sure she could do. No, that would be too much for her. Desiree thought about how she would choose her son over Bradford any day and that too made her heart sink.

"I'll pick you up then, say in about an hour?"

"Okay Bradford, I'll see what I can do about a sitter." Desiree hung up the phone and called a young girl that lived down the block that she had used for emergencies and was in luck. She was so tired from the bottle of wine she had drank the night before and the restless dreams that had kept her tossing and turning, that she would need a shower and a cup of coffee before he arrived. Her mind was scattered with thoughts of angels and birds and John, Benjamin and even Bradford. She felt that she needed to separate each person and try to make sense of the havoc inside her brain. She walked to the front door and peered up at the sky that had turned an awesome pink and gold and searched for any bird upon the horizon. Then she headed to the bathroom to shower and get ready. She pulled back the shower curtain and let her clothes fall in a heap on the tile floor. The warm water sprayed upon her face and she closed her eyes.

"God what are you up to this time?" She said it as if he were there watching her, his eyes resting upon her and patiently waiting for her to let all her bitterness, self-pity, anger and hatred for Benjamin Stewart to flow down through the drain, along with the pure water that cleaned her.

Lovely Lilly

Chapter 64

Marcie walked up the porch that was adorned with white wicker furniture and an array of potted plants and hanging ferns. There was a glass vase with large sunflowers falling over the rim and just above her door was the house numbers, each number was a mosaic ceramic mold that held a southwestern vibe. Her front door was painted a rustic red and adorned with a large brass door knocker. Marcie raised the lever and tap, tap, tapped.

"Marcie, dear!"

"Hello, Grams." Her Grandmother Lilly had pale yellow hair kissed with white. Her eyes twinkled and her voice was filled with genuine excitement, this always made Marcie feel warm inside.

"Well, hello dearest, how are you? Come in, come in. Is everything okay dear, you look a little scattered."

"I'm okay Grams, just was wondering if maybe I could stay with you for a little while?"

"Marcie, you know my home is always open to you, goodness gracious." Her arms hugged Marcie and told her to follow her to the kitchen.

Her grandma loved making healthy foods and often foods from other countries. On this particular night she had tofu in a spicy peanut sauce with noodles and a cucumber salad with seaweed and ginger sauce. "Smells wonderful, Grams." Marcie realized it had been quite a while since she'd had anything in her stomach other than alcohol and she was tired. She was tired of the drinking and the hands that she had let touch her, invade her and take from her very soul. She was tired of the bruises and the rejection that seemed to follow her. She was tired of breathing. She tried to dodge the mental clips of Steve and his vulgar comments that kept shooting through her head and desperately tried to focus on her grandmother. But there were more clips of Benjamin and then a sharp pain that seemed to shoot through her eyes and out her head.

She listened as Lilly spilled off her latest Korean recipe of kimchi and a beef and vegetable dish called bibimbop. More tales of the church social and the latest fund raiser for the needy. "That's wonderful Grams, and the food sounds delicious. I can't wait to try it."

"Well, I sure love cooking and growing fresh herbs and vegetables. Maybe I could teach you some gardening tips while you're here or how to cook with a wok?" She smiled at Marcie, who could only think of all the mistakes she kept making.

"Marcie, what's wrong? Is it a boyfriend that's got you so haggard and depressed?" Marcie chewed her meal robotically and took a drink of iced tea.

Lilly looked at her young granddaughter and knew she had been given all the material things a child could ever dream of, but when it came to time and attention, affection and love, her parents were too busy living their American dream. Lilly sighed, and took Marcie's hand. "Let's go in the sitting room and talk about it, you can bring your plate in there."

Marcie obeyed and decided for once to confide some truth to her Grams and see what advice she could give her. She slinked sluggishly to the overstuffed chair and propped her feet up under her.

"Okay shoot, I'm all ears."

"Well, it's rather complicated." Marcie didn't know really where to begin. "I met a man, well, he told me he was in a bad car wreck and that he was driving and hit somebody head on killing his fiancé. He explained that now he walked everywhere and that now he drank to forget the life that he took, his love."

"Oh dear, that is a wretched story! Oh how horrible, what a sad, sad, story."

"Wait a minute Gram, it gets more complex. See, I fell in love with this man, but came to find out, he didn't kill his fiancé but was driving drunk and killed a husband and father of two. He lied to me about the whole thing and he keeps pushing me away and then pulling me back."

Lilly studied Marcie for a second and thought carefully before speaking. "You are in an unhealthy relationship that won't get any better until the two of you get help. I say that

467

out of love." Marcie looked in her eyes and knew she meant what she said.

"You have felt rejected since you were a small child and now you continue seeking out those that will hurt you the most. Marcie, you need counseling and this young man sure could use it. He will have to live with the guilt and shame of taking another man's life for the rest of his. He will have to learn to forgive himself. I believe that is why he lied to you. He probably thought if he told you the truth, you would never give him the time of day." Her grandmother walked across the room and put her arms around Marcie. She held her and patted her head in silence. Marcie wished she could feel, but she had become so numb and so lifeless lately.

"Marcie dear, start working on you, began to paint again and sketch and listen to music that makes you feel alive, return to school and finish your degree. Focus on you Marcie, and healing yourself, then pursue a man. I think though until you are whole, I regret to say, each attempt at a relationship will end in doom."

Marcie realized she needed sleep, sunshine and teacups with warm honey lemon. She needed to listen to her grandmother and try and heal. Her heart hurt so deeply and her mind was tired of analyzing Benjamin's next move, or hers rather. Did he know she spent the night at the hotel? Did he miss her? Would he ever call her again? Were her parents aware that she was even alive?

Marcie was jolted once again out of her dazed state by another question. "Marcie, are you working anywhere?"

"No Grams, I have been being quite a sloth lately."

"What about your art work?"

"Haven't touched a pencil or paint brush in months." Marcie peered up at Lilly and realized she missed her art, it was therapeutic and staying here awhile and painting might be just what she needed, fresh air, fresh food and Grams lovely face. When she thought about how her father had come from this precious woman's womb, she was boggled. How could such evil be birthed from the very womb where such love lived? "Grams, can you call Daddy and let him know I am going to be here for a bit, I need a bath?"

"Of course dear, why he is so busy with that company he probably doesn't even know you're missing! Oops, sorry dear, you know what I mean." Boy, did she ever. Lilly shook her head back and forth and made a tsking sound with her tongue.

Marcie finished her tofu and headed for the bathroom. There were candles and flowers everywhere. The scent of floral filled the air and the large claw foot tub looked so inviting. Marcie grabbed the bath salts and bubbles, allowing the water to get extra hot. Then she laid her head back and closed her eyes. She wasn't one for praying, but for some reason she felt like talking to him.

"God, if you're real and you can hear me, I need help. I'm sorry for all the bad things I've done and I really need forgiveness. I'm tired of riding this roller coaster and I'm tired of men treating me like garbage and God, I'm tired of not knowing why I'm here and what I am supposed to do here on this planet called earth. There has to be more to living than this! If you could bend down your ear and hear me, I need help."

A silent tear travelled down her cheek as she ran the soft washcloth over her broken body, finally resting below where Steve had left an ache of invasion, roughly using her to fulfill his lust, she began to choke up.

"Do you hear me, God?" another glistening droplet fell into the water. "Oh God, please bend your ear and hear me!" At that moment unawares to Marcie, He heard.

Reunion

Chapter 65

Walter stood up and looked out at the gray sky, familiar ground he thought. He missed home, even the area of town looked engaging to him. It was where he raised his children, where he raised his pigeons and where he had met Ruthie. "Yes, the air even smells differently," he said, as he inhaled deeply. But although the air was fresh with familiarity, Walter wasn't feeling like himself. He was clammy and the urgency in his bladder was screaming for relief. He walked off the path of gravestones to a treed area to relieve himself. This was something that was becoming more and more difficult to do. His mouth was exceedingly dry and he realized he'd had no medicine for his diabetes for days. Walter wasn't sure how he could physically walk all the way to the police station to turn himself in. Up ahead he heard cars in the distance and then two vehicles emerging straight towards the grave site, both looked hauntingly familiar to Walter. Walter walked back towards them, his eyes following the vehicles. And yet Walter didn't feel so well. He coughed several times and peered at the cars making their way towards the side street next to the row of tombs where Ruthie laid. Was he dreaming? Then the sound of car doors opening and voices that were calling to him, echoing his name seemed enormously surreal.

They were over five hundred feet away, but he knew the sound of his children. Yes, he'd know their voices anywhere. Before he knew it his grandchildren were running toward him and the face of his daughter, her eyes peering into his from a distance. "Daddy, Daddy is that you?" He heard her call for him, it was his carrot top and then his son Daniel's joyous face running towards him. They were drawing closer and closer. But Walter stood frozen and still. What could he possibly say or do to fix everything? He had been nothing but a coward, he had left them and lived as a vagabond while they worried, while they cared for his sick wife, his responsibility. Walter looked out at the figures coming towards him and he began to tremble and he began to cry from his belly, an inward shaking of humbleness and grief in the highest of forms.

Walter had tried to be strong for so long. He had tried so hard to be tough and not feel the emotions that laid dormant underneath like a breath of winter hidden from reach. He had tried to sleep any and everywhere and never ask for pity or assistance. Even the bread he stole from Desiree was repaid by repairs and handy-work. He had tried not to cry or become angry at God over the hand that was dealt to him, but all of a sudden every emotion from Ruthie's spirit leaving this earth, along with her mind, was coming down upon him. Every face and every smile he had longed to touch and feel were headed toward him and all Walter could do was sob and moan as his whole body began to shake. And yet as worthless as he felt about what he had done, he stretched out his arms, to take in any that would still have him. His body rippling with emotions, racked from anguish was shaken.

He then heard a sound that was almost as precious as his children and his grandchildren, it was a cooing sound and a sound of feathers brushing the skies. Walter looked above him and the sight of Jackie gave birth to even more joy mixed with tears. His chest and throat felt swollen and his heart tightened with each breath. Walter tried to run to meet them, but wave after wave of feeling caused him to stand and sob like a baby. Then he began to cry out to them. "Oh God, I am so sorry I left you! Oh God, I'm so very sorry." His eyes were meeting theirs, pleading for forgiveness. "Oh how I've missed you all, can you ever forgive me? Can you ever forgive me?" His words were cracking and slurring with pain.

Walter fell to his knees right in front of Ruthie's tombstone and continued to sob. And suddenly they were all before him, his beautiful family; eyes locking and arms and hands reaching towards him. "Daddy, we've missed you so. Are you okay, Dad?" But there was a humming sound in his ears and a far away feeling Walter couldn't shake. And as he rose up to meet them, something happened to Walters balance, and there was that tightening gripping his chest and numbness in his arm, then a blackness. And yet Walter heard the sound of his name being sung out over and over, except as hard as he tried to reach them he could not. Then he began to travel swiftly through a tunnel filled with light and suddenly the voices and the faces were completely obsolete.

Distance

Chapter 66

Bradford pulled in the driveway and walked up the porch and let himself in through the front door. Desiree met his eyes and wanted to simply run to him, just put her arms around him and let him hold her until the world melted away. She didn't want to fight anymore or let anything come between them. Now with Benjamin in the picture, her heart felt mangled and twisted again.

"Truce?" He said. His smile was irresistible and she couldn't help but smile back.

"Yes, truce." She answered. Desiree walked up and embraced him with a hug that was over too quickly for her. She then went to kiss the kids and double check with the sitter about the rules, grabbed her purse and cell phone and looked at Bradford. "Well, where is it that you are taking me that's so mysterious?"

"You'll see, are we ready?"

"Yes sir, whenever you are."

"Right this way, my lady, your carriage waits."

"Bye Josh, Bye Tabitha, be good for Crystal." Desiree yelled from the front room as she and Bradford made their way out the door. Desiree hopped in Bradford's Jeep and soon they were off for an adventure that seemed perplexing. If Desiree hadn't witnessed Benjamin firsthand the night before she could just act as if everything was normal, and that Bradford's biological son hadn't really killed her husband. She could pretend they were off on a date and that everything was blissful. But inside she was scared.

After several minutes Bradford was getting off the expressway at an area of town known for drug deals, projects and poverty. Desiree looked out the window at the shotgun houses that lined the streets. There was a rather vicious looking dog tied to a tree, very inhumane she thought as they breezed by. Across the street an assortment of children were playing ball and jumping rope, their eyes oblivious to the trash and debris that seemed to litter the street and sidewalks.

There was a car up on blocks and several houses had broken down looking vehicles layered about the yard. "Where are we going?" She turned to Bradford her facial expression revealing her confusions as to why anyone would want to be in this part of town.

Bradford eased down an alley and pulled the Jeep in front of a shotgun house with a ripped screen door and a yard full of brown grass. "We're here," he turned and looked at her, analyzing her response.

"Okay, and where is that actually?" Desiree's forehead was crinkled and she was confused to say the least.

"I wanted to try and explain the chain of events that led to a horrible tragedy for the two people I love."

Desiree was intrigued. "Go on," she said, motioning with her hand.

"Well, first I need for you to knock on the door of the house we're parked in front of and meet a man named Larry. Just pretend you have the wrong house and get back in the Jeep. I won't let anything happen to you."

"Bradford, I don't want to just go up to some strangers door and knock on it. Come on?"

"Desiree, can you just do it for me? Anyway, it's not some stranger, it's the man who raised my son."

"In this area of town, I know you said it was bad, but gosh, Brad."

"I know," Bradford sighed, "I felt completely shocked when I saw it. I prayed there had been some sort of a mistake."

Desiree was starting to get a vivid picture of what this young boy's life must have been like. And with the atmosphere of poverty before her she decided to take an even closer look inside the young man's life who had taken John's. "Okay Bradford, I'll be right back."

Desiree eased out of the Jeep and walked up the sidewalk littered by cigarettes butts and empty beer cans. She made her way up the porch and knocked on the green trimmed screen door. In the distance she heard a voice yell something that she couldn't make out and nervously looked back towards the Jeep. After what seemed like eons the screen door swung open abruptly.

A little scrawny man with a cigar in-between his fingers opened the door. He had beady eyes and reeked of body odor and alcohol. He looked Desiree up and down lustfully and then smiled up at her only to reveal a mouth missing several teeth. "Hey doll, what brings you my way?"

"Uhhh, I must have the wrong house," Desiree said hurriedly and turned quickly, heading back down the porch as fast as she could.

"Where you going in such a hurry," he called after her. Desiree jerked the Jeep door open and hopped inside and Bradford took off as quickly as he could.

"See why I wanted you to meet the man who raised my son."

"Oh God Bradford, that was horrific."

"I know Des, I'm still flabbergasted. Patty and I gave up our son, and all the while I thought he was being raised in some nice home in the suburbs, going to good schools and playing sports; meanwhile back at the ranch! I have never had so much guilt in my life. While I ate at 5 star restaurants and travelled the world, my son was getting the crap beat out of him and the worst forms of verbal abuse you can imagine from that man. To top it all off, he watched his mother die of cancer. I thought if I showed you this place and where he came from, you might be able to understand better why he was drinking and driving at 17. I am by no means trying to make an excuse for what he has done to you and your children. I know that what he did was wrong, but I wanted you to try and see what life must have been like for my son. Just for one minute, can you please just try and do that for me?" Bradford was choking up inside.

Desiree sat in silence. So many things and such pain filled her heart for Bradford. Knowing how much she loved her children and wanted to protect them, she knew it must have hurt him terribly to see what kind of life his son had lived and know that it didn't have to be that way. She wanted to forgive him, but something seemed to pull her back to the cemetery and Joshua standing by her in his little suit coat crying. How could she ever rid herself of the hatred that had consumed her? Now at least she understood why Benjamin had done the things he had. At least she had peered into his world from a distance.

"I'm so sorry Bradford. I know this must have wounded you deeply. I'm sorry your son was raised in such an environment as this. I feel bad for any child who has to go through abuse. Thank you for allowing me to see inside Benjamin's life more clearly."

She looked at him sincerely. "I just don't know if I can ever get over what he did to my family. I wish I could tell you I was ready to forgive him and that I was mature enough to, but I just don't know if I can do that. And I know I can never forget, no, I will never forget what he did."

Bradford looked at Desiree intently, "He will never forget either." There was a long pause before Bradford continued. "My son will live the rest of his life rehashing a ride he took one night after hospice came in and removed his mother's body. He will never forget a ride he took to get away from a father named Larry who was the spawn of Satan himself. He will relive the sounds of that crash for the rest of his life. He will relive the smell of blood and death and he will replay in his mind every 'what if' over and over until he is crazed by mental disturbance. What if I hadn't drunk so much? What if I hadn't driven? What if I had just taken a walk instead? Don't you understand, Des? Don't you get it?"

Desiree was crying now and sobbing uncontrollably. She tried to stop by sniffing, and continuously wiping her eyes that were streaming. But the tears along with her mascara kept coming.

Bradford pulled into the parking lot of a restaurant and pulled Desiree into his arms. He laid her head on his chest and tried to calm her. "This is going to take some time Des, but if you will work on it, I know eventually you will do the right thing. If you search your heart and mind and think about what kind of effect this is all having on you and your children, I know you will forgive him."

Desiree didn't know why, but she felt like a child curled up on his chest and the sound of his heart beating in her ear and the smell of his shirt all made her feel safe. She knew she would miss this man and she knew that she had to walk away because of Benjamin, she also knew that she would regret it for the rest of her life. "I'll do whatever it takes, Brad. I promise," she said, as she wiped the smudges of mascara from beneath her eyes. "I'm going to try and get better for me and especially for my children. I'm going to miss you." She looked at him and felt saddened by the turn of events.

Bradford took her hand and squeezed it. "We'll always be friends Desiree, and we will be in touch at work and you know that if you or the children need anything, you can call me. Anytime, you can call, just right now I have to focus on my son and what's best for him." Desiree nodded and squeezed his hand in a return fashion. Then they travelled through the dark streets with their silence and their many thoughts that ran as fast as the road beneath them.

Tears of Forgiveness

Chapter 67

Walter stepped through the lighted tunnel to a place where he felt joy like a river. He had no fear whatsoever. He was ageless. It was as if he was spiritual and not physical. A celestial body had taken the place of his physical one. He heard songs that were so full of energy and peace; yet, the instruments used to make the sound of them was foreign to him. Flowers danced on hills and beckoned him to colors he could not name. Trees waved leaves that resembled nothing he'd ever seen and the fruit of them was large and bright with hues unknown. And there past a river that was crystal clear stood his beloved, Ruthie. She was so young and so beautiful, Walter could scarcely breathe. All at once he realized he had been created for this place. This place was where he belonged and everything seemed too blissful to comprehend. Yes, he had always been meant to live here in this captivating land. He held out his hand and Ruthie took it.

"You're early, Walter," she mouthed. Walter tried to decipher what she meant and then it dawned on him, he was in heaven. He was at the place where time stands still and yet he was early?

"Walter, you've come early dear," she smiled repeating herself. "Oh Walter, how wonderful this place is!" She twirled around laughing with joy, her eyes dancing and Walter wondered if this was real. Was he dreaming?

"How do you know I'm early, Ruthie?" Walter did not want to leave. This is what he had been longing for all along, to be with her and enjoy his Ruthie with a strong celestial body and a sound mind. How could he be early?

"There are things left undone, strings left unwound. Yes Walter, you are so very close, but the time is not exact. I'll be waiting Walter, and don't worry, you will understand when you return." Suddenly a bright light shone around them and Walter questioned what this light was.

The Holy One! Yes, Walter knew him well. Oh how could he stand before the most Holy One? Walter wanted to feel sad inside, but he couldn't, he couldn't even cry. This place was too magnificent. He searched for words to describe it and perceive it and grasp it, but none could be found. It grabbed your soul and filled it with good things, tangible, liquid love and a freshness that he had never experienced.

"Does it involve our dear children, Ruthie?"

"Walter, all the earth is filled with God's children. You will be back in no time, as you may know there is no time here, no sickness, no tears. Walter, it's everything and more than you could ever imagine!"

Again there came a brightness and then a creature walked into the mist and knelt before them. It was a little lamb that appeared to have been slain, and the lamb's eyes pierced Walter. Walter fell to his knees before the Lamb and cried out, "You are holy, oh so holy," before he even knew the words would come upon his lips.

Then as quickly as the lamb appeared, he swiftly vanished, leaving Walter in awe of His glory. Ruthie reached up and touched his heart with her hand and imparted a strength Walter had not known. "I love you, Walter. Finish the race strong!" Her eyes twinkled and Walter mouthed the same 'I love you' to her, his hand upon hers.

Suddenly Walter was traveling as fast through that tunnel as he had came. Abruptly he was coming to a place where everything he had felt left him and noise and beeping and voices filled his senses. Someone shouted in the distance, "We've got a heartbeat!" Then Walter heard clapping and cheering and a pain in his chest that knocked the breath out of him. Another hand held his instead of Ruthie's, and then a voice ever so softly that he recognized. It was his carrot top.

"Daddy, we love you, it's going to be okay; hold on Daddy, don't leave us again. I have so much to tell you, Daddy." Then Walter felt a wet substance dripping on his hand and realized it was Brenda's tears. 'She has forgiven me', he thought and so has the Lamb. Walter tried to open his eyes, but he was so exhausted he could not. Peace washed over him and he slept with the assurance that Brenda's hand was entwined with his, so was Ruthie's and so was His Lord's!

<u>*One Year Later*</u>

Benjamin hung the last of his shirts in the closet and studied the room. It was the nicest room Benjamin had ever known, from the king size bed adorned with a plush comforter, to the plasma screen television mounted above the opposite wall. Not only did he have his own computer, but a full bathroom. Living with Bradford certainly had its benefits. He looked out the window at the fountain and garden area and wondered how he ever survived life up to this point. He could still hear the shrill of Larry's voice sometimes, but it had become much quieter in the past few months, so had the nightmares and the memory of that horrific night that had changed his life forever. Sometimes he still felt horrendous guilt over what he had done to

Desiree and her family, but he had come to a place of moving forward.

Benjamin had finished a 28 day program and his mind had never been clearer. Sure, he was still puffing on cigarettes, but everything else had diminished with the past. He was going to college and working on an autobiography. Write what you know, that's what Mark Twain had said after all. He picked up the notebook from his end table where he had been jotting down titles for his manuscript. One seemed to stand out above the rest. 'Some of the Greatest Men were Murderers'. Benjamin wouldn't have known this if he hadn't picked up a Bible that year. Moses and King David had renewed his hope that maybe, just maybe he could start over and get that second chance he needed.

Benjamin would never have dreamed he would be so level headed or so free. He wasn't sure why God had given him a second chance, but he was thankful that he had. His counselor had enlightened him on some spiritual beliefs that he'd never forgotten. Sure, his old friends had drifted away with the booze, drugs and deceit, but he'd made some new ones that seemed to be just fine for him. Bradford had taught him things regarding becoming a man that he'd not known.

But then again, he'd never been around a real man. He'd learned words like honor, respect, integrity, and trust, the last one being the hardest.

Benjamin picked up the ink dot drawing that he'd framed and positioned on his desk. He missed Marcie, but he had a feeling their paths would cross again. Sometimes at night he could hear her laughter and remember the apricot scent of her hair. Every so often when he closed his eyes, he could remember their bodies entangled together, trying to hold each other's pain and sometimes when the birds were singing in the morning, he could still hear his mother's voice. And for the first time in his life, he could hear his own voice and it felt jubilating. He put down the drawing and walked to the door taking one last look around, he sighed and pulled his shoulders back. Benjamin not only had a new home and a new start, he had a new name. Benjamin Stiltz, son of Bradford. He stood with a sense of confidence and vision and a new mind set. Closing the door behind him, he made his way down the hall to his father's room.

Marcie

Marcie held her sides and laughed from a deep place. Her ribs ached and she was squeezing her bladder, trying to not pee herself. Her grandmother, Lilly was dancing around the room singing and mimicking Lucille Ball. She'd made a whole tray of fudge and was shoving it into her mouth and replaying the classic chocolate episode. Her mouth was so full Marcie couldn't understand what she was saying, but they had the giggles that day. It started early that morning with their hair that seemed to stick up and Marcie's mascara that had left black smudges under her eyes. Marcie had pointed at Lilly's hair and shrieked, "Grams, go look in the mirror!" But of course her grandmother's wit came shining through she had pranced out of the bathroom with it sticking up worse and her eyes crossed. "Go look in the mirror yourself, missy," she squealed, "you look like a linebacker!"

Marcie was so happy here, this place she'd found inside Lilly's home and inside her soul. She thought about how far she had come and in the midst of the laughter she wanted to cry. She'd cry for the little girl, Marcie who needed saving. It had been a year since she'd even been with a guy and she felt her spirit healing. Yes, one full year since she'd shown up at Lilly's door with her demons and her essence that needed restoring. She glanced back on the evening in the bathtub and her hands trying to scrub off the fingerprints of men and miles of pain and she hardly recognized herself. She'd reached a place where she wasn't so starved for attention from men, not even approval and most surely not from her father.

She had been holding paint brushes and chalk and charcoal and things made of clay. Things that had therapeutic qualities and she'd been holding the earth. Lilly had her planting herbs, vegetables and flower beds, and she loved every minute of it. Watching the seeds grow and become something so beautiful, something she could feel and touch and even eat. At the first of the year her artwork would be on display at a local gallery. It was clearly a dream come true. Sometimes at night she could hear the whippoorwills, the katydids and a sound coming from a place where the little girl inside her was becoming whole. Her heart was mending and most all the leaks and gaps that had once oozed were covered in a balm of anointed oil.

Her grandmother took a drink of tea, grabbed her hands and began dancing her around the room. Dizzy Gillespie's scat hailed in the background and Marcie shuffled her feet to the beat. How did I end up here in this place? She thought, looking deep into the eyes of this incredible woman, who she hoped to be half as great as. She felt freedom and peace and also a sense of knowing who she was and what she wanted from this life, this life that had battered her and left her scarred and frightened to trust anyone.

Sometimes at night she remembered the man with the dark hair and small teeth who held her in his arms and wanted to love her, but didn't know how and sometimes she wondered if she would ever see him again. She wondered if his soul had healed and his demons had vanished and she silently prayed, "God, help Benjamin become this free." She crossed her feet and twirled under her grandmother's arm, her feet dancing to a whole new tempo! She reached for a piece of fresh fudge, it melted under her tongue and savored her taste buds. Life is good she thought, life is good.

<u>*Walter*</u>

Walter sat in the brown easy chair and held the newest arrival, Annabella. She was delicate and soft, with puffs of carroty red hair, but her smile is what caught Walter's attention. He would recognize that smile anywhere, for his Ruthie had one just like it. The twins played at his feet and laughter and bustle fell all around the kitchen, as his children and their spouses set the table. It was just 4 days until Christmas and the tree lit up almost as brightly as Walter's brown eyes that day. He studied the lights and reminisced about flowers and trees with colors he had no words to describe. 'Ruthie, are you watching me from above?' He pondered his experience and had dared not tell anyone for fear of them thinking him mental. But still he could not shake how real it all had seemed.

The doorbell rang and Brenda's German shepherd let out a bark from the other room. Walter put Annabella down in her carrier seat and opened the door. The lovely woman who greeted him, he'd not seen since he was wearing the clothes of her deceased husband and there beside her stood his little Josh. His eyes were smiling and his legs running to Walter. He grabbed him and held on. "Walter, Walter!"

"Well, well Josh, my how you've grown, come in, come in. Everyone welcome!" Walter had barely got their coats and introduced everyone, when he heard the doorbell ring again.

Bradford came in next, the man who had gone to court for him and managed to clear him of all his charges, while he recovered from open heart surgery. The hand written note from Josh and the fact that Desiree had refused to press charges, made it quite simple it seemed. Yes, he owed them so much. Desiree greeted Bradford and then hurried past them, back outside to retrieve the last member of her family. She carried in a cage and there inside cooed one of Walter's greatest friends, Jackie, who had kept him company on many a cold night and listened intently as he cried over his loss.

495

"Oh Jackie, my friend, how have you been?" Jackie bounced up and down and seemed to coo only for Walter. Walter felt as if he might burst inside from joy.

Tabitha rushed past the scene and stared down at Annabella. "Hi, lil baby," she said as she patted her hand. "You are a good baby, aren't you?"

"Welcome, welcome," Walter said, his eyes tearing up at how God had worked everything out so smoothly. He had taken him from sleeping in the elements and being hunted by the police, to a place of comfort and peace. Under the Christmas tree Walter eyed the gift he'd wrapped earlier that morning, inside held a gift Walter had hand carved for Josh. He pondered why he was still here and felt the scar that ran across his breast where the doctors had sawed his chest in half for bypass surgery. He had been dead when they got him to the ER for a total of six minutes.

"How you been, Josh?" Walter patted his head. "Have you been taking good care of Jackie?"

Josh began talking a mile a minute, filling him in on all his endeavors. He even told him of the morning Jackie crossed the sky and came back home to him. Desiree placed their gifts under the tree. Daniel and Brenda welcomed them in and offered them drinks and embraced these new found friends that had become a part of their lives.

Walter thought about the phone call he'd received from Josh, and how he told him all about the angel who demanded he must release the bird and how scared he was that Jackie would not return. Walter knew that bird should have flown straight to his old home and not the cemetery that day, but then again God could change anyone's direction, hadn't he surely changed his?

A brisk knock on the door amongst the bustle got Walter's heart beating in his chest. Out of all the people he wanted to see on this special occasion, this one meant so much. He opened the door and there stood Buddy, pulling on his beard and that eye tooth glistening in the sunlight.

"Buddy, come in, come in!"

"Hey old timer, it's been too long!" Soon they were embracing and hands were patting backs and their eyes held the love and the tears they each tried to stop from flowing.

Walter wondered how he'd gotten his life back and how along with it he'd gotten a whole new family. He could still see Ruthie by the crystal river and he could still feel her soft hand, but he was content and happy for the first time in a long time. He wasn't sure why he'd arrived early that day, but that was better than late, he thought with a chuckle. He felt good inside. Walter reached under the tree and picked up the gift for Josh.

"I want to let Josh go ahead and open one of his gifts, if that's okay with everyone?" Walter reached down and held it out towards Josh. "Here Josh, this is for you, a special reward for saving my life!"

Josh's eyes lit up and everyone gathered around the room waiting for the unleashing of Walters special gift. Josh knelt down and began to tear the paper, his little hands pulling off ribbon and pieces of tape. In the distance he heard a faint voice that tinkled like china, "You must release her, Josh. Once you complete the mission you will be rewarded!" Josh guessed his time had come, but he had already been rewarded with getting Jackie back and Walter making it through his surgery and not dying and going away like Daddy did. Josh tore the last of the paper and then opened the box. A faint gasp could be heard as he reached inside. The workmanship was impeccable. The hand carved replica of Belinda with her flowing hair and delicate wings was breath taking. And if one were to look ever so closely, they would see in her hand a clutch bag purse and nestled inside lay a bird, a bird that had brought hope and healing and even life, Jackie.

"It's Belinda! How did you know she carried a purse?"

Walter winked at Desiree, who smiled at this warm man she had once wanted dead and wondered how everything had turned out so incredibly perfect. But then she knew that the same God who wanted her to forgive Benjamin, had a sense of humor and his own way of doing things. Who would have thought that a bird and an angel and a homeless man could change so much of their lives?

Walter and the others gathered around the table and looked at all the fixings. Each person had come so far in just one year. Each life had held another, and each person had healed more of their heart by forgiving. After all the plates were passed and each one was filled with ham and turkey and all the trimmings, they soon were transfixed by an old man with grey hair and a beard that was just coming back in. He tapped his glass with a knife and cleared his voice.

"I just want to say thank you to each and everyone here. I am so filled with joy on this day, and so blessed to sit here with each one of you. First, I'd like to thank my children and their spouses for forgiving me for leaving you at a time when you needed me the most." He looked in the eyes of Daniel, Brenda, Sandra and Burt. Then he scanned the table his eyes falling on Buddy, "Buddy, my dear ole friend, how could I ever repay you, for all you gave me? Food and shelter and rest from the cold, a listening ear and a heart as big as Texas. I cherish you my friend." Walter then directed his attention towards Desiree, "I want to thank you for feeding me and sheltering me as well, even though you had no idea you were and for believing in me and trusting me that I would never hurt your son, whom I love." Walters's eyes were glistening with tears and his throat had grown scratchy. "Bradford, my friend what can I say? If it wasn't for you I'd probably be rotting away in a prison cell somewhere eating a miserable turkey dinner." He grinned through the tears. Walter paused for a moment and then looked at Josh intently, "Josh my boy, I like to think we come from the same stock, you and I lost people we loved dearly. And you Josh, listened to an angel and took a risk on something you loved and let it go, having faith that it would

500

return to you. As bad as you didn't want to release Jackie and set her free, you obeyed that still small voice and because of that, I am alive today. But most of all, I have to thank my God, my Lord, who gave his only son Jesus, for my soul and died for me and for each of you. He became a living sacrifice and because of His great sacrifices, one day I will see my Ruthie again and Josh you will see your father as well. Merry Christmas everyone!" The table cheered and laughter filled the house and somewhere far above the clouds Ruthie Kendal clapped her hands with glee. "Well done, Walter! Well done!"

Notes

Parker, Dorothy. "Resume." Portable Dorothy Parker. Copyright 1954.

http://www.poetryfoundation.org/poem/174101

"Fallen Leaves" as recorded by Primitive Quartet. Author unknown.

As Recorded by Primitive Quartet

Primitive Quartet does not own the copyright to FALLEN LEAVES. They did record it many years ago, but they put on their recording, "Author Unknown".

"Homing Pigeons." *Wikipedia: The Free Encyclopedia.* Wikimedia Foundation, Inc. June 2009. Web.

<http://en.wikipedia.org/wiki/Homing_pigeon >